The Mermaid
and
The Bear

by

Ailish Sinclair

GWL
PUBLISHING

First Published in 2019
by GWL Publishing
an imprint of Great War Literature Publishing LLP

Produced in United Kingdom

ISBN 978-1-910603-73-4 Paperback Edition

GWL Publishing
Forum House
Sterling Road
Chichester PO19 7DN

www.gwlpublishing.co.uk

Dedication

For Davie, Daniel and Charlotte

Acknowledgements

Thank you to my husband and children for putting up with, and actively encouraging, my obsessive writing habits. To Davie, for never failing to champion my ideas, whether they are building medieval herb gardens or writing novels. To Daniel, for his encyclopaedic knowledge of history, and his generous willingness to share it whenever needed. And to Charlotte, for always being my first editor, plot detangler and writing mentor.

I would also like to thank Wendy at GWL for her insightful comments that have made this book shine so much more brightly.

Gratitude also goes out to the friends who have been there for me during this writing journey, those who walked with me, talked with me, and counselled me. You know who you are Quines!

Part One:
The Mermaid
and The Bear

The Beginning

September 1596

The first time the sea killed me, my brother brought me back to life. I bore him no gratitude, awakening to fresh nausea, throat raw and bones bruised from his efforts of re-enlivening.

Our seafaring nightmare was ongoing: the rise and fall of the world, the rocking floor, the rough drag of the ropes on the mast above, and the creaking, the relentless creaking of wood. Waves crashed against the outside of the boat, as if they would shatter its fragile hull. I retched over a bucket while Jasper spoke what he imagined to be words of comfort.

"'Tis but a short voyage," he said. "Maybe only one or two weeks if the wind is with us, and then, such adventures await, my dear. Remember the tale you spun? Of mountains and forests, magical pools and mists, big hairy men with rough accents and strange ways? And don't forget the castle. Our grand new home."

Story-telling felt like an activity from another age, a time long gone and almost forgotten. "How long was I dead?"

"You were not dead, Bell. You choked on your own vomit, is all."

"You mean it is the same day?"

It was the same day. The first day of the escape, the first day of the great journey, and the beginning of the terrible stench, for that started very quickly. It grew worse each moment, each minute and hour, that dense odour of human confinement that was at once sickly and sweet and sour. There were but a few passengers on the trading ship, but no clean air passed through the murk of the hold to lift the gathering sludge from our lungs.

The boys went up above sometimes, but I had to remain below. The boys went ashore sometimes, but I had to remain on board. Their concern that I might be recognised by my long golden curls and short, rotund stature was truly founded, but I cared less for the fact as time went by. In my enforced confinement I daydreamed of the sun and the wind and the stars and the moon. Through the dreams drifted words from nearby, some loud and well enunciated by the boys while entertaining the other passengers with speeches from plays. Others were softly spoken, surreptitious and secret: maybe our great plan would all go wrong; maybe we would be discovered. Then the beautiful and gentle Ian would marry the poor creature I had become. Out of kindness. Out of pity.

I squirmed into nightmares that were of the sea, always the sea to start with, and then him: the man with the manic eyes and devilish laugh; the man who wed and tortured and killed women.

Maybe he would have done quickly what the sea was doing slowly. Maybe he would catch up with us anyway. Maybe it was all for naught.

"Stop it," ordered my bright-eyed brother when I gave this fear voice. "He would have put you through unthinkable terrors. Remember his first wife? You were right. This is better. This is safe. This is how we all stay together."

So I clung to my bucket. I came to know every crack in its wooden slats; my thumbs formed new indentations on its edges as my strength drained away. I took to lying limp on the shifting floor. I learned all its lines and knots and scrubbed clean hollows. I awaited death's salvation; I longed for a place with no bad smells and a floor that didn't shift beneath me. It was time to go to The Lord. Eighteen was plenty years to have lived on the earth. Heaven would be filled with roses and lavender and thyme. A breeze would bring sweet scents as I lay upon a soft bed. There would be angels with wings. And trumpets. Sweet music. Sweet air. Sunlight. Being shaken awake.

"You have to eat something," said Jasper, holding out what seemed to be a sweetmeat of some sort.

"She's too weak," noted Ian. "There's a lot less of her than there was when we set sail."

It was true. My dress hung like a billowing curtain on a stage when someone had left an outside door open. It was dirty. Damp. I suspected mildew. Nothing about the venture had been properly thought through.

"We should go back, find another way," I said, wondering why I had not insisted upon such a course of action earlier. The voyage, the escape, they were all part of my own plan, and a person could change their own plan.

"Bell, we're here," said Jasper.

"Here? Scotland? Castle? Forests? Clean air?"

The strength to stand arrived all in a rush and I stood, feet wide, suddenly stable on the unstable floor. I climbed the ladder before the boys and sucked in night air that was full of salt and seaweed and distant smoke and land. A dark mass was visible to the left. Craggy cliffs. Mysterious beaches. Motionless and solid all!

I crammed the sweet pastry into my mouth as men readied a small boat and threw our trunk into it, along with other boxes and barrels. They helped me in with as much ceremony.

Sitting between Jasper and Ian, squashed in the middle, I squinted to see. The lantern at the front of the boat illuminated only mist and nearby swirling waves; the man who rowed hummed as he made his way into a black and inky cave. It could indeed be a place of enchantment and magic and faeries and monsters. I shivered with a mixture of excitement and fear.

"Out you come," said the burly sailor and he lifted me over the boat's side as if I weighed nothing at all.

The sloshing water came up to my knees and was astonishingly cold. A screech escaped my mouth and the sound carried and repeated all around the high pink roof of the cave, as if I were shouting back at myself.

"Whisht Lassie," said the man. "We dinna like to draw attention here. Ye're te carry yon up to the castle." He threw the rest of the cargo onto the rocks that lay beyond the water's edge.

We slipped and slid our way out of the sea while the man just sat there. He didn't row away. He had given us a small lamp and a lot of things for three people to carry.

"There it is," said Ian, eyes looking to the back of the cave. "Up the tunnel we go."

They found this most amusing, did Ian and Jasper. I, burdened with two heavy sacks, did not. They walked ahead with the light and our trunk, while I shuffled along behind. They laughed and talked. I stayed silent.

"Look up, Isobell," Ian called back, indicating the high crevice of a roof above us. "Some stories to be made out of that, eh?"

The truth was that caves and tunnels were more fun when told of at a fireside, in dry clothes with a full belly. The reality of them – the cold, the wet, the dripping and the echoing, and the smell of decay – was only startling. The roof looked as if a huge ogre had wielded a knife inside the cliffs, cutting and carving to his heart's content, but the idea contained no mirth, nor even any interest. And what lay ahead in this new life of ours? Surely that was the most terrifying thought of all. At least back home in London, we knew what perils were set before us and could prepare accordingly. Here, anything could happen. New horrors could jump out of the dark and old ones could follow.

The boys shooshed each other and stopped. Up ahead, a strange orange light glowed, not from a friendly welcoming room in a cosy castle, but from behind a large rock in the tunnel wall. The stone seemed lined with fire and there was accompanying sound. A monotonous intoning. Small hairs stood up on the back of my neck. The deep voice of a man could be heard from beyond the boulder. He was speaking in an unknown language. Scots? Gaelic? Pictish? Latin? Was English not an option in this place?

There began a grinding noise like millstones, rock against rock, and the track of orange light widened on one side. We three scuttled further along the tunnel and hid in the shadows as a rough doorway opened and the air was filled with a smoky perfume and a light so bright it must have come from a multitude of candles or lanterns. Two men emerged from the opening in the wall, carrying a large wooden box between them. They were silhouetted against the illuminated doorway like a painting. A small woman, cloaked and half hidden, peered out after them. "Take care of her," she said, her voice cracking as if in sorrow.

The men confirmed that they would do this in gruff speech, the only word I caught was 'aye'. And then, so strange, a robed priest came out, carrying a large silver censer, the source of the scented smoke. He walked down the way we had come, chanting in what I was sure was Latin, swinging the censer, while the men with the box followed. We all stared after them, us three travellers and the woman who did not see us. Once the odd procession had vanished, the woman crossed her chest in a most popish fashion and returned to the strange room, and the grinding noise began again.

We stayed still until we were once again in darkness, the light having shrunk back to one line around a boulder, and then Jasper touched my arm and pulled my sleeve. We had not yet reached our destination. Of course we had not. We continued on up the tunnel in total darkness, the boys having pinched out our own light during the peculiar event. The surroundings became dryer, almost dusty. I felt dizzy but determined not to trip, not to be pitiful again. Brave Isobell. Strong Isobell. Isobell who had fallen somewhat behind, but could go no faster.

My slowness mattered not. The boys were waiting up ahead in an area filled to the roof with barrels, bottles, casks and kegs. Wooden steps led up to a hatch above. On this they were knocking, not for the first time, and debating whether we were definitely expected.

After some time the hatch lifted and a large woman looked down upon us, cross and forbidding, her shawled attire suggesting she had been abed.

"Aye," she said, looking us over. "A pretty catch the sea's sent us this night! Up ye come, up ye come."

Up we came, and stood within the grey stone walls of the castle while the woman bustled about. The boys were to go directly to the farm, and after sorting their things from mine, so they did. Too tired for tears, I knew I would see them again soon. And I had been shown a bed, a bed that was as soft as my own at home and sweeter smelling. Lady's bedstraw, that must be it, a herb that held the air of summer in its stalk and the heaven of sleep in its leaf. I was surrounded and comforted and knew no more till morning.

The Kitchen

The girl poured water into a brown bowl and laid cloths beside it, then turned to stare at me in the half light of the bedchamber. I took her to be young, about my age, but slim, little and pretty with narrowed eyes that gave the impression of missing nothing.

"To clean yourself of the dirt of travelling," she said, indeed having missed nothing.

"Thank you," I replied, sitting up in the bed and looking around. We were in a small room with two narrow beds and no window.

"You're come up all the way from London?" the girl asked. "You must have seen some grand places."

"Well, yes," I said, thinking of the Theatre and the Thames, and even the large house of my father, but then forming my speech to fit our story. "Grand kitchens, you know."

"Aye," she replied, standing taller. "Well, I'll have to leave you. I've got to see to the young master. I'm Agnes, the governess here at the castle. We'll be sharing this room."

Left on my own, I made best use of the water and cloths; there was even a small lump of soap, though I found myself longing for a warm bath. Servants would not carry water for me anymore. Would I have to do that for the ladies of the castle? The men? No, surely not. That would not be the task of a kitchen servant. Banishing the idea of scrubbing the back of some elderly gentleman while trying not to look at anything, I rummaged in the trunk. Agnes had been dressed in something basic and dark, so I chose my plainest gown, a midnight blue with hardly any embroidery, and hoped it would be good enough. It was certainly large enough after the starvation of the voyage. I fastened a belt round the middle of it, pulled a comb through my tangled hair and tied it back.

So what to do next? Find my employer? I opened the heavy door and stepped out into a dim and curving passageway, then setting off along it. Perhaps I might happen upon Jasper and Ian and we would enjoy wholesome Scottish food and fresh air and mountains—

"She has arisen!" announced the woman from the night before, who seemed less formidable in the morning light. She was large, both tall and round, and quite old, grandmotherly, but there was a friendliness in her face that I had been too tired to detect the previous evening. "Through ye come, Lassie, and hae a sup o' breakfast. There's fresh bannocks..." She trailed off as I joined her in the kitchen and she, like Agnes, stared.

Was I such an oddity in this place? I was rather an oddity in most places, really. So short. So wide, less so than before, but still, wide. Such uncontrollable hair. While she took her fill of my appearance, I took in the huge fireplace archway with a large pot already hanging over the flames, various blackened implements of cooking which did not seem to match the ones I'd painstakingly read about, and an enormous table with a big pink joint of meat laid on a board.

I stared at the dark grey slates of the floor but could not avoid the woman's gaze forever, and braced myself for disdain as I met her eye. The friendliness had diminished somewhat. She appeared stern. Sceptical. Cross again. It was not a good start.

"Fit's this?" she said, touching my sleeve and then rubbing some of the cloth between her finger and thumb.

"Is it not suitable? I have other gowns, maybe I should—"

"Sit doon," she ordered. "I'll get us a wee morning drink."

My legs bent automatically and lowered me to the bench as the woman poured hot water from a pot into two cups and added bits of herb and spice from various jars and bottles to the mix. She stirred and sniffed and added a little more, and then joined me at the table.

"I think you'll like this," she said, placing a steaming cup in front of me.

I took a sip of the fragrant drink. It was sweet, a little lemony, a local herbal decoction perhaps? "Nice," I said, hoping things could be better between us again.

"Right," she said in a business-like voice. "I'm Bessie Thom. I'm the Housekeeper, though I mainly cook. And I thought I was getting a little kitchen helper."

"Yes." I nodded, keen to please, but then muddling words in worry. "That's what also I believed my duties to be."

"Quiney." She laughed. "Nobody's goin' to believe you're a kitchen maid in that frock. So tell me the truth and be quick aboot it, afore I put you out of the castle and send you on your way."

Dismayed to be discovered so soon, and horrified at the idea of being put outside for anyone to find, I opened my mouth to deny Bessie Thom's words and tell the planned story, but then didn't. Only facts escaped my mouth. I told her about Wicked Richard, the man I was supposed to marry, and all that was said of him, and how he scared me. I took a deep gulp of the sweet beverage before continuing, "There was no arguing with my father; it was a good match, he said, and my brother John agreed. He likes Richard. They drink together. Jasper says they would have drunk my whole dowry away within a month."

Bessie tutted but said nothing else, so I went on. And on.

By the time I'd reached the grainy dregs of my cup, Bessie knew all about my great plan and Ian's cousin here at the farm, and how sick I was on the boat, and how I'd read pamphlets on cooking and tried to sneak into our kitchens at home to watch the cook and the maids at work. Under the watchful eye of the castle housekeeper, I even poured out the guilt I felt about the boys giving up their lives in London, and how Ian had said he'd marry me if it all went wrong; how Jasper and I had already taken his surname to add to our disguise. "I persuaded them, you see, with stories of how wondrous and magical Scotland would be."

She listened quietly all the while I spoke. Then she got up and put some butter and round bread things before me.

"As I see it," she said, buttering one of the bready cakes herself, "you've done the best thing. Us women can take a lot o' suffering, a lot of pain in our lives. We have to. But imagine if you had bairns, children, and yon cruel manny rained down his abuses on them. No, Lassie, fit else could ye de? Aye," she said, studying my face. "You've known some cruelty; you've been made to feel less worthy than the others around you; being a gentlewoman disna spare you that. But it'll help you now. You'll adjust to your new life quick enough. And dinna worry aboot those loons; that's two boys on a grand adventure if ever I saw. Yer twins? I thought so, bright yellow curls, the pair of you."

So Bessie was in on the lie, though she stipulated that it would be only us two that knew. "Ye'll hae to keep your head down, stay oot o' trouble. Folks dinna take kindly to women coming up with plans to improve their lot, especially when it involves disobeying the men around them. Dinna confide in Agnes, fitever ye de," she warned. "Noo, let's get you something better to wear."

It was a dark blue sack. And sack though it was, I had to admit it fitted rather better than my recently baggy dress. We added a girdle and a shawl and some ribbon bits for my hair and there was a promise of Bessie's daughter Janet donating more clothes, at least one more sack anyway, when she came to do the baking, and possibly a bonnet to hide my hair, as it might prove too recognisable if anyone did come searching.

"As to the cooking, ye'll pick up the basics. We'll make do. You can say goodbye to these bonny soft hands though." Bessie threw her head back and roared with laughter before composing herself and patting my bonny soft hand. "Ye're affa well-spoken, but we'll explain that by ye bein' English. Now, I'd better show you aroon."

The Woods

The castle was pink. The stone blocks of the building sparkled as if they had been hewed from a magical rock face somewhere in Faeryland. The outside of the building was much brighter than the inside; that had seemed rather bereft of soft wall hangings and rugs and too totally made up of grey stone.

Bessie had shown me the great hall, a huge room that put one in mind of a church. Sunlight fell through twelve windows, making narrow shapes on the earthen floor of that place, as if the twelve apostles themselves were pointing towards the various long tables that took up a large portion of the room, the fire at their side. The grandest of these, the top table, was where the Laird, a very well-educated and very well-travelled man, currently away becoming more so, held barony court and sorted out feuds and wrongdoings with unsurpassed fairness and justice. To do this, he sat on an immense chair, like a throne, with lions' heads carved into the arms. We would all eat together in the great hall, servants along with the family of the castle, but only when the Laird was at home. In his absence only the family ate in the hall, and Christen Michell, his late wife's mother, ruled the roost and gave Bessie no end of bother.

"There's always something funcy the woman wants," Bessie told me. "French wine, French sauces for the fish, spices like they eat in France. She was a great admirer of Queen Mary, as were we all, but michty-me, the trouble she does cause! But there's terrible sadness and regret in her; come let me show you."

So, before I was sent on my way to "explore and get to know the lay of the land", I was shown a bedchamber, a room kept as a shrine to Christen Michell's daughter Mary, the Laird's dearly departed wife. A portrait of the young woman looked down from the wall as Bessie held a lantern aloft to display a room in which the drapes were never drawn. Mary had been beautiful, slight and dark haired, but, like my own mother, not strong enough to survive the birth of her child. It was so sad, my eyes swelled with water.

"There, there, Lassie, it's a chance we all take," said Bessie before sending me off outside. And outside I was very glad to be. It was stench-less, not that the castle had been smelly in a bad way, just of food and new wood and smoke from the fire, but given that I was still aware of a hint of the boat journey upon me, the fresh air was most welcome. And outside there were no clouds of sorrow locked away in dark rooms. The day was bright and sparkly, just like the pink exterior of the castle. And I was free to explore all morning. Bessie had recognised my tiredness and the strangeness of the place to me and had done this great kindness. How blessed I was to have come to such a country and to have found such a woman to work for. What a blessing it was also that it was only she that had discovered our secret, and she would help keep it from leaking out any further.

I walked round the castle. The architecture was quite different to what I was used to seeing, but it was obviously modern, well thought out and purposefully built. I noted its huge, heavy studded door, its high strong walls, the many narrow windows and the sheer size of the structure. It dominated the land around it like a giant, the trees of the forest like dwarves gathered to admire the mighty fortress. In among those leafy dwarves I went and found myself in yet another world. It was shady, yes, but greener; so green, I wanted to dance for the beauty and joy of it. There was no one around to see or complain, so I skipped along the winding path between lichen covered branches and trunks. The entry into a faery tale felt complete when I came upon red mushrooms dotted with white. A sitting gnome was easy to imagine. Faeries dancing and singing easier yet. And then: a pool!

The enchanting pool was surrounded by silver stemmed trees. Tiny golden leaves hung around their more coppery branches like precious jewels and were reflected in the water. I crouched beside and wondered if anyone ever came this way. There might be no hot baths in Isobell's future but bathing in this pretty lake would be no hardship. I didn't mind cold. I didn't mind mud. If there were fish or eels I would welcome their dance in my bath.

However, to be observed would be most unfortunate. I would quiz Bessie about the coming and goings of the castle people later, and see if the idea were a possibility. In the meantime, I set off round the banks and continued along the path that led further into the woods. Shortly, I came upon a small house. It was stone built, as if it were a tiny baby of the castle, with the same pink sparkle to its walls. Oh, it was so dear! I could easily imagine living in it, perhaps improving the plain walls by growing flowers up them. Inside would be so cosy, there would be a log fire, a small kitchen and a soft and comfy bed. Lots of wall hangings, not just painted ones but proper tapestries, and many rugs and cushions would furnish the warm little abode.

However, it was somebody's home, so maybe I should not stand in what might be their garden, gawping at their house? I made my way back through the wood, stopping to admire the biggest tree I'd ever seen. The leaves of the ancient oak were just turning for autumn, the brighter green of summer giving way to delicate yellows and oranges. High up, dark against the blue sky, I thought I spied mistletoe boughs. I heard an owl, or what I thought was an owl, and a large shape landed in the tree above, sending a shower of small leaves and twigs down upon me. There were many bird sounds in the wood, little tweets and more aggressive caws and the gentle cooing of a pigeon. And yet it was the quietest, calmest place I'd ever stood in.

It was much less shaded round the back of the castle in the walled garden. There, the intense heat of the autumn sun was gloriously apparent as I bent low to pick some parsley from the herb plot, the only task I had been assigned. It had still been summer when we left London, with all the unpleasant smells that season brought to the city. It would have been different here. Scents of fruit and blossoms would have filled the air, while brightly coloured vegetables were plucked from the earth and carried inside to the huge kitchen table. There were rose bushes and apple trees trained up the walls of the garden, the flowers long past, but small apples and rosehips were still growing rosy and red in the sunshine.

The trifling memory of London was enough to have me hurry round to the back door of the castle and scuttle inside. We might still be followed. We might still be found.

Back in the relative dim and calm of the kitchen, Bessie was finishing the preparation of the broth. She plopped sliced meat into an enormous pot that bubbled over the fire. This we were to eat with barley bread and cheese. She left me at the table while she served the family in the great hall, before returning for her own meal. The broth was salty and delicious; it contained vegetables and herbs and the succulent pieces of meat. It would be my duty to start this soup cooking each morning and to make bannocks over the fire, porridge too when the Laird was home. That would be simple enough to start with, Bessie assured me. Just some chopping and stirring and baking, all tasks which were impossible to get wrong.

The Table

Scrubbing the table with salt was a satisfying task, if hard on the arms. And what a fine piece of furniture it was. Bessie had told the tale of how it came to be: the previous winter, a huge oak, much like the one I'd seen in the woods near the little house, had been taken down by gales at the edge of the forest. The Laird, always full of good ideas, had proclaimed that it must be used for special items in the castle, so after seasoning all summer, his grand court chair had been made and this fine, thick table for the kitchen. Formed of five wide boards of oak, it stood triumphant, eclipsed only in power and size by the fireplace.

Over the fire, the water for broth already heated. A manservant had carried buckets from the well for that, and helped me lift the huge black pot onto its hanging hook. Bessie had explained my work for the morning while she plucked three small chickens, handed in at the door by a tenant farmer as part of his rent. I realised now I had been more interested in hearing about the farmer's wife and their five children, one of whom suffered from permanent sore ears, than in paying attention to the cooking instructions. Bessie had given the man some oil for the child's ears before he left.

What exactly was I to do with a pile of vegetables, soaked grains and three chickens? Well, how difficult could it be? Indeed, Agnes had told me my work would be easy compared to hers: looking after a devil-child. She had come to her bed late the previous night, exhausted almost to the point of passing out, so long had it taken to settle the boy to sleep. I had yet to meet the child, or "wee bairn" as Bessie called him, and was interested to see what he looked like, whether evil could be discerned from outward appearance. Wicked Richard looked quite fair, in a swarthy sort of way. It was his words and facial expressions that revealed him for what he was. And his hands. His grip— But enough of that.

Onions. I cut them into chunks and plopped them into the pot, like I had seen Bessie do with the meat the day before. My eyes smarted and stung, both from the accursed vegetables and the smoke of the fire. Carrots got dealt with too, and then parsnips. I spent some time wiping my eyes. It soon became clear that the vegetable knife was no match for the slimy pink chickens and I located a large bladed implement on a back shelf. It was heavy and hard to hold, but I was sure it would get the job done, although I would need to swing it like a woodsman. Up it went, and down towards the chickens, and then it was stuck fast in the table. Oh no! The beautiful new table. I pulled and pulled, but the blade would not budge.

My eyes watered again. This would be the end of my employment. Bessie had uncovered the secret and gone along with it, but this would be too much. The pride she had shown in the table. The Laird's grand oak tree. I tried pushing the handle of the cutting device, which had by now taken on the look of an executioner's tool, but pushing it in the opposite direction caused a crack to appear in the new wood of the table, and then touching it at all only made the crack grow longer.

"In a bit o' a pickle?" said a man's voice from the doorway.

A young, dark haired man stood there laughing. How infuriating! Who was this impudent wretch, and how dare he laugh at my predicament? So handsome there in his fine clothes, finer than my sacking anyway, and finding humour in the unfortunate dilemmas of those less fortunate than himself?

As if sensing my attitude, he approached in a tentative manner and took hold of the handle. "Let's see if I can help." He pulled. He pushed. "It's stuck fast," he admitted. Eventually, he leant his whole weight on it and the knife was freed from the table, along with a sizeable wedge of wood. This he made merry of again, chuckling and using his foot to free the knife from the triangular segment of oak tree he had removed.

"Dinna worry, quine," he said. "I'll tell Bessie I did it. She's much taken with me; there'll be no trouble."

Then he used the knife, or cleaver as he said it was, to chop the chickens into pieces. My heart warmed. What a fine young man he was. While he worked, he informed me that he was Duncan McCulloch, Greeve of the castle, a title that meant he organised every little thing that needed doing in the building and grounds. He was Christen Michell's nephew. And that was his little house in the woods. I gave him some of Bessie's bannocks and the best bits of cheese and butter I could find, and put the bowl of plums, fresh from the trees of the walled garden, before him.

When Bessie returned from seeing her daughter in the bake house, she found much to be merry about too. "See, Lassie," she said once Duncan had gone, "I telt you you'd learn best on yer own!" She yelled with loud laughter. "You should have peeled the onions though…"

Bessie removed the onion skins before serving the broth to the family in the great hall and we sat and ate our own in the kitchen. And then, a great surprise…

"Good Morrow, fair sister. Good Morrow!"

Jasper and Ian!

I regretted giving Duncan the best bits once I saw those two handsome faces, already losing the palid appearance of the journey, and showing a healthy glow from their outside work. Bessie said we could take another cheese from the larder, though, and all was well, so very well, in the little world of the castle kitchen. Even the letter that Jasper handed me to read, from his friend back home, didn't lessen the joy for more than a moment. So our father and brother and Wicked Richard were angered by our disappearance? That was to be expected. So they were looking for us? They were still in London, so their search was hardly going to be productive, was it? The great fire turned the letter to ashes as I likewise banished it from my mind, instead focusing on the boys' tales of the harvest, or 'hairst' as it was called. Then I sat down at the table and told them my broth woes.

"So," said Jasper, placing his elbows on the table and his fingertips together under his chin, "on your first day in the castle you run amock in the woods, and on the second day you take an axe to the Laird's new table? Bell! What will you do tomorrow, I wonder?"

The Pool

The water was so still, like a looking glass of the clearest and most expensive type. I smiled at my cheeky round face, took off my shoes and stuck a toe in. It was cold, but inviting. Oh, to be properly all-over clean. Bath clean. Pre-voyage clean. Cloths and water had not removed the remnants of the boat to my satisfaction; it would be sublime to know that my body was cleansed entirely of it. The morning was yet new, the sun not properly up, and Duncan, the only other person to walk by the pool on a regular basis, was already safely within the sparkly pink walls of the castle.

I looked round in all directions and strained my ears to hear. No footsteps. No people. Only the birds, and they were naked as the day they had hatched and would care not if I were too. Off came my clothes, and quick as a duck, I stepped into the water. The cold was greater than anticipated − it had a bitter bite − but I waded into the deep, bent my knees and bobbed there, feeling twigs and branches under my feet as my skin adjusted to the new temperature. I stretched out my arms and floated for a moment before tipping my head back and soaking my hair.

There was a bang in the distance, probably just the castle door, but still, I scrambled out of the pool and into my clothes, and wrung my hair out as best I could. It would dry while I prepared the broth. I ran back along the path through tweety, birdy, mossy Faeryland, and into the kitchen where my hair absorbed the smell of (peeled) onions and smoke.

I managed much better than the previous morning. No parts of the table got removed and I made a batch of bannocks that were only black on one side. Duncan said they were good when he visited to see how things were going in the kitchen. Bessie found some hilarity in that, but I was quickly learning that she had a powerful and loud sense of humour to go with her good heart, and a habit of seeing comedy where others did not.

I was permitted to help serve in the great hall, and so met Christen Michell, a forbidding looking woman dressed all in black and wearing an old fashioned headdress, and Wee Thomas, the Laird's son, who looked very small and sweet and not devilish at all. I curtseyed to them. Christen Michell appreciated that, Bessie told me later. The little boy seemed interested in the curtsey, until Agnes began pulling at him and trying to persuade him to eat. He didn't look very happy, and I said as much to Bessie back in the kitchen.

"You notice such things too, Isobell, like me. I'm sure Agnes pinches him out of spite but I've yet to catch her in the act. When I do, I will be telling the Laird. Noo, tell me aboot yer brother, yer twin. I thought *you* were well-spoken, but he's something else altogether! What's with the funcy talk and strange wee speeches? 'Yea, from the table of my memory'? I've never heard the like."

"Oh, Jasper and Ian are actors in the Theatre; those are words from a play they were in, and he was making fun of..." I indicated the hole in the table edge. "Will the Laird be very angry, do you think?"

"Ach, no. Dinna worry yersel aboot that. This is a working table; you just made the first mark of toil on it. There'll be many more."

There were. The very next day I laid a hot pot of stewed kale upon the table, which seared a deep black ring into the beautiful wood. Duncan said it was decorative, and Bessie laughed her marvellous laugh.

So the days found rhythm. They usually started and ended with a tale of wrongdoing from Agnes in our shared room. There were dairymaids who'd got themselves in trouble and ended up destitute, farmers who'd lost all their money and ultimately their farms and families too, and then Agnes's favourite: women accused of witchcraft; one from Perth was even to be examined by the king himself. These most evil of people were usually burnt till there was nothing left of them. In the end, all the stories had the same moral: everybody was wicked and deserving of their bad fortune, except Agnes. And me. Maybe me. She knew I had met Duncan and did not seem pleased for the fact. She told me she knew the truth of how the table got damaged, Duncan being a very dear friend of hers. So, maybe not me.

Most mornings I found time to visit the pool, or Castle Loch, as Bessie said it was called. I loved its ever changing appearance and feel; some days there were little lapping waves and the water took on a blue colour like the sky, other times tiny yellow leaves swirled here and there around me. When rain fell, all went dark in the depths, and circles blossomed all over the surface. I loved to completely submerge and watch the storm from below, from the calm of the pool floor, the raindrops causing small explosions in the water.

"Best watch yersel, Quinie," warned Bessie, who seemed to have discerned the direction of my walks. "There'll be frost soon. It'll be affa bonny, but most affa cold. Ye'll be the colour o' yer fine blue gown!" Her chuckle resounded round the white painted walls of the kitchen.

I got better at making bannocks, though they still often burned while I stirred the broth pot. Oat cakes were worse still. They earned me a, "'Tis burnt; and so is all the meat. Where is the rascal cook?" from Ian, thinking he was being terribly clever. He ate some with strawberry preserve from the summer and said it tasted well enough though.

Wee Thomas danced into the kitchen one day and readily accepted a bannock with butter and berry preserve. He smiled up at me, red all round his mouth, a halo of soft and fair hair round his face, before Agnes came running in, shrieking that sweet foods were not good for him and he was a bad boy for taking it. Later, in our room, she explained her behaviour as being the fault of Wee Thomas and his evil ways. He had to be kept in check. Sugar made him more devilish than ever. I found myself siding with Bessie on the subject and said nothing.

The Bear

I was actually standing in a faery tale. White mist swirled around the surface of the pool like magic about to take form. There was absolutely no chance of being seen in such conditions, so I flung my clothes down on the damp bank and waded in. Feeling especially daring, I pulled myself up onto the large, flat topped stone that lay to one side of the loch. But it was cold up in the air with the floating clouds of icy fog, so I soon slipped back into the water for a final swim and a little bit of a sing.

I'd noticed before that the birds went quiet when I sang, but this time they did not start again on the cessation of song. I sank soundlessly below the surface in case I had scared them with my splashing and diving. Let them open their lungs again. Let their call make music in the forest. All was still under the water; there was only the roar of my own blood pumping through my body, only light above.

I peeked out, letting naught but my eyes raise above water level. Still silent. Well, if the birds were sulking with me, I'd give them something to be frightened of. Back below the water, I swam over to the rock and then sprang out onto it, whipping my head back, water flying from my hair. It felt so delightful, so free, that I laughed, the sound almost competing with Bessie's full chuckles.

Straightening up, I began to wring my hair out and looked through the mist to where a big brown shape stood on the bank. It was vast and hairy and misshapen. Mist continued to travel around the loch, preventing me from getting a proper look at the creature but its eyes were wide: wide and wild. A bear!

I landed in the loch with a splash and crouched on the muddy floor. Would it go away and leave me alone if I waited long enough? Or would it bide its time and eat me when I emerged? Maybe it had already eaten. I held on until it felt as if my lungs would burst and then tipped my head back so only my nose and mouth came out to breathe. Nothing happened. All seemed quiet. Eyes and ears out. Nothing happened. All was still. Head properly out, looking all around, I could find no trace of the bear.

I'd never dressed so quickly. But where to go? What to do? Should I climb a tree? I stood very still and listened. Was that a sound up the castle path? Had it gone that way? The walls of the great building were strong; its occupants would be safe, and no doubt more used to bears than I. Why had no one warned me? 'Watch out to not get eaten by a bear,' would have been wise advice. I planned to have words with both Bessie and Agnes. Agnes especially, always full of tales of others' errant ways, and her knowing of everything that went on around the castle, could have spared a few breaths to speak of carnivorous wildlife in the woods. Had none of the naughty farmers or fallen dairymaids ever been chased by a bear? None of the witches transformed themselves into one?

Anger gave me power to walk, to walk towards the castle, even with the risk of bears and who knew what else? Wolves? Dragons? Unicorns? That last would be rather nice; I could imagine myself atop a pretty white unicorn riding sedately through the forest.

Bessie was the first person I encountered upon entering the castle and I quickly availed her of my adventure, while standing by the fire. She didn't seem to treat the situation with the appropriate level of gravitas at all; in fact it appeared as if she were holding in one of her wonderful laughs.

I looked up as someone else entered the kitchen, a highly unusual occurrence at that time of the morning, and then I stared. Before me, in a loose necked white shirt, drying his face on a cloth, was the most beautiful man I had ever seen. No, not the most beautiful man, the most beautiful anything I had ever set eyes on. What made him so was hard to discern; his face was pinkened from removing his beard; I recognised the symptoms from when I had seen Jasper do the same. His hair was light like mine and wee Thomas's. He was tall and broad, a man of muscle and hard work, but he gave off some sort of radiance that filled the kitchen with light. He was like a biblical vision appeared before the fire, the salt of the earth and the light of the world, all rolled into one. I discerned a subtle and wholesome aroma, like that of the ripening oats up at the farm when the autumn sun hit them full force. And his eyes, well his eyes were—

I clapped my hand over my mouth in a mixture of shock, horror and embarrassment.

"Now," said Bessie in a stern voice, "there'll be no more talk of bears or mermaids from anyone. It's been a long time since either creature has been seen in these parts." A tiny part of her laugh leaked out. "Isobell, you get some porridge put on for the Laird, who's just come home. This is my new kitchen maid, who likes to walk in the woods," she told the Laird, for that was who he plainly was. To me she said, "And this is your employer, Thomas Manteith, the third Laird o' the castle, who has just come home, through the woods."

There was only one thing I could do. I dropped into a deep curtsey, so deep it hid my face, so deep I nearly fell over, and said, "My Lord."

He mumbled something about there being no need for such an action and took his leave of the room. His voice had been deep. His face had been young, so much younger than I expected a Laird's to be, but his eyes had been wild.

My cheeks were on fire; I could have cooked the broth on them.

"Oats," said Bessie. "Best get them bubbling. You could go and fetch some cream too, from the dairy. He likes that, and he's had a bit o' a scare this morning." Her mirth was finally set free. "Oh Lassie," she said, between howls. "Dinna worry. Nobody's ever bin pulled up in front o' the court for being naked in the forest!" She sobered as she looked at me. "Ach, it was misty, I'm sure he didna even get a clear view. And you thought he was a bear!" Peals of laughter rang out again.

I made the Laird's porridge. I didn't burn it. Bessie served it to him through in the great hall. My burning face and I stayed in the kitchen.

The Stones

Despite managing to avoid meeting the Laird again on his brief visit home, there was no escaping mention of him. Duncan was delighted that court was to be held and various local disputes were to be, it would seem almost magically, resolved. Jasper was beside himself in admiration for the man too, the Laird having been up to the farm after breakfast.

"He travels to London sometimes. He's attended the Theatre. He doesn't think I was there that day, or he would've remembered me, he said. Oh, Bell, he's a very fine gentleman, most cultured for a man of only twenty-four years. He's not high and mighty with it though; he mucked in and helped out with the hairst today. But what is this awkwardness I sense? What ails you, sister?"

I could see he couldn't decide on horror or humour for a moment after the telling of my story. "He thought you a mermaid?"

"So Bessie says."

"Ha!" Humour won. "You must take the best from this, Bell. You're lucky he didn't take you for a whale in a wig!"

Bessie did not join him in laughter. "That's quite enough out of you, young Jasper, I'm sure Isobell made a very fine sight. The Laird wisna horrified, in fact if anything... well, he was surprised to see a magical creature leap from the water."

"I just meant with the mist," my twin assured us. "He probably only saw a vague watery shape with golden hair."

"Aye, well you've got work to be doing, I'm sure."

27

And so Jasper was dismissed and I turned back to the preparations for the main meal of the day. We were all to sit in the great hall with the family, with the Laird. It should have been exciting and thrilling. Instead I bent my head in steamy shame over the muckle pot. At least I could do this one thing right, at least I could make sure the grains did not stick to the bottom and burn, as so often happened when I was in charge of the broth.

"Here ye go, Lassie," said Bessie, handing me a cloth-wrapped parcel. "I've been thinking it's wrong how you never have any time off, and there's places you might like, other than that loch." She gave me a long look. "Aye, you take this food and have yerself a wee break. Come on noo, let me show you."

She led me round the side of the castle and then pointed toward the thickest part of the forest where I had never wandered, having been so taken with the pool. A narrow path was just visible between thick trunks and hanging branches. I started to thank her for the reprieve, but she shooed me away towards the trees and hurried back inside.

The pathway was much less dark than I had expected; in fact it seemed to glow with a green-silver sort of light, brighter in places where the trees thinned at the top. Underfoot was mossy with little stones in quite a number, as if a proper walkway had been made long ago but greened over by nature.

The trail led uphill but felt easy, light; my feet wanted to go this way. Quite suddenly, but with no surprise, as it felt like I had known I was coming to it, I stepped out into the golden light of a wide glade. I knew I was on top of a hill and I knew I was looking at the most perfect sight of my life, this morning in the kitchen excepted.

It was as if God had looked down and thought to himself, 'What would be beautiful there on that hillside? I know, I'll just take these stones…' For they were huge and they were ancient, and though men must have put them there, their guidance had been Divine. They were tall menhirs, like the London Stone in Candlewick Street, said to have been raised by Brutus himself when he founded Britain, but the arrangement and situation of these stones made them so different, so sacred.

It was too soon to step within the circle, I sensed that. I had to grow used to them; they had to accept me in. I laid my food parcel down on the ground and, head bent in reverence, walked the outer ring, through the long grass, feeling my skirt grow damp. As I came to each stone, I stopped to lay a hand on, to meet and greet, as it were. Two hands were required for the enormous boulder that was secured between the two tallest stones. How had anyone lifted it? Maybe it had always been there. It mattered not. All was perfect in the circle of stone.

Finally it was time to set foot inside and there was an instant change in atmosphere as I did so. I had to dance. And sing. Round and round I went, respectful behaviour having been banished from the place; all I could express was joy. I leapt onto a fallen stone, even it seemed harmoniously placed, reminding me a little of the sitting rock in the pool and I laughed about that too. In the larger journey of life, what was one 'mistaken for a mermaid' incident? How could it trouble anyone for long?

I sat down on the stone; it felt warm, as the sun filtered gently through the thinning mist, making the circle glow and smile, or so it seemed. I ate my package of barley bread and soft cheese and a perfect apple from the perfect orchard behind the castle. How blessed was I? How fortunate? I could have been a beaten wife by now, waiting on a wicked husband. Instead I was here, in Scotland, among beautiful stones and men and food and sunshine, and my life was as good as any life could ever be.

I stayed many hours there, mainly lying on the flat stone but also exploring, noting how the day's mist hung above and around the circle but the air between the stones felt warm and dry. I wanted to paint it. What a backdrop it would make for one of Jasper's plays.

I curtseyed to the stone circle before I left, and as I skipped back down the forest path, I knew I could cope with anything, with everything that was coming, and that all would be well in the end.

The Elfin Blade

The glow of happiness from the circle spread out like a raindrop fallen in the pool, and pleasant events kept happening for the rest of the day. In the evening, Jasper visited the kitchen in a contrite mood. I knew he had meant nothing mean-spirited by his earlier whale comment, but he had made me a corn dolly, shaped a little like a mermaid, "A beautiful Mermaid," as he was keen to stress to Bessie.

"Aye well, that is affa bonny," she conceded and put a bannock and some cold meat before him. She also gave him a tiny pot of ointment for his harvest blisters and all was cosy and good round the oaken table of the kitchen.

Bessie informed me that the Laird was only spending one night at home. He would be leaving at the break of dawn on business, so I would not face the embarrassment of meeting him again soon.

Duncan commented that he would be happy to show me round his house if I fancied to walk that way in the forest when he was at home. And no bitterness poured out of Agnes that night as we prepared for bed in our small room; in fact she was uncommonly soft spoken, merely asking after my day, remarking on the fact that I had now met the Laird too, and then telling me how he had talked to her most kindly when he came to see Wee Thomas.

I drifted off to sleep in a mist of dreamy happiness, only to wake again after what felt like a short while. Someone had spoken. Someone had said something foul. They had said that Mermaid was a word for whore. Which it was. I had heard it used to describe Queen Elizabeth by John and his drinking friends when they were speaking in a most uncouth way of her. Wicked Richard! Was he here? My eyes searched the darkness. My ears strained to hear, but there was only the sound of Agnes's deep breathing. The air of the castle was still, undisturbed by bad men. So I had dreamt the voice and the words.

I lay awake for a long time, twitching alert at every little creak, imagined or otherwise, and woke bleary eyed and tired from it all in the morning. Agnes was up and gone long before me. I found my clothes and my shoes and then… oh! My shoe bit me! Really bit me. My heel was wet with blood. I hobbled out into the passageway and through to the better light of the kitchen to discern what had happened. I sat on the bench and examined my cut heel and then my shoe, and was totally mystified.

There was something in my shoe. Was it a strange insect? Or some sort of plant, like a fierce stinging nettle? But no, it was hard and sharp and pointed, and it seemed to be a thin stone, stuck fast into the lining of the sole.

"Fit's a do, quiney?" asked Bessie, coming into the kitchen.

"I really don't know," I told her. "I've cut my foot on something in my shoe."

She took the shoe and squinted into it. "Well, well," she said. "It's a long time since I've seen one of these."

"One of what? What is it Bessie?" Had I, indeed, been bitten by some exotic form of bed bug? One with a hard shell perhaps?

"It's an elfin blade," she said. "An arrow said to fall from the sky, used by faery folk to harm cattle. So they say." And she plucked it from the shoe. "I dinna think it was a faery who set it upright in wax for you to step on Isobell, do you?"

She held out the misused footwear for me to see where a circle of thick red wax had held the blade in place. It made me think of how a seal looked on a letter. A letter with information about John and Richard. And my fear in the night. And the words I had heard. Mayhap that had not been a dream after all. I had thought there could be bad men in the castle at that moment and I babbled the information out to Bessie who shook her head at the idea.

"If such as them had arrived, I doubt this would be their way of announcing themselves. No, I think you can look within the existing household of the castle to find the mischief maker. But firstly, we need to treat you. You've been elf shot."

The treatment for being shot with an elfin blade was tea made from pointed leaves, shaped like arrows themselves. Feverfew went into the brew and some other herbs I did not know. It was bitter. But not as bitter as my thoughts as I tried to think who could have done this to me. Indeed, there were not many contenders; I had met so few people at the castle as yet, and no one seemed very likely.

"What did you and Agnes talk about last night as you prepared for bed?" asked Bessie as she doused my foot in the same tea. It stung.

"Oh, just about how I had met the Laird and—"

"The manner of the meeting?"

"Oh. No. I did not tell her of that."

"You did not need to."

"You mean people already know?" I said, flushing.

"In a place like this, aye," said Bessie. "Of course they know. And you know who is most interested in devilish and witchful ways hereabouts?"

"Oh Bessie, it cannot have been Agnes. The two of us are becoming friends."

"I hope that's true, Bell. Two young quines like yourselves should be friends, looking out for each other in this world. Agnes didna have an easy childhood. I ken you didna either, but yours was helped by having a twin on your side." Bessie thought for a moment, rubbing the elf arrow between her finger and thumb. "I mind a case, many years back, when Janet was just a wee lassie, where a woman made two clay images of people she wanted to kill and shot arrows like this at them. It is well known throughout Scotland. But you watch the folk of this place today, Bell. See who looks to see if you've been hurt. And who disna turn an eye to notice anything."

Bessie bandaged my foot with some feverfew in among the cloth and told me how some fine ladies paid many a penny for elf arrows and had them set in silver to use as a charm against evil.

"Do they really fall from the sky?" I asked, thinking it seemed an unlikely event.

"They look to me like things as has been carved," said Bessie, rubbing the small blade with her fingers again. "Something old and not understood. But you've your own mystery to solve today, Lassie. Look sharp and put your shoe on, here comes Duncan." And the elf arrow disappeared into Bessie skirts.

The Love Cakes

Duncan had nothing to do with the elf arrow whatsoever. I knew this in my heart without seeing how absolutely normal and everyday he behaved with me in the kitchen, more interested in seeking a bannock than looking to see if I had sustained an injury. After Duncan, various maids, bake house people, manservants and more appeared in the kitchen. They were all busy with their work, not one of them wondering if their blade had found its mark. My morning did not go well. Tiredness and mystery combined to create a nasty and confused atmosphere in the kitchen as I looked with suspicion at all who entered. I burnt the bannocks, spilt hot broth on my hand and cut my finger with the vegetable knife.

I thought back to the previous day, looking for clues there as well. Agnes, of course, had actually been full of a new story at bedtime, but it was one she was not going to tell me, and Duncan had probably already been a recipient of it when he invited me to his house. Had he been alluding to the fact that I sometimes walked in the woods? Was he under the belief that I paraded about naked between the trees, or some other nonsensical exaggeration? And he thought this would make me an amenable and delightful visitor to his home? The thought was enraging, and so it was that I was already angry when Agnes and Wee Thomas came into the kitchen in the late morning, an unusual event in itself.

"And how are you today, Isobell?" asked Agnes as she scrutinised me, giving especial attention to my feet.

I was so angry I could not speak. I just glared back at her and it was only Wee Thomas's demands for berry preserve that broke the stare. I spread the sugary preserve on the least burnt bannock for him, mentally daring Agnes to naysay it. But she didn't, too interested was she in me for that.

I ignored her and spoke to the wee boy instead. "What have you been up to today, Thomas?"

"Playing my drum that faether brung me," he told me with a wide fruity smile. "Agnes disna like it."

"It's always good to make music," I said.

"Aye, well, we'd better let Isobell alone," said Agnes. "She has much work ahead of her to prepare our meal for us."

And they went, Agnes looking back for one more examination as she walked away.

"It was Agnes," I told Bessie when she came back with the bread for the meal.

"Aye," she said, showing no surprise at all. "But we're going to treat this with honey, nae spite."

"What?" I said, feeling the pain in my foot, and having been quite looking forward to Agnes being in trouble for it.

"Let's make a batch of honey cakes," said Bessie. "And we'll put all the best bits in them: raisins and cinnamon, rare spices from the locked pantry even." She jangled her keys.

It was pleasant work, the mixing and the scent of the food stuffs, but: "Are these to be for Agnes?"

"Nae just Agnes. These are love cakes. You can give them to Jasper and Ian, Duncan too, if you've a mind. What a shame the Laird is not home." Bessie filled the kitchen with one of her large laughs. "Look." She took the mixing spoon from me. "With every fold over of the mix, think on things you love, people you love. Ask God to bless them all. It all goes in, all gets soaked up by the fruit and the honey and the sugar and spice. And then the fire of the oven sets it fast. Whoever eats it will feel it. Works the other way round too; you dinna want to go eating the broth I make if I'm in a temper!"

Later in the day I took cakes up to the farm for Jasper and Ian, and ate one there myself, sat in a fragrant pile of fresh straw with them. We reminisced about our lives in London, for though there had been much unhappiness there, Jasper and myself being disdained and disrespected often in our own house, there had been joy and love too. We recalled the fun we had had, at the Theatre, and even sometimes in our home when it was just the three of us there, talking, singing and telling stories.

Back in the kitchen, I insisted that Bessie sit down and enjoy a cake, and ate another one myself then too. They were a rare and delicious treat that put you in mind of summer skies and butterflies and the prettiest of flowers and Scottish lochs, and even bears. Bessie remembered how bonny and sweet a bairn Janet had been when she was wee and then, like a young girl herself, she fair skipped off to the bake house to give her daughter a cake.

But now: the great test. The reason for the cakes' making. Would they re-forge the friendship between Agnes and myself? I was not sure how it had gone sour. Bessie believed Agnes felt threatened, unaccustomed as she was to having another lassie her age so close by. I laid the best looking cake from the batch on Agnes's bed and climbed into my own, leaving the candle on so the gift would be seen.

It seemed a long time until Agnes appeared but I, belly full from cake, amused myself with thoughts of how happy together we all were in the castle. And now Agnes and I would be reconciled, the strange elf arrow put behind us, no need to mention it even.

She walked in.

I smiled.

She stopped. She pointed at the cake on her bed. "What is that?"

"It's for you, Agnes, a gift; the best of the cakes we made today, and a hope that we can be firm friends."

"You and Bessie Thom made this? Together? For me?" she asked, picking up the cake.

I nodded.

Agnes took the cake and held it in front of my face. Then she crushed it in her fist. It broke between her fingers and fell all in crumbles and raisins about the floor.

"I'll nae be enchanted by your witches' pie!" she shouted. "You winna get me that way!"

The Quines' Fight

"Agnes, no!" I said, horrified by her assumption. "It's just a cake. We've all been eating them today. We've given them to Jasper and Ian, and Janet too. How can you see witchcraft in a cake?"

"Why are you saying you want us to be friends?" she demanded. "Are we not friends already?"

"Maybe not as good as we should be."

"And who told you that? Who has been saying things about me?"

I tried to think what to say. Without mentioning the elf arrow, it was difficult, and so I was not quick enough.

"Bessie Thom, that's who!" shrieked Agnes. "Oh you dinna want to go listening to her, Isobell. Or telling her things either. Did she give you an enchanted drink when you first got here? To get all your secrets out from inside you?"

"No! Bessie has been nothing but a good friend to me."

"Is that right? It's well kent in these parts that she murdered her husband! Poisoned him to death with one of her witch's brews."

"Agnes, what nonsense. If she had done such a thing she wouldn't be here. She would have stood trial and—"

"No! No!" Agnes's eye's had gone wide, her whole face frenzied and strange. "That's nae fit happens aroon Bessie Thom. She gets everyone twisted round to her way of thinking, gets you all running about doing her bidding. And now she's got it in for me!"

"Agnes," I said, getting up out of the bed, wanting to calm her. "That's not what's going on at all. These are 'love cakes'; they're the very opposite of anything bad."

"Love cakes? So you put a spell in them?" And she made to punch me in the throat, which was a great mistake.

I may have seemed sweet and mild and tender to people when they met me – indeed I was those things at most times – but I had grown up in a house with brothers, one of them rather a rogue, and I could stand my own in a fight, especially a fight with a wee bit of a girl like Agnes who really didn't know how to throw a punch. I caught her fist in my hand before it connected with my neck and then I twisted her arm round behind her. I kicked her legs out from under her and sat on her back.

However, Agnes had some learning of her own, maybe from other fights with girls. She managed to reach round and grab my hair and that did hurt something awful. My grip on her arm weakened for a moment and she spun, scratching at my face. I went for her neck, not as she had done, with a weak and easy to block punch, but with the outside of my hand, used like a cleaving knife on meat, brought down fast and hard.

And then we were pulled apart. I was lifted right off Agnes and back up onto my feet. Agnes continued to lie upon the floor, breathless from the cleaver style attack. I resisted the urge to put my foot on her neck as John would have done in such a situation if it had been me on the ground.

"You twa!" said Bessie Thom, the finisher of the fight. "Fit's all this about?"

"Agnes did not much like the cake we made for her," I said.

Agnes just glared from the floor, her hand upon her neck.

"You quines will be friends yet," said Bessie, serious determination detectable in her voice. "Come with me to the kitchen and be quick smart about it."

We two followed, neither looking at nor speaking to one another. Bessie sent me to a back room to fetch two pails and two brushes which Agnes was then ordered to fill with water.

"A bucket and brush each," said Bessie and I knew she was holding in a laugh as we followed her through the great hall and out into the entrance hall. "You'll start at the bottom here," she said, pointing at the stone steps of the tower. "And you'll go all the way up. I'll be looking in on you to check, so nae mair fighting. And if you're not friends by the time you get to the top, you start there and come all the way back down again, clean step by clean step. You can go up and doon all night if you want."

It was unpleasant work, very quickly making the hands wet and cold and sore, and the arms ache. Neither of us was used to it. But we were quiet and we ignored each other.

There was only the sound of brushes, scrubby, scrubby, scrubby, as we pushed them back and forth on the steps.

This was all Agnes's fault. She had started the quarrel, and not even with her anger about the cake and her punch, but with the elf arrow in the very beginning. I felt like swinging the heavy wooden brush and knocking Agnes down the steps with it, so enraged was I. She was already being punished of course, but then so was I. The unfairness of it!

"I dinna believe this!"

We both turned, Agnes and I, to see Duncan on the steps below us. His face was full of mirth, the situation obviously giving him great entertainment. I threw my brush at him but he dodged it and laughed.

"You've not been fighting over me, have ye lassies?"

"Why would we fight over a glaiket whore like you?" shouted Agnes.

I had no idea what glaiket meant but it did put me in mind of the curses and bad calling of folk that got put into plays. So I joined in. "A knotty-pated fool such as you is of no interest to us!"

"Fit?" said Duncan, clearly not understanding my words.

"Oh, away and boil yer thick heid!" Agnes told him.

"Quines, quines," he replied. "You need to calm doon." He held his arms out wide. "There's plenty of me to go aroon."

Oh the cheek! Agnes flung the water from her pail in his direction and he backed away down the stairs.

"Away with you," I shouted. "You poisonous bunch backed toad!"

Duncan's retreat was all of a sudden so hilarious that we did roar with laughter, there in the wet and the cold of the tower, until a door, someway further up, opened and Christen Michell entered into the scene.

"What is with all this collieshangie?" she demanded and it was quite the funniest word I had ever heard. If I ever met Master Shakespeare again, I would have to tell him of it.

"We are just finishing up a task for Bessie Thom," said Agnes, herself struggling not to laugh, I could see.

"Well, be quick and quiet about it," advised the old lady before disappearing into her room again.

As soon as the door closed, we both fell about laughing again, but in a more held in way which threatened to explode now and again.

"I think we've finished," I said to Agnes, holding out my hand to her.

"Aye, I think we have," she said, taking my hand.

"What does collieshangie mean?" I asked as we gathered our buckets and brushes.

"Oh, ye ken: noise, uproar," she said and we ran down the stairs, slipping and sliding some of the way, in an effort not to let Christen Michell hear our laughter.

So that is how Agnes and I became fast friends. For about twelve hours.

The Scream

The new day was as good as the previous day had been bad. Agnes and I said kind words to each other in our bed chamber, before parting ways to go to our own work. She hoped the broth didn't burn and I wished for Wee Thomas to be happy and good.

Through in the kitchen, as I started the broth off and got the bannocks going, I wondered if I should take it as a compliment that Agnes saw me as such a threat that she had taken to cursing me with a magical arrow.

"Well," said Bessie, on being told of the thought. "If it helps you feel friendly towards one another, I suppose you could think of it that way. But you're a bonny quine, Isobell. Agnes kens it; so should you."

Duncan peeked a sheepish face round the door mid-morning. "Is it safe for me to come in?" he asked.

"I reckon it is," I said. "You are maybe not quite as bunch backed a toad as I said last night."

"Aye, well, I shouldn't have been so cheeky. Agnes is nae speaking to me at all."

So I gave him a bannock and some cheese. And then I gave the same to Wee Thomas and Agnes when they came through.

"I dinna want cheese," said the wee boy, his eyes very bright and wide. "I want strawberry preserve."

"No sugar," said Agnes. "He's wild this morning."

"Ah, but this is magical cheese," I told him, slicing it thin and laying it out in a circle on top of the bannock. "It'll make you really strong."

He took a bite but was off again at once, unable to sit still or be quiet, running away back through to the great hall, banging his drum.

"Oh my heid!" said Agnes, shaking her head and following him.

I sliced the ham to go with the broth. I looked out the bowls and the spoons. And decided my lot was really quite good. I might be only a kitchen maid but there was kindness and friendship in my life. There was no more brutality, no more daily disdain from my father or John. The only sour note was the recent elfin blade incident, and that was all surely over now. The cut on my foot was healing fast.

A loud scream cut through my thoughts; it held such a note of anguish and sorrow and pain that my heart leapt in my chest. I rushed to the door of the kitchen and met Bessie running the same way. The sound had come from the great hall, and we both ran the curving passageway to the vast room to discover Agnes holding the drum high in the air and Wee Thomas crying and wailing and stamping his feet.

"He bit me!" shrieked Agnes. "He bit my hand!"

"Is that the drum his father gave him?" demanded Bessie. "Did you take it fae him?"

"Well, he canna beat it all day, it's worse than the dancing, and that was bad enough," said Agnes. "It's givin' me a sore heid. And now ma hand." She held out the injured part, which looked to have no injury at all.

But to me there was something strange and wrong about the scene, and something strange and familiar about the look of Wee Thomas. I knelt down beside him and took his hands, which were hot, in mine. He stopped crying but swayed on his feet. "Bessie," I said in concern, and we both carried him to the bench by the long table.

"Makin' a fuss o' him winna help," started Agnes, only to be whisht at by Bessie.

"He's fevered," said Bessie.

"Look at his face," I added. "So sudden a change since he was through in the kitchen. Flushed all over, white round the mouth. I remember Jasper looking like this when we were little and we both had Scarlatina." I stopped. Jasper had nearly died and Wee Thomas looked worse even than my brother had. There was a slimy greyness to his skin that seemed to warn of a young life slipping away.

"Bell," moaned Wee Thomas and held his arms out to me. How he'd come to learn my brother's name for me on so small an acquaintance I didn't know, but I took him onto my lap there on the bench and rocked him to and fro, humming a lulling song I remembered from childhood.

"Maybe he's been bewitched," said Agnes.

"Ach, away with your nonsense," scoffed Bessie. "Go fetch Christen Michell till we see what's to be done."

By the time his grandmother arrived in the room, Wee Thomas was fast asleep in my arms.

Bessie wiped his face with a damp cloth. "It could be Scarlatina, Mistress," she explained to the old lady. "I've checked, and he does have an angry rash on his belly. The doctor should be summoned, but I would like your permission to treat him also."

"Aye," said Christen Michell at once, sitting down beside us and touching the little boy's face and damp hair. "He's burning up. I cannot lose another one, Bessie. First my husband, then my daughter; not Wee Thomas as well." She crossed her breast as she spoke, then fingered a bejewelled golden cross that hung about her neck. "I'll send word to Father Daniel for a Mass to be said for him. We will all do what we can."

Bessie and Christen Michell decided it all between them. Messages were sent to the doctor, the priest and to the Laird to come home. The latter was some distance away, so getting the letter sent out to him quickly was of great urgency. Bessie suggested that I should be the one to stay with and care for Wee Thomas up in his nursery, a room halfway up the tower.

"She's a natural way with him," Bessie told Christen Michell. "He likes her and she was the one to notice he was ill; she recognised the malady at once, having suffered from it herself as a wee lassie."

The older woman nodded. "Well then, Agnes can go to the kitchen."

The Illness

I listened to the wee boy's breathing as it rasped and dragged like a saw through rough wood, but at least he still had breath. Bessie came with fragrant oils for his chest and bitter herbs for him to drink; at first he would have none but I administered them with gentle songs and then he fell into fitful spates of sleep as if he were full of bad dreams. He called for his mother twice; something that surprised and saddened me, for he had never known her.

I comforted him as best I could and knelt by his bed and prayed. It was all that was left to do. The doctor had left a bottle of what smelt like poison which had done nothing but make the boy vomit. Bessie's herbal draughts calmed him, though he still sweated and burned with the fever. So I prayed. I begged God to spare the small child's life, to let him have a happy time on earth out in the sunshine. I would take him for walks by the pool with no thought of my own embarrassment, for what a trifling nothing being mistaken for a mermaid seemed, when death wavered by the door. We would also go up to the circle of stones when he was better. This I promised God. I would feed Wee Thomas the best of any food to be found in the castle; he was small and frail and thin, maybe taking after his mother. I would do my best to remedy that, once he was able to eat again. And let the Laird return home soon, I prayed. I knew he had been far away, but surely he would ride at full speed to see his son? It would certainly help the boy, perhaps even raise him from his fever, to know his father was there.

I pushed back on my arms against the bed, back stiff from so long kneeling, to find Christen Michell standing in the room observing me.

She nodded in approval and, with some difficulty and stiffness of her own, got down on her knees in her black gown beside me. She took my hand and we prayed together, as equals on the floor before God. Father Daniel, an elderly, and somehow vaguely familiar priest, came and said a blessing over the child. In Latin. This all seemed rather odd, but I was too exhausted to analyse or think such things through. Bessie dosed me too, with strengthening drinks and fortifying flowers from the walled garden.

The room quickly became the whole world, the entirety of existence, the little boy's life entwined with my own. Sometimes as I dozed by his bedside it felt that there was another presence in the room and that his breathing grew more even when it was there. Was it the Laird, returned at last? But no, in my dozing state I saw an image of his beautiful, dark haired mother cradling him, lifting him. Not to Heaven! Not yet! I jerked awake. But he was still with us, still the same, hot and restless and suffering.

Christen Michell brought a bit of dry bread, Panis Benedictus she said it was. She soaked it in a little wine and I fed it to him when he roused enough to take it. This pleased her; it brought her some relief, I could see that.

I took to singing whenever he was awake, he seemed comforted by that, and we all needed comfort; it was what we longed for during those long, long nights and days that were filled with the dread of losing the wee boy. I sang songs from Jasper's plays, and songs my own nurse had sung to me, and some that I invented as I went along, of unicorns and faeries and a magical pool and enchanted stones placed on the earth by God to gladden our hearts and fill our souls with His love.

"I want to see the stones." He'd spoken. Wee Thomas had spoken. He spoke again: "I'm most affa hungry."

His forehead was cool and his eyes clear, and soon he had some dry bread and broth which he ate with the most wondrous eagerness.

"I want Bell's preserve, the strawberry one."

We all laughed, us three women together, for the joy and relief of it. We grasped hands and gave thanks that this healing had come to pass. Agnes appeared for the first time to see how the patient was faring, but

Christen Michell sent her back to the kitchen at once, which did leave me feeling uneasy, although there was no time to dwell on the situation as my little charge grew stronger and chattier each day. We enjoyed songs and stories together with pictures that I drew; Jasper delivered some parchment and charcoal and soon we had a collection of horses and knights. Wee Thomas's favourite tales were of King Arthur and his companions. I told him all about the Spanish Armada and the fire ships, and other stories of kings and queens of old, but always he wanted to return to Arthur. The idea of the sword in the stone intrigued him most of all.

The news of the young master's recovery travelled around the castle and surrounding farms, and Wee Thomas was sent the best everyone could give him. He ate the cheek of a pig, the largest goose eggs and the first cream of the day's milking in his porridge. Bessie took nuts and dried fruits from the special store and these were ground and added to his meals. It was not long before his face took on a new roundedness and glow and we all smiled again, full of gratitude and joy.

Duncan delivered a wooden sword and shield, painted up with unicorns like the family crest; many people had lent a hand to the making of these, and their new owner was much thrilled with the pieces, and excited to be well enough to play with them outside.

He wanted me with him all the time so a small bed was moved into his room. "It can be shifted through there," said Christen Michell, indicating the adjoining room, "once he is fully recovered. Bessie has informed me that you are a learned young woman, capable of providing a level of education and care that Agnes could not," she added, lifting one of our story etchings to study. "You will accept the position of governess?"

"But... Agnes?" I said, calling to mind the image of the girl's face when she had been sent away downstairs. Her expression had been hard, eyes narrowed, mouth thin.

"Agnes was more concerned that she herself did not contract the infection than she was with helping my grandson," said Christen Michell. "And she was never appointed governess; it was a title she gave herself. I took her into our household when she was a child, as a kindness to her and to provide companionship for Mary. 'Lady's Maid' was another title she took for herself." A sadness settled over us in the room for a moment, before Christen Michell clapped her hands and said, "So, Isobell. Shall we do the best for Wee Thomas together?"

I nodded, at once overjoyed to be caring for the child, a task that hardly seemed to be work, especially when compared to scrubbing tables and butchering chickens, though also knowing I must speak to Agnes soon and assure her this was not something I had planned. But then maybe she would not be too aggrieved; she had not enjoyed her time with the boy, they had not warmed to one another and, Christen Michell assured me, she would be put to work elsewhere in the castle. She was not to be made destitute.

After many nights of sleeplessness, I was still tired and prone to fall into a deep slumber when Wee Thomas slept, so I was not sure if the huge shape bending over the boy was a dream when I woke in the night. I raised my body up onto one elbow. It was no nightmare and no phantom, but a great big man! I grabbed the nearest weapon I could find, the toy sword from the floor, and lunged at the intruder. His hand grabbed the wooden blade before it found its mark and he turned to me, the light of a lantern displaying his handsome features quite clearly.

So my second face-to-face meeting with the Laird was no more auspicious than the first, but at least I was fully clothed, albeit in a nightgown; that was a small mercy to be thankful for.

The Porridge Pot

It must have been a dream. Obviously it had been; after the Laird had grabbed the sword, which still lay upon the floor when I woke in the morning, I could remember no speaking; he had simply disappeared. Well, that was a relief. I helped Wee Thomas on with his clothes, and smoothed down my own new gown. A governess did not have to dress in a sack, and Christen Michell had been quick to arrange two new dresses for me. They were black, like hers, but plainer.

We headed down the wide curve of the stairs and crossed the two halls, to the kitchen. Wee Thomas was making good progress in his recuperation. For the last two days we had breakfasted at the kitchen table, the boy showing a good appetite for mine and Bessie's fortifying food ideas, and then we had sat at the back door in the autumn sunshine for a short while before retiring for a rest. He still ate the main meal in bed and I had mine up there too.

Today I had promised him bacon and eggs, a mixture that had intrigued both Bessie and Duncan when I told them of it. The thinly sliced ham was ready to go on a skillet and I hung it over the flames to cook. There was a pot of porridge ready to eat, so I dished up a small helping for Wee Thomas while he waited, enriching the bowl with raisins and hazelnuts and a fresh plum which he ate with gratifying gusto.

Then, all of a sudden, it appeared that the most embarrassing day ever was happening all over again: there was the Laird, coming into the room drying his face after removing his beard, but this time he laughed when he saw us. "Why, it's my bonny loon and his staunch defender!" he declared with a mischievous twinkle of blue in his eyes.

"Faether!" cried Wee Thomas.

The Laird lifted him and spun him round, a move that I hoped would not induce vomiting. It did not, and he soon replaced the child back at the table by his breakfast.

"And fit's this yer eating?" asked the Laird, examining our meal.

I explained the reasoning for the foods, remembering to turn the meat and add the eggs, as I spoke. Indeed, it was a relief to look away from the man towards whom I had recently wielded a sword, if only a wooden one. There was no sign that he retained any bad feeling from the event and he joined us in our repast, discovering a great liking for the bacon and eggs too, a fact I found almost as pleasing as I found his eyes fascinating. I had thought them grey or brown like a wild bear, but they were a very clear blue like those of his son.

It was good to be able to look at the Laird in a more normal situation. He was no biblical vision or bear, though his face was perfectly structured in the way that people asked artists to make them look in portraits, a fact I discerned by taking small glances between mouthfuls of porridge. His chiselled chin had a small cleft in it. His cheekbones were high and shapely. He had no flush across his face from the excesses of drink, like my brother John. Thomas Manteith was an artist's dream.

"Well, isn't this a bonny scene?" remarked Bessie, coming into the room with Agnes, finding us all happily eating at the table.

"Aye, it is that, Bessie Thom, it is," said the Laird and we all laughed, even Agnes, who I had not seen since our change in circumstances.

"How do you fare, friend?" I asked her. "And would you like to try the bacon and eggs?"

"I fare very well indeed, Isobell," she said, with a wide smile which seemed directed more at the Laird than at me. "But I am far too busy to sit and eat." And with a swish of her old frock, which now had some kitchen sacking worn on top, she walked happily, or so it seemed, out of the kitchen.

The return of his father to the castle was the best medicine Wee Thomas could have had. From that day on he managed a good walk every morning, with only a short nap after the main meal, a meal I finally took in the great hall, a meal served to us by Bessie and Agnes before they sat down too. It was interesting to observe the Laird's behaviour in the room. He started by sitting beside his son, asking where our daily walk had led us. My cheeks warmed as Wee Thomas described the pool, but the Laird seemed to think nothing amiss of it.

The large man then spent some time at different parts of the long tables talking with the different members of the castle's society. From the visiting laundress, to stone masons and carpenters, dairy maids, fallen and otherwise, and various servants, it appeared that Thomas Manteith considered none beneath him, which I found most impressive.

Also impressive was the large amount of food and pennies given away to the poor at the back door of the castle. I was not aware of it until Bessie expressed a concern that, without my daily burning of the bannocks, the poor were surely going to starve. It was in jest only; I enjoyed handing out the alms and food with Wee Thomas and the Laird one morning. All sorts of people came to the castle in need; farmers, blacksmiths, butchers and labourers, and they were all treated with respect. Any that had injury or ailments were sent to Bessie for a salve or tincture. Bessie's patients came from all walks of life but usually entered via the back door, desiring either their visit or their ailment to be kept secret.

Agnes often tried sore to find out why a certain fine lady or a rich gentleman had met with Bessie near the bake house or in the walled garden beside the herbs, but Bessie revealed nothing, other than annoyance at the questioning, and sent Agnes away to tend to beds in the tower, or wet down the dairy floor. I saw the sour thin line of Agnes's mouth at times like those; her smiles were kept only for when the Laird was in the room and she never had time to stop and speak with me.

The biggest change in our lives at the castle was really that breakfast became the most exciting time of day for Wee Thomas and myself. The Laird, at home for an extended stay, always joined us. One morning he was there early, an expression on his face like that of his son when up to some mischief, the porridge pot on the table with some small bowls beside.

"This is something I had once with my own father," he explained. "We were visiting a family who lived in a grand old Dun, a dry-stane tower, on the West of Scotland, and this was their breakfast. I thought you might like to try it. We all stand round the pot, a spoon each." We obediently picked up our wooden spoons. "Then," the Laird continued, "you take a dip o' porridge, and ones of cream, whisky and honey as you fancy."

We tried the combinations. Wee Thomas, standing on a chair to reach, spluttered over the whisky and stuck to cream and honey, but I rather liked the burn of the golden liquid and the mild euphoria it produced. Bessie was none-too pleased to discover the Laird had laid the pot bare and hot upon the table and burned a black circle into the surface. But that did not stop it being our jolliest breakfast yet, and it was followed by the happiest visit to the stone circle that had ever happened in the history of all time, I was sure. Then there was the longest nap Wee Thomas had ever taken since recovery, which meant a long rest for me too, lazing upon my bed. Life had transformed into something beautifully good and pleasant, and it had occurred so fast, such was the way of change within the thick pink walls of the castle.

The Mothers

The bond between Wee Thomas and I grew as we discussed that neither of us had known our mothers. I told him I believed my own looked down upon me and Jasper from heaven and the child quite happily took to the idea that his did too.

"Can we visit her now?" he requested.

At first I was confused as to whether a trip to the cemetery was in order, but no, it was to her old room that we went. It seemed he was in the habit of speaking to her; something I wasn't sure was quite healthy but, seeing how happy it made him, quickly came to approve of. He told her everything we had been doing: our walks, my songs, the bacon and eggs, the Laird and his pot of porridge and the stories I told; his new sword and shield were proudly brandished. He hoped it was sunny in heaven. So did I. And I found myself mentally reassuring the gentle looking Mary that I would care for her son as best I could.

"That's Mother's special stone," said the small boy, pointing out a detail in the portrait that I had not noticed before. Mary held a rounded pink crystalline stone, half hidden in the palm of her hand. "We are to give it to grandmother if we find it; it is lost," he added.

Bessie dismissed the story of the stone as nothing more than an old lady wanting any keepsake of her daughter she could find, and continued her detailed explanation of every item required in a birthing kit, stopping now and again to check I had paid attention and remembered everything.

The truth was that I who, like Wee Thomas, had never known a mother, suddenly had two, three if I was to count the mother in the portrait. The other two were far less quiet. They had both read much into the recovery of the Laird's son while in my care. Bessie sensed she had found a fellow healer, while Christen Michell believed my gifts to be spiritual.

So, while Janet watched Wee Thomas, I attended childbeds occasionally with Bessie, sharing the pain and horror of the birthing chamber and then the delight and joy of the baby. There I wiped away blood.

With Christen Michell I watched others drink the blood of Christ and eat his body, in the form of wine and bread. The serious decision of whether I were to become Catholic myself, something the older woman assumed I would want, was to be left to the future, after much careful thought and study of the Sacraments and Catechism.

It perplexed me greatly. Christen Michell spoke as if such a thing were a normal and acceptable practice. But I knew Scotland had been through reformation too, and asked Bessie about it early one morning before the Laird arrived in the kitchen.

"Aye, she's a Papist, and in this wee bitty o' Scotland here, we turn a blind eye. It's the true religion to her; you'll have noticed she disna attend the village church wi' the rest o' us of a Sunday? Always makes some excuse? But you tak fit learning you can fae it, Lassie. You never know what will come in useful in yer life. And yer getting to go to the Goddess Chamber. That's a place far older than ony religion, like the stones above it, I widna mind a lookie in there myself!"

It was true. The location of Father Daniel's underground Mass was… well, underground. It was round and curved and stony, like sitting inside a huge rock. We came to it to via the same tunnel Jasper and Ian and I had travelled to come to the castle from the sea, and entered through the mysterious glowing door we had seen then too. But there were other ways in. Duncan walked down a passageway from his house to open the way for us. He also lit the candles in each of the holy recesses and prepared the place for Father Daniel. In the calm of the underground setting, and in a well-rested state this time, I realised why the old priest had seemed familiar when he came to pray for Wee Thomas. It was him I had seen swinging the censor on the evening of our arrival; he had been coming out of this very place. I decided not to mention the fact, understanding that I had witnessed some important and secret event that night.

A small number of others attended Mass with us; women and men and a few children. Some came by boat and up the tunnel from the cave, others set off through the door towards Duncan's house at the time of leaving.

After the first Mass I attended, Christen Michell showed me the detail of the cross about her neck. It was etched with a map of the underground tunnel system which she maintained had been built in ancient times to allow true worship to take place in Scotland; rubies marked the entry points to the tunnels on her cross. But I knew the carving of angels and hearts and the Manteith coat of arms in the stone chamber were very recent. Bessie had told me of the stone masons' work down there. They were currently working on more angels for the ceiling of the castle entrance hall, though the small chapel off the same hall had been closed up to show obedience to the new religion.

The Laird knew of our exploits too. "Dinna let yourself be led down paths you don't want to go," he advised. "Religion is largely determined by the family and culture we are born into. What matters is our own connection with God, and no one else can dictate that. And dinna believe all the stories you're told either; those tunnels were originally for smuggling. How do you think we get all the stolen sweetmeats and wine up to the castle?"

Amusing as that was, and the Laird was most amusing at times, his eyes always showing a particularly bright blue when he was in jest, there truly was something magical about the underground chamber and what took place there. The smell of incense and tallow from the candles combined with the music of voices singing and the intoning of Father Daniel in Latin, to create a deep peace beyond any I'd ever known. The stone walls cradled and augmented the sounds and scents, making it easy to believe that the wine in the great goblet and the bread had actually become the real presence of Our Lord.

I was surrounded with beautiful and mysterious places and practices. While Wee Thomas and I played among the circle of stones in the day, pulling the sword from between two of the larger ones, and declaring ourselves "Kings and Queens of All England! And Scotland! And the World!" Bessie used the space for more sober activity.

"It's a women's place," she explained, after a truly difficult labour had led to a healthy baby boy and a happy mother. "Some call them Druids' Stones, but that is a misunderstanding, an ignorance, for this is ground marked for us to give thanks and make sacrifice."

We poured wine on the earth and thanked the Goddess for blessing the work of our night.

But my favourite time, the best bit of every day, remained, perhaps, the simplest: breakfast round the new, slightly spoiled, oak table with the Laird and Wee Thomas. Bessie and Agnes came and went from the room all but unnoticed, as we three laughed and ate together. It was humorous, and sometimes embarrassing, that nothing of our days could be kept secret with a small child around. Wee Thomas told Big Thomas every detail of every word I sang, every story I told, and every person we saw.

"Have you always liked to sing, Ishbell?" the Laird asked.

I, liking the way he said my name, was keen to tell him of my love for music. "Yes, I used to play the harp at home—" I stopped, for in the free and happy moment I had been enjoying, the truth that I was essentially living a lie in the Laird's castle had all but been forgotten. "That is, in the house where I used to live, I was permitted to play the harp." That the instrument had been my mother's, I could not say.

"It saddens you to speak of this," noted the Laird, and we spoke of it no more.

The Snow

"Aye, mak the best o' it today," advised Bessie as Wee Thomas and I wrapped up to go out. "Snaw'll be here by tomorrow. Ye'll no be going anywhere then."

"Snow?" I asked, sceptical, standing on the back door step, face upturned to the warm November sun.

Granted, as we made our way through the woods there was a slight nip in the breeze that ran across the water of the pool towards us; we imagined it to be the wake of a sea monster, trapped in our own castle loch. Wee Thomas was Sir Gawain questing through the woods, sword at the ready as we reached the stone circle. I played the part of the dragon quite well, leaping back and forth over the flat stone as he tried to catch me, then sitting upon it to catch my own breath.

The sunshine was soothing, the small boy happy, going from stone to stone, challenging each as if it were a knight. So, I lay, and let my fingers trace the faded markings on the stone, recognising it for the same pattern as was on Christen Michell's cross, made long ago by someone unknown. The makers of the underground pathways? The builders of the circle? How many years had these places been there as they were now? How many generations of Manteiths had walked their ways? And who would come after us? From us? I felt dizzy with the crossing paths of time, the subject having expanded into something too large to be understood.

"Bell!" Wee Thomas summoned me back to the present, standing with his sturdy wee legs wide and hands held out. "Snaw!"

Snow was, indeed, falling between the tall stones and all around us. I had never before encountered such flakes. They were huge, square shaped, falling softly and in silence, already making the ground white. It was mesmerising to stare up into the sky and watch the snowflakes rushing towards us like a wintry army of ice faeries.

The walk home to the castle was still green but the light between the trees had taken on an iridescent glow of the weather. By the time we reached the end of the path, the castle and surrounding ground were covered. The top of the high tower sparkled in the bright air, painted white against a now dark and stormy sky.

"In ye come and nae get cold," ordered Bessie. "Broth's ready!"

The next morning, our way to the kitchen was impeded by a crowd of people in the great hall. There had been a disaster in the night. Such a quantity of snow had fallen that the roof of the farm workers' sleeping quarters had collapsed. They were being housed in the castle, down below in a large storage area. I was dearly glad that Jasper and Ian were safe and well and cosy with us all under the secure roof, but felt the loss of our usual quiet breakfast time. We all ate in the hall together and then everyone mucked in to set up bedding in the downstairs storage areas of the castle.

I was exempted from the task, being in charge of Wee Thomas. Agnes paused beside us and our story writing in the great hall, much folded bedding in her arms. "It must be strange to you to have your own room," she remarked.

"And you," I noted, smiling in an effort to remove the sting of her tone.

"It was my own chamber before you came. Long before you came," she said and marched off.

The bitter taste of the exchange was soon removed by Bessie. "There's to be a feast!" she informed us. "The Laird's declared it a holiday and we're all to eat like Kings and Queens! Isobell, do you hiv any ideas of fine dishes we could do as extras?"

I described the grandest foods I had heard of. Wee Thomas's eyes widened in surprise and delighted anticipation, but pies with birds flying out of them would be a bit difficult to arrange. Pigeon and rabbit ones were to be made though, and ham too.

"The Bishop of London is said to have eaten a pastry castle once, at a banquet," I remembered, "with a moat of custard. We could make that!"

Wee Thomas and I set to work. We crafted a pastry tower and great hall and entrance hall and kitchen, and then we placed a moat round it.

"Needs crocodiles," suggested Jasper on a visit to the kitchen. This provoked an investigation into what crocodiles looked like. We asked Duncan and the Laird and Bessie and Father Daniel, who was staying as Christen Michell's guest. We made round heads and long jaws and big teeth. The boy who turned the spit by the fire thought they had big ears too which made them look like dragons. That pleased Wee Thomas, and into the bread oven our creation went along with Janet's loaves and pies.

The custard finished it off nicely, and we added red berry preserve to the crocodiles' mouths before the tart went through to the top table to sit in front of the Laird, who was most taken with the dish. He took his son on his knee and they had a long conversation about the details of the castle and the crocodiles.

"It's a good thing you've done there," said Bessie as I helped her carry dishes of vegetables through to the other tables. "He's always been an attentive father, bringing the wee loon gifts and paying him attention, but there's niver been this ease between them before. It's natural. Beautiful, really. Look at them."

They did make a happy picture, a man and boy so alike, my heart warmed to look upon them as they laughed and talked and made merry.

"Of course, nae to take credit away from you completely, Bell, but it could have much to do with the removal of Agnes from the scene. That's a lassie likes to poison the waters between folks, put them in doubt of each other. I'm nae always sure how she does it, but she disna like to see happiness or success in others, and she'll stop it if she can."

I'd never thought Agnes was quite as nasty as all that, but as the meal got underway, the Laird called for me to come sit beside Wee Thomas, and in the fun of the moment I ended up sitting on the Laird's right and his son on his left, and I saw her eyes. They were narrowed, one closed more than the other, and one side of her mouth was lifted in contempt. She whispered something to the maid next to her, who turned her head sharply to look at us, her eyes widened with surprise but not from any tale of birds flying out of pies.

The Play

The wine we drank that night was richer than the small ale I was used to. It was fruity and delicious and made me feel dreamy and content and then wistful and sad. Earlier, Bessie and I had descended the wooden steps to the cellar area to fetch the kegs of fine wine at the Laird's request. It had been cold and strange to be down there again, in the place I'd passed through on my way into the castle. I'd shivered in the dark.

"Aye, ye sense it too, Lassie," said Bessie. "I thought ye might. Come. Let me show you."

She led the way round a curved passageway to more steps, stone ones this time, which led down into a greater darkness. She held the lantern aloft, but the tiny light within struggled to infiltrate the dense gloom, and it took a moment or two for my eyes to adjust and see. I could make out chains on the walls and a table with cruel looking implements placed upon it. A Dungeon! A torturer's domain. It made my feet want to fly back up the steps.

"Oh dinna worry," assured Bessie. "Naebody's bin kept doon here since the Laird's grandfather's time. He was an angry man. Christen Michell's nae the first zealot to bide here in the castle. But this is fit I wanted to show ye; look up."

She raised the light high and indicated the stony ceiling. One huge block stood out from the others, and not just because it was a hundred times their size. It seemed familiar but I couldn't think why.

"It's the missing stone," she said, as if this made sense. "Fae the circle. He had it built in here to show Christianity's dominance over the old ways. My grandmother cursed him for it. 'The family o' the castle will know pain and suffering through the childbed till the ancient stone is putten back.' But then who disna? It's a curse that can never be disproven!"

Bessie's great laugh had echoed round the underground cavern in a shuddering way, as if it might bring down the stone and put an end to the curse. I'd been most pleased to climb the steps and be above ground again, clutching a keg of the Laird's best wine for the feast.

Agnes, in the dairy talking to the women who were working in there, had seen me carrying the keg up the narrow passageway towards the great hall. "Are you sure you can fit through there wi' that?" she'd called after me and then sounds of much giggling and hilarity did come from the dairy.

Obviously Agnes and I were never going to be friends. But on that day, it mattered not. Here I was, sat by the Laird at the top table, drinking fine wine and eating a pastry castle. Everyone had been impressed with Wee Thomas's crocodiles but there were only seven of them and not enough to go round, so we promised to make more next time.

"I gave Jasper permission to put on a play," said the Laird in my ear, bringing me back from thoughts of dark places. "See, they are readying the stage."

Several men were arranging three of the long tables together, laughing as they went. Props were made ready too: a stone and a few tree branches; some blue fabric was laid down as if to symbolise water. I experienced an unfortunate feeling of foreboding.

Jasper appeared, normally dressed – well, normally for here in his role as farm hand. He invited us to watch and to laugh and to be filled with wonders. He told how the great hall so resembled the Theatre in London, with its earthen floor and high ceiling, though it was good that this roof was closed to the elements unlike the one in London, and how it was the perfect venue for the play that was about to take place. This last he said with a lightning flash of a smile in our direction. Why, soon became clear.

Jasper transformed into a pretty mermaid in a golden wig, winding some of the blue fabric round his legs. He combed his hair with an enormous comb and knocked his wig askew. The room roared with laughter. He then gave a speech on the nature of beauty, a rather familiar sounding speech. And there was Ian, Ian in a fur! Ian peered through the trees, and also spoke fair and familiar about beauty.

It was time to interrupt. I stood and called over to Jasper: "These words you speak do seem to have been heard before, brother!"

"Do they, sweet Isobell, do they?" beamed my tormentor.

"Master Shakespeare did write them, did he not?"

"Well, that really is a question!" he replied.

"Who is this Shakespeare?" asked the Laird, standing beside me, adding his height and frame to my cause.

"A playwright," I informed.

"An actor, a simple village lad," corrected Jasper. "And one who does wish to know our sweet Isobell better."

"Brother, you are in your cups!" I said, incensed. "Master Shakespeare is a married man."

"Shame he can never seem to remember it," quipped Ian and both boys fell into convulsions of laughter, the golden wig falling off entirely.

"I think it's time this play became bigger," said the Laird taking me by the hand and stepping forward. We walked the short way through the audience, as everyone had become, and joined the naughty boys on the stage. My cheeks grew hot as the Laird's strong arms lifted me with such ease onto the tables.

"I," said my rescuer, "will play Jasper. Perhaps Ishbell can be Ian?"

What a plan! The Laird mimed using a hammer but once and developing a tiny blister which he thought would kill him. I acted eating a burnt bannock and told everyone that it might kill me, while I secretly enjoyed it all the time, helping myself to more preserve when I thought no one was looking.

"I'm King Arthur!" came Wee Thomas's call from the ground and soon he was lifted up with us all too. Many others joined in and carried the play forward in various nonsensical ways before we all sat down, well entertained, well fed and most happy with ourselves.

That night I dreamed of the Laird's big, strong hands as they had held me, before my mind became confused and I fell through scents of oats and salt and was lost in the dark of the dungeon. And then it seemed I was in the circle, standing in the place of the missing stone, speaking to Wee Thomas's mother, the Laird's beautiful wife, one who had suffered at the hands of the curse. We had to break it together, her and I. We were Goddesses met in the circle, women all together; there were many, so many of us, standing across time, through the years, the centuries, standing strong and true. United in our blood and our love. And then there were flowers, tiny pink and white flowers, with drops of dew and bright sunlight. They made sparkling crowns for us all.

The Plaid

"Tell us more of this Shakespeare," requested the Laird at breakfast the next morning as we all enjoyed bacon and eggs and barley bread with butter through in the kitchen.

"Aye," agreed Bessie. "I take it he's an admirer of yours, Bell?"

"No, not at all," I began before being spoken over by Jasper, who was prone to popping in at any time while the snow was still too deep for normal farm work to resume.

"Yes he is," he said, sitting down and breaking off some bread for himself. "Our little Isobell is blind to what is right in front of her at times."

"Jasper, that's not true!"

"But I often see you speaking with him, dear sister, when you frequent the Theatre... unless... yes! May it be true! There are rumours..." He lowered in voice to a dramatic whisper and leant on the table, fist under his chin, surreptitiously pointing a finger in my direction as he spoke his next words. "They say that Master Shakespeare has someone else write the plays for him. It would have to be someone clever. Someone who can read and write, obviously. Someone who likes to tell stories and spin tales of Faeryland and magic..."

Bessie roared with laughter as I scoffed.

"Who's to say it's not a woman?" mused Jasper.

"What woman would have the time?" asked Bessie, askance.

"One that is not as talented at the tasks of cooking and cleaning as she ought to be, due to the time spent secretly writing plays!" declared my irrepressible twin, then adding: "Look how quickly my own dear sister did recognise her own dear words last night. She could not be published under her own name, could not be taken seriously, but Bell! You could have used my name. I would have put it around that it was you who penned the works and not have taken all the credit unto myself as he has done."

I shook my head, deciding not to encourage the nonsense any, and focused on wiping Wee Thomas's mouth free of breakfast.

"I've always thought women might be better managers of the world than men," said the Laird. "We have made a terrible mess of it. Why should they not be writers too? But, tell me, do you get snow such as we have here, in London?"

Jasper answered him, telling how the Thames had frozen the previous year, and we had both walked and skated on it and people had even taken sleds out onto the ice.

"We could do this," announced the Laird, looking more like his little boy than ever, in blue-eyed excitement. "There is an old sledge out in the brew house; let's see if it can be made fit for a family outing."

Wee Thomas jumped up and down with his own excitement when the news came that the sled was ready to go. I dressed him up warm in his coat and hat with extra woollens, and pulled my shawl as tight as it could go round my shoulders.

"You'll be needing a cloak, Isobell," advised Bessie.

"I don't think I've got anything quite fitting," I told her, trying to convey what I meant with my eyes, aware of both sets of Manteith eyes on me. I had a warm black cloak, but it was made of far too fine a stuff for a governess to own, let alone a person who was so recently a kitchen maid.

"Ah, but I have the perfect thing," said the Laird and off he ran, away up the kitchen passage.

"Aye, abody's acting like wee bairns today," laughed Bessie.

Soon I was being wrapped round in the warmest item of clothing I had ever encountered. It was thick and woollen and woven in colours of purple and blue. It held a scent of lavender about its folds. Bessie showed me how to arrange the 'Plaid' and how to utilise part of it as a hood.

"And now, look, to hold it in place," said the Laird, still shining with happiness and enthusiasm. "A brooch." The pin was a silver ring with a cross bar that had been worked with two sparkling stones of purple, matching the colours in the plaid.

Bessie and I both looked at him in enquiry as he pinned it to my shoulder. "Aye," he said, a little gruffly. "It wis my mother's; it'll be good to see it put to use again."

"M—My Lord," I stuttered. "I cannot possibly accept—"

"Aye ye can, Lassie. Come on noo, nae fussing. The governess needs to accompany her charge on an outing; I'm providing the necessary equipment."

"Well, ye canna argue wi that," said Bessie, possibly repressing a laugh.

There was no time to argue. The Laird whisked us up the hallway to the back door. "Ye need a plaid to live here, Ishbell," he explained. "That was a brown travelling plaid I was wearing the first time you met me."

I flushed, but found myself laughing as he unlocked the door's many bolts and then I gasped at the sight of the large sled and even larger horse that was to pull it.

"Oh, he's beautiful," I said, walking over and reaching up to place my hand on the animal's nose. He was nervous, unused to being worked in such a way, and I murmured reassurances as I stroked his glossy brown face and neck, and tickled his hairy nose. His big dark eyes reminded me of a pony I had ridden at my father's estate in the north of England. John broke the pony's leg in a hunting accident and then ended its life. Jasper said it was deliberate, that John could not bear me to have anything good or nice. But this was a happier day. And this was a much bigger horse, I realised as I measured the size of its head with my hands.

"You know horses too," remarked the Laird, before encouraging us to climb aboard the sled and putting a blanket round our legs, and then… off we went!

I clung to Wee Thomas in fear that he might fall out, his father seemingly intent on going as fast as possible down the castle track and out onto the road. But then we slowed and could look out at a countryside transformed. There was so much snow! It lay deeply piled at the sides of the road and the white world seemed to stretch forever, encompassing hills and forests and cottages and farms. A white hare with black tipped ears ran across the wintry expanse of a field, causing myself and Wee Thomas to cry out in delight.

We turned into a woodland track shortly, bushes and trees high at either side of us, and then there was Duncan's 'wee hoosie' as he called it, similarly transformed with snow, and, before I knew which snow-dusted tree to stare at first, we had come to the pool, the place of our first meeting, and it was changed almost beyond recognition.

The Pipes

At first the pool appeared to have shrunk, snow having gathered round its banks and edges making a soft and fluffy frame for the ice. For that was what the water had become. It wasn't glassy, but thick and frosted and silver and white, small bubbles visible just below the surface. It was made up of flowers, large circular and wavy flowers that had formed in the body of water as it solidified; such a pretty picture they did make.

"No, no!" ordered The Laird, as I had been about to descend from the sled to inspect the frozen flowers. "Naebody walks on the ice till I have tested the safety of it."

He stood, majestic, in the centre of the wintry vista, a magical winter king reigning supreme over his snowy realm, and stamped a black-booted foot. He turned and repeated the action several times in several different places. Not a crack appeared, nor did the ice show any sign of shifting under his feet. The trees behind the Laird were contrastingly dark and dramatic, the snow on their tops making the spaces between trunks and branches shadowy and strange, though not in any way forbidding. Here and there, tiny golden leaves could still be spotted, little lights of yellow left from the previous season.

Thomas Manteith held his arms out and we scampered from the cosy carriage like 'wee bairns', as Bessie would have said.

I stepped over the bank of snow and onto the slippery surface of the pool, then turned back and held Wee Thomas's hands as I transported him over to his father.

"Will ye show us how you skated on the Thames, Ishbell?" asked the Laird, gesturing with a hand like an actor on the stage.

"Like so," I said, moving backwards and turning on the ice as I went.

"Me, me, me, me!" shouted the small boy and I led him around, slowly at first, then faster, then too fast, and we both landed in a giggling heap.

The Laird did not skate, he merely watched and encouraged and helped us up when needed. I dearly wished to take his hand and lead him into enjoyment of the ice too, but I was a governess, there to help Wee Thomas, not to continually be doing and saying inappropriate things in front of my employer. The details of the last time the two of us had graced this place was something I would not think of, else I would fall down in embarrassment; but no impropriety could take place there again.

"It's good to see such colour in two young faces," said the Laird, helping us up for perhaps the hundredth time. "But, we must go home. Fret not, Wee Thomas, there will be more revelry in the hall tonight."

Back from our adventures, we were warmed by both broth and fire in the great hall. The Laird had ordered the logs built high for this last day of holiday. The snow had stopped falling, tracks had been cleared and work could continue the next day. Mending the roof at the farm would take some weeks, so the castle would continue to house many extra bodies for the time being.

The feast was not so grand as the previous night; there was no pastry castle. But the entertainment was impressive, and far gentler on the emotions. So many people among the castle workers were musicians; I was amazed by both the variety of instruments and the skill of the players.

"Well, what else do we simple farm boys have to do of a night, except fiddle away and play with our pipes?" said Jasper, causing much mirth around him as he often did.

"Enough of that!" said Christen Michell, in an angry voice. "This is a Christian household and there are ladies present, and I urge you all to remember that if you wish to remain under this roof!"

I looked at her, shocked, not understanding what had caused her distress. "Don't worry, Isobell," she said. "It is no fault of yours. Men will be men after all." She studied me then, and fingered the brooch at my shoulder. "You sometimes make me think of my daughter," she said. "Mary would have loved this music and also your brother's play last night."

"Would she?" asked the Laird, from where he sat on the other side of Wee Thomas, the fun of our prior seating arrangements, sadly, not having been repeated tonight.

"Oh yes," answered Christen Michell with a slow nod, turning her attention back to the musicians.

I listened to the sounds of the pipes and the small stringed fiddles, and watched as some of the farm workers started to dance, but I had no inclination to join them. I was beset with a mixture of sadness and confusion about the family of the castle. Did they not know one another well? How could that be? Wee Thomas was four years old. The Laird and Christen Michell must have been known to each other at least a year longer than that, surely? And Mary to have died so young; that was such a tragedy, but how could her husband not have been aware of the pastimes she enjoyed? If the Laird had been the kind of man Wicked Richard was, that would be understandable, but he was the very opposite! So kind and interested in everyone. It made no sense at all.

"Isobell," said Bessie, approaching and startling me out of the reverie. "Come and meet my grandchildren." And the evening took on a much jollier bent.

Janet had told her seven children about my stories and pictures and much time was spent enjoying both. It was good to see Wee Thomas playing with others near his own age, laughing and joking, as drawing skills were compared and improved upon in competition. Every person contributed to a wild tale of an ice monster that grew out of the pool in the woods and then came to life, at first appearing terrifying but then showing itself as gentle, visiting each and every one of them with what turned out to be an ice gift. Such fun was had dreaming up what each person would receive: Wee Thomas decided he would have a crown, the Laird said I needed gloves as my hands had been quite blue after falling on them so many times, but what use would they be if made of ice? There was much merriment when I pointed that out. Agnes started a story about a wicked witch who stole the things belonging to others, such as employment, plaids and brooches, but Christen Michell interrupted her to contribute an idea of her own: a great ice crucifix left behind long after the ice giant was gone, a holy miracle that no fire could melt.

The Chapel Perilous

My bowl of porridge was full, but it felt empty. The fire blazed in the huge hearth, but the room was cold, as if the snow had not melted after all, had not filled the woodland pool to overflowing and opened the roads for travel. Wee Thomas was forlorn also, his appetite less than I had seen it since his illness.

"Ach, fit are the two of you like?" remarked Bessie, taking in our moping faces. "He'll soon be back and then it'll be Christmas. What a time we'll have then. You think yon party was fun wi' the snow, but ye've seen nothing like Christmas. Twelve days of it to keep hersel happy, there's different folks invited on different nights, music, games, feasting. You wait, Isobell, happy times are acoming."

But the castle was a changed place without the Laird. It was too quiet, though he was not a loud man; maybe he just evoked cheer in others.

We continued to go below ground to the night time Mass, but I felt disconsolate; why did I even attend the services? I wasn't going to convert to the religion of the past. Why would I? I didn't understand the Latin; my education had not included the old languages. The previous peace I'd experienced in the underground chamber had turned to something akin to boredom. I hoped that wasn't too serious a sin. The Laird didn't go down there under the earth. He was satisfied with the Sunday worship in the church, where his presence fair lit up the place. Everyone felt it. Everyone smiled when the party from the castle arrived of a Sunday, and he was the reason.

So the days continued. Wee Thomas brightened them often by saying some funny thing, or by my noticing how quickly he learned his letters. How clever the boy was. How like his father.

"Isobell."

I jerked away from my dream of what Christmas in Scotland might look like, and looked instead at the serious face of Christen Michell.

"Come. I have something to show you."

What could she want with me? I would rather have stayed with Wee Thomas and Bessie in the kitchen, but through the entrance hall we travelled and over towards the tower. Christen Michell made a great show of taking a big old key out of her pocket and looking around, lest someone might see us. My interest piqued. We were obviously about to enter the locked chapel.

It was dark. It was musty smelling. And then she lit a candle to reveal the secrets that had lain hidden there, safe from the axes and hammers of the reformers. "The Virgin Mary," said Christen Michell, indicating a perfect statue of mother and child, both with ornate silver crowns, the Lady's open at the top, the child's closed. "Our Lady of Aberdeen is associated with miracles of success. She will help correct what is wrong or lacking in your life."

We stood in silent wonder for a time, gazing up at the serenity of the Lady's face, and then moved on past a golden angel and a tall crucifix, and many golden candlesticks and painted panels depicting saints and sinners and stories I did not know. Their faces flickered in the candle light. "There is a coloured window also, but it is boarded on the outside," she told me, raising the flame to show, "The Archangel Michael with his sword of truth."

Even without proper illumination, the window was magnificent; the angel stood tall in knight's clothing, sword aloft, wings spread out in all the colours of the universe. I could imagine the brilliance of the window if the sun were to shine through it and said so.

"Oh yes," she agreed with some fervour. "I once felt the holy spirit enter me when I looked upon that. That window lets in far more than the light of the sun. But it is I who must wield the sword of truth now, my dear. Let us sit."

We sat on a carved wooden pew and Christen Michell laid down her candle, increasing the shadowy nature of the chapel, and took my hand in both of hers.

"You must know, Isobell, that you have brought healing to my heart since you arrived. The emptiness I have felt since the loss of my daughter has been eased – not mended, for that will never be so – but comforted in part. The cross I bear has lightened a little. You are like her. Sometimes you bring her to mind so strongly. You are another innocent in this world of evil, this world of men, Isobell; you know of what I speak?"

"I am glad to have brought you comfort, Madame. You have welcomed me and…" Truth was all around us in the holy place. It felt wrong to let a lie sit between us. "I came here to escape an arranged marriage to a man who was not good."

"I thought there was something of this sort," she answered, not asking for any more detail. "However, we must make sure a worse fate still does not befall you. Affection can sometimes lead a woman down more dangerous paths than the lack of it. I will not sit by and see you fall, Isobell."

"I don't understand." At the word 'fall', I recalled the Laird as he had helped me up on the ice. His big hands. His strong arms.

"The Laird," she said, as if thinking of the same thing. "You must know he is growing extremely fond of you."

"Oh. No. Really?" I was glad of the dark; it hid my burning face.

"Lassie," she said as if I were being very slow. "We all see it. Even wee Agnes with her spiteful story the other night was alluding to this. And your returned affection for the man could make it difficult for you to refuse him."

"Refuse him?" I said, indeed feeling very slow.

"Oh, not in marriage, Isobell. You don't harbour such an idea?"

"No." Of course I didn't. I hadn't thought of such a thing… What a thing it would be though. My whole body flushed at the idea.

"He cannot marry beneath his class, you know that. But your pretty ways and smile are a sore temptation which, being hot-blooded like the rest of his sex, he will not resist much longer."

"Madame. Christen Michell. I can assure you that nothing untoward—"

"Not yet. But you are in danger, Isobell. He is a man."

"The Laird is a good man. He has never—"

"A man, just the same. Be at peace. I meant to accuse no one. Sometimes sin can be avoided before it occurs. I have friends who seek a governess. They are much impressed by what I have told them of yourself. They have five children, aged between three and twelve years, and would like them to learn to read and write. They are good Christian people. You will be safe there. They are situated in Inverness, so some distance away, but I'm sure your brother could visit you sometimes."

So it was arranged. I watched Christen Michell snuff out the candle as we left the chapel, and I witnessed the darkness descend. I heard the great lock turn as she used the key to shut away beauty from the world.

The Blackened Cloot

The changing expressions on Bessie's face as I recounted what had taken place in the chapel revealed that she had many thoughts competing to be heard. They burst out of her in fast succession: "Oh, there's mair to this than meets the eye. I dinna think it's aboot fit she's saying it's aboot. As if—! You're the best thing to happen to yon wee loon, to the castle, aye to the Laird too, though nae how she's meanin'. What a thing to suggest. Ye're nae like Agnes, lifting her skirts for any man she thinks useful. By God, I have to have my say." And with that, she marched out of the kitchen, almost colliding with Jasper and Wee Thomas as they came in.

"Bessie's in a bit of a bustle this morning," remarked my brother as I sat down with the Laird's son who, on Christen Michell's orders, was to know nothing of my leaving until the day itself. This made explaining the situation to Jasper rather difficult, and I also didn't want him to create a big scene or fuss over it. This departure, unlike the last, was not of my own choosing. I was being dismissed by my employer. To fight against such an action would only draw unwanted attention and perhaps endanger us all. It could be hoped that the trail had gone cold while Wicked Richard and our brother John soused their anger in the drinking houses and clubs of London. But we could not be sure. *Head down, Isobell. Avoid trouble, Isobell.*

I encouraged Wee Thomas to eat, filling his bowl with sweet delicacies to nourish and delight. That I could do, though I could eat none myself. It was hard to tell stories, though I managed at his insistence.

"When?" demanded Jasper, once he had discerned the main points of what was happening, his actor's voice shaking the pots over the fire. "And why? Did you do something to displease her, Bell? Is it because of my coarse words the other night?"

"No, no," I said and stared at the table, unable to say more in front of Wee Thomas.

Jasper flounced off after Bessie, out of the kitchen, away from me.

The fire crackled and spluttered as Wee Thomas ate and swung his little legs under the table. The wood made more smoke than usual; it stung my eyes and caused them to water, as I explained to the little boy. Soon voices were heard in the passageway and Bessie and Jasper returned full of the story of the day.

"It is slanderous, Bell, what she is saying," said Jasper. "There's been no hint of— Has there? You must tell me, sister."

"Of course not," I said, frowning at his mention of things that should not be mentioned in the company of the child.

"Oh the wee loon winna understand, Bell, dinna worry," said Bessie. "I reckon it's all really about Mary, and it's connected to the ceiling angels, for the entrance hallway, remember?"

I remembered, but I knew Wee Thomas understood a great deal of what the adults around him said, though I, myself, was having trouble understanding how the carving of angels related to my leaving the castle in any way.

"Work on them has stopped," Bessie went on. "Money's nae unlimited in a place like this, as folks often think it is," she explained. "The money that had been allocated to the angels is now being spent on the farm roof instead and hersel was right upset about it when she was telt the other night."

"So?" said Jasper. "How is that Bell's doing?"

"It's not, and nobody is saying it is. But, well, the Laird is a good man. You must have seen how many tenants pay their rent in chickens and eggs? And some pay not at all. He winna put them oot. Oh, he dis other business to bring some in, but stone angels are an extravagance too far at this time. But she's been going on about them since just after Mary died. I think they were intended as some sort of monument to the girl, though I never heard such a thing spoken out loud. But if she canna hae the angels? The Laird is going to stand in for them, kept as a shrine like the blue bedroom, his love for Mary pure and strong, and he's never to look at any other quine again."

They both looked at me.

"Really?" said Jasper, before turning back to Bessie. "She admitted all this to you?"

"No. Dinna be daft. She's full of the tale of 'doing fit's right for the wee lassie'."

They spoke on, in riddles to hide their meaning from a child, but they befuddled me too. Only later, sitting in the stone circle, did I realise that whatever the whole truth of the matter, some of Christen Michell's words to me had been very true indeed. The Laird would never marry me. And I knew it was, indeed, best I was going. For though I had never let the thought fully form, never spoken it our loud, like Christen Michell with her angels, the idea had settled inside me somehow and a deep fondness for the man was growing. That he would even entertain such a notion was a nonsense greater than any I had seen on stage. I was short and wide and wanted in marriage only by an evil man for some evil purpose. Or maybe only my dowry. I didn't know. I didn't care.

Leaving my wee boy, though; that was a different pain, a wrench augmented by the fact I knew it would hurt him too. So from that moment, every activity we partook of together, every outing into the Scottish countryside, became seeped in sorrow, like bread in milk, soaked all through with the salt of many tears added to the mix. I made my focus Wee Thomas's education, his letters. I would try to teach him them all before I departed, before Christmas, so something of worth would be left behind, along with my brother, my twin; the good Christian household in Inverness had no need of him or Ian.

"Perhaps it is for the best, just for now," said Jasper, holding out another letter from London. Wicked Richard and John had journeyed north to York in their search for us. "With you in Inverness and me here, we are not together, not so conspicuous, and you are even further away. It will not be forever, Bell, it will not."

Agnes, aware of my impending departure, became, at last, friendly. She kept telling tales she considered amusing in an attempt to cheer me up. When she came upon me with a blackened cloth trying to improve the appearance of the burnt part of the table, she clapped in delight. "Oh, you better watch yersel, Isobell. Remember Christian Stewart?"

I did not and continued my task, futile as it was.

"The witch from Perth I telt you about? She's been executed! Found guilty of bewitching a man to death with a black cloot!"

"I'll gi you a cloot, Agnes Milne," said Bessie, coming into the kitchen. "Roon the lug. Wagging tongues like yours is what gets folk accused of such things. That, and displeasing the people around them. This land has known plague and famine in recent years. Simple minded souls are looking for something to blame, something to hate. Think on it while you carry this through to the great hall."

The weight of the broth pot was beyond the abilities of Agnes, so I took the other side and together we ferried it down the passageway and into the great hall.

I thought about Wee Thomas and how he would fare when I was gone. Would another governess be appointed? Would Agnes reclaim the role? That worried me something terrible. But Bessie would still be here. And Jasper, who was fond of the lad too. And, of course, the Laird, but I tried not to think about him at all.

But then the very next morning, there he was in front of me as if materialised out of the air of the kitchen. It made no sense. One moment I was stirring the porridge for breakfast, gazing into its depths, grey like everything else. And then he was smiling, blue eyes twinkling. With a beard. My bear from the woods, from the pool. His smile did not last long.

"Ishbell, what has happened? Have you been ill?"

His hands were on my face. I had to not think about that, or about him, about all I was feeling, and instead answer sensibly. Everything sensibly. "I am quite well, sir."

He seemed determined to keep his hands upon my face. I shut my eyes for fear of falling, not how Christen Michell meant; that had never been true, never been an actual possibility, but literally falling onto the large grey flagstones in front of the Laird, who should not be there. I was meant to be gone before he was there. That had been decided, set on as a fact.

"I will see a smile on your face yet," he said and took my hands.

The Harp

He pulled me out of my sorrow. He pulled me down the kitchen passageway to the great hall, talking of presents and music and good times to come. There, stood beside the fire, where it would quickly untune, was an enormous harp. It was taller than me, carved of some light and fragrant wood, and, "Double stringed!" I noted in delight, running my hands over the strings, hearing their magic fill the air, imagining the stories that could flow from it in song. "I've never played one like it."

"And now you shall," said the Laird. "It is for you to play at Christmas."

There was incongruity between his words and what could actually come to pass. I felt myself shrinking back into accustomed sadness.

"I will not be here, My Lord. I am to start a new position before Christmas. We are just waiting to hear that the road to Inverness is clear."

It was as if I had struck him. He stepped back from me, all happiness and excitement about the harp gone. "You are leaving? Ishbell… Isobell," he corrected, as if to speak more formally. "You have not been happy here? Has something happened in my absence? Some cruelty? Of course it has, I should have known by your faded appearance when I saw you."

I shook my head, unable to speak.

"Your brother, he goes too?"

"No."

"I wish to know what has happened here in my castle, Ishbell. Will you not tell me?"

How could I? How could I recount Christen Michell's words about him, to him? I struggled to find what truth I could speak. "It was thought best—"

"So it was not your own idea. Return to the kitchen and be warm by the fire, Lassie. I will go and seek out the whole truth of this."

The kitchen was in somewhat of an uproar. "He's back?" asked Bessie, though it was obviously not an actual question. "That man never lets me ken when he's comin'. But you had porridge on anyway for the wee lad. Dis he ken? The Laird? Aboot ye leavin'?"

I nodded.

"Aye. Well. We'll see noo," was all she said before going to issue commands to the castle's food producing servants.

"I've just been in the bake house," said Agnes, carrying a water pail into the room. "They're saying that the Laird's come hame early to dismiss you, and see you on your way to Inverness, because folks has found out the real reason for your grand new position. Well, I have to say—"

"You will say nothing, Agnes Milne, if you value your own position." The Laird stood in the doorway of the kitchen, filling it with his size and his wrath. His eyes were wild again, but with some other fire than when I'd first seen him. "Remove yourself from my sight and hearing," he said to her and she scurried away.

"Sit doon, quine," he said to me, his voice and demeanour returned to gentleness, "and hae something to eat. Fit is there?"

I watched with much disallowed fondness as the large man searched out a bowl and filled it with porridge, then adding some of Wee Thomas's nuts and dried fruit to the mix.

"Now," he said, placing the food before me. "I'm hoping you'll let me renegotiate the terms of your employment here. Things were not arranged as they should have been. Your pay was never adjusted from that of a kitchen maid. If I put that right, will you stay?"

"My Lord, that was not the reason—"

"Oh, I ken it wasn't the reason. You have been a victim of your own youth and beauty."

My cheeks warmed. Did he know the fullness of what Christen Michell had said and thought about him?

"Aye," said Bessie, taking her turn in filling the doorway, amusement written all over her face. "I'm glad you seen it too."

"The castle is nae Christen Michell's to run as she sees fit," he declared to the two of us. "I've telt her as much this morning. I want you to stay, Ishbell. Will you?"

I managed a nod and the earlier excitement returned to his face in a smile.

"I'd also dearly love you to stop calling me 'My Lord'. And to eat your breakfast."

Bessie laughed. "One thing at a time, My Lord!"

"Dinna you start, Bessie Thom. Noo, where's the cream? The lassie needs building up; ye've been letting her waste away while I've been gone."

"She's managing to eat noo," noted Bessie as I ate the porridge the Laird had prepared. "I'll send Agnes for the cream... no, I'll get it myself. Her face'll turn it sour this morning." She paused, looking serious. "And let's nae hae anything else turning sour here in the castle. To lose a bairn is a terrible thing, no matter what age it happens at, and some folks never get over it. Not really. Grief makes them do and say many a strange thing. Whatever else she is, Christen Michell is a poor old lady with much regret in her heart." She clapped her hands and returned to her smiling self. "And here's the wee master, who disna even ken anything was amiss." She added this last meaningfully, in case anything wrong should be said.

But it wasn't. Wrongs had been righted. The kitchen was full of warmth and happiness again. Wee Thomas wolfed his own food, so keen was he to see and hear the new harp in use.

I sung a ballad about a man who got lost in Faeryland and emerged years later to find his children grown and old, while he himself had stayed young. Christen Michell entered the room as I sang of The Faery Queen and her tricks and wiles, and she sat to take breakfast at the topmost long table. How things would stand between us now, I did not know. I bore her no grudge, understanding her sorrow about Mary, but would she be cross about my staying? As I sat helping Wee Thomas write out his letters, the old lady approached.

"In my heart I am glad you are to remain," she said, then in a lower voice, "but you must now be strong, Isobell. In more ways than one. I think, in time, it would be good for the boy to be sent to school as the Laird was. He will come to an age where he needs toughening up in ways that women cannot provide. But let us enjoy our time together here, as women of God. There must be some hymns to be played upon the new instrument?"

The Holly and the Ivy

Another phase of life began at the castle: the preparations for the coming twelve days of Christmas. There was happy anticipation, there was a lot of hard work, and wonderful scents and sights were to be found everywhere.

It was one of the happiest times I had ever known. Gone was all the despair of the last weeks, for I was to stay. Gone too, was what little faith I had had in the things Christen Michell said to me. I could see her eye was jaded; the pain of the past imprinted her opinion and fed her negative view of life and men. About some things she was right: one day Wee Thomas would have no need of a governess; one day the Laird might send him away to school. But none of that was happening yet. I had changed and adapted to avoid unhappiness before, and I would do it again.

So I threw myself into the delighted atmosphere of the moment with great joy. The Laird looked every day, before breakfast even, for a shipment of goods he had arranged for Christmas. Finally it arrived and was pulled up the wooden stairs from the tunnel below. "I hope to keep all my ladies happy," he said, with a wide smile, "and my wee laddie!"

There was fine French wine for Christen Michell, exotic herbs for Bessie, and white wheat flour for me. "I thought you would be used to softer bread in London," he explained. Bessie described the purchase as 'a piece of nonsense', but as with all things at that time, it was said with a smile.

Wee Thomas and I flitted throughout the festive busyness of the castle, stopping as we fancied, helping, or sometimes hindering, various people with various tasks. The extra cooks from the farm were still housed in the castle and the kitchen was generally a crowded place, but one day we found Agnes alone crying over a bucket of eels. They were slimy and she was supposed to prepare them for pickling. "Oh pickled eels are lovely," I told her.

"Aye, the Laird said it was a dish you would have had," she snapped as if the unpleasant job were my doing.

Memory stirred: a page from the small book of cooking advice I had read before coming to Scotland. "They are freshwater eels?" I asked, and she shrugged. "Salt. That's what's needed." The salt worked a treat, and soon the long fishies, as Wee Thomas called them, were free of their slime, though much of it was on the boy and myself.

Descending from the tower, dressed in fresh clothing, we encountered Duncan and some more of the men carrying fragrant and bushy greenery into the entrance hall. Bessie and Christen Michell issued orders and we watched as holly and ivy and mistletoe and green fir branches were dragged across the floor into the great hall.

Bessie told us how the prickly holly represented the power of the male and the softly curved ivy, the female. Mistletoe was where they reconciled. This year the holly branches outnumbered the boughs of ivy and she thought that was a good thing. "Certain hens need to remember they dinna rule this roost!" she said with her customary chuckle.

Ladders were brought in and the roof was soon alive with activity as the foliage was hung where the stone walls met the timber roof. Everywhere there was rustling of branches as in the forest, and the scent of the fir trees dominated the air. Christen Michell told us how the holly leaves represented the crown of thorns worn by Christ, and the berries, his blood. Wee Thomas touched a berry, a mixture of wonder and fear showing in his face.

Jasper became highly animated when he saw the mistletoe. "The Kissing Tree!" he cried and proceeded to spread round a story about how maidens could be kissed if they were found to be standing under the white berried plant. "Only on the cheek," he specified as Duncan approached with a bunch of the stuff. "And only if the lady stands there of her own free will. You cannot just run around with a piece of it, McCulloch."

"If Bell will give us some music to work by, we will take care nae to hang any above her," said Duncan with a laugh.

The great hall took on a great sense of the festive as I played. Some improvisation was needed: I couldn't remember all the details of each and every Christmas song. I sang of holly and ivy, a Merry Christmas, bells on high and the Christ Child. Bessie nodded in approval: "Something for everyone," she said.

Wee Thomas danced to the music and revelled in the applause that came from the men up by the roof and those on the earthen floor.

"Here is a scene I could watch forever!" boomed the Laird from where he stood by the top table, how long he'd been standing there unclear. "The Faerie Queene at her harp with her wee imp in attendance."

"Am I the wee imp?" asked Wee Thomas.

"Of course you are, laddie, of course you are," confirmed the Laird, picking up his son, and the festive merriment increased beneath the high ceiling of the great hall.

The Daft Days

"Good fun as the Twelve Days are, I'll be sad to see the end of Advent," confided Bessie. "The auld Ladybird has bin much easier to feed without all her funcy sauces and different meats."

"Maybe she'll be in a better mood now she's getting more to eat?" I wondered aloud.

"Aye, well, her crusty countenance is nae just caused by the food, Bell. You must ken that. She's been on about her angels again and the Laird's nae budging. Though he is becoming a wee bit vexed, I think. Come, we'll give him something else to think about; it does a man good to be teased sometimes," she said with a wicked laugh. "And this is the last breakfast before Christmas. We'll be all grand with everybody through there after this; you pay heed, Lassie, learn fae the best."

Bemused, I sat back down with Wee Thomas. My goal for his education had stretched as my time in the castle had expanded. I was determined to have him knowing both italic and black-letter scripts. It was good to make that my focus and not what the future might bring.

"The Daft Days are upon us, ladies," declared the Laird on entering the kitchen. "Are you all ready for them, Bessie? We are to feast and make merry into the New Year?"

"Aye, Thomas, we are," she said.

I looked at her, askance; should she be addressing him by his given name like that? But she was about to explain.

"Aye," she continued. "It's at times like these that you look back over the years, and forward too. I remember well when you yersel were Wee Thomas."

The Laird smiled good-naturedly as he helped himself to bacon and sat down, pausing to look at his son's writing before starting to eat.

"And look, here, noo," continued Bessie. "The next generation is learning to read. And young Bell, she's eighteen years young, surely ripe for wedding and bedding, don't you agree, Thomas?"

I choked on my barley bread. Bessie bashed me on the back and gave my shoulder a squeeze. The Laird said nothing and I did not dare look up to see his face.

"Come now, sir," Bessie continued. "You must know many young lads as would make a good match for our lassie here."

It was mortifying. I wanted to run down the tunnel to the sea. Screaming. Instead, I peeked up at the Laird to see what his reaction was.

"What would a great oaf like me know of such things?" he said, looking and sounding quite put out.

"Ach, what nonsense," said Bessie, then turning to me. "Twelve days of revelry lie ahead, and many young men will visit the castle. There's a special feast for the tenant farmers and their families, and one for the merchants, and another for the workers. Oh Aye, a body roon aboot as has anything to do with the castle will be traipsing through the halls and making merry. Very merry. Dancin' and drinkin'. It's a time to be social and meet folks."

"Bessie," said the Laird with some firmness, "ye ken as well as I, there's some uncouth lads about, nae culture about them at all. Not like this." He indicated our writing on the table. "And have you seen what is happening with the young eens now? They're all for wearing their plaids belted and high up their bare legs, some new fashion taken from the dress of soldiers. Ishbell disna want to be bothered wi' idiots like that."

"It's Christmas," said Bessie as if this bested his argument. "And you dinna ken fit us ladies want to be bothered with. We might like to see a bit o' leg." And with that, her laughter resounded around, raising the spirit and mood of the kitchen.

"Dinna you let Bessie Thom bully you into dancing with anybody you don't want to dance with," advised the Laird in some seriousness which only made us laugh more.

"She can dance with me," offered Wee Thomas.

"And me," said Jasper, coming in and commandeering the conversation from that point. He was very excited. People had been giving him accounts of Christmas at the castle. He sought permission for plays and games and various other diversions, all of which the Laird agreed to readily.

It was a task to settle Wee Thomas for the night, but then once he was finally asleep, I found I could not rest either. Exhilaration was running too high; it danced through every room of the castle like a frosty and naughty woodland sprite, stirring us all with thoughts of the days to come. When my eyelids finally relented, my dreams were filled with Christmas puddings and oats and salt and presents and dancing and plaids belted too high and sparkling holly up high near the roof and merriment all around. Round and round in the stone circle, round and round down below in the chamber and round and round the castle.

I woke with a start from something dark and terrible that I was sure had involved the dungeon. But that was silly. Daft even. For it was Christmas!

The First Day

Bessie was right, we were all grand through in the great hall for breakfast, though it was no grander a meal than usual; in fact for the Laird, Wee Thomas and myself it was plainer. We had oatmeal brose and barley bread and weak ale. No cream, no bacon, no eggs, no honey or dried fruit and no preserves. It was a day for celebrating the birth of Christ, a day for church, though Christen Michell got out of that as usual by claiming infirmity and old age had made her tired on this day of days.

Instead of our customary walk through the woods and along the road, the Laird had Bessie, myself and Wee Thomas travel to church with him in his coach, a transport I had not known the castle boasted. During the short journey in the comfortable seats, while Wee Thomas peered out of the windows and made handprints on the glass, time off work was discussed. The twelve days were meant to be free from our usual labours, but Wee Thomas would still need care, and food still had to be prepared. It was arranged that Janet's eldest daughter, Jane, would take over for me at getting my charge to bed most evenings, so I could join the night time revels. Bessie would likewise get time off to celebrate with us; she and the farm cook would take turns being in charge of the castle kitchens.

After a lengthy service sitting in the hard and wooden Manteith family pew, with its ornately carved loft above, it was back to the relative comfort of the coach and its two horses. I regretted not bringing a single carrot or apple for the animals but contented myself with speaking soft and stroking their faces and manes and enjoying their indignant snorts at the lack of treats. Wee Thomas's fondness of the horses warmed my heart as I thought about my gift for him. A lot of evening sewing time had gone into it and his face repaid me manifold as we sat by the huge, blazing fire in the great hall, before the feast of the day.

"A white horse! Like King Arthur rode!" he declared in delight at the poppet, perfectly understanding and appreciating the intent behind the gift.

I had sewn presents for everyone, trying to treat all equally, but as I gave out the pocket kerchiefs it was obvious, hopefully only to me, that the Laird, Bessie and Jasper's gifts had received much more work than the others. In that order. Jasper lifted an eyebrow as he compared the amount of embroidery on each piece. That I could not refer to my employer by only his first name was not my fault but it meant Bessie and Jasper had one embroidered letter each while Thomas Manteith had two.

Christen Michell gave me a white lace collar for my dress, Bessie some balm that smelled of roses, and Jasper a carved wooden mermaid which I quickly pocketed away out of sight.

The Laird's presents to his household were most lavish and generous. Bessie got a large pestle, Christen Michell, a new Latin bible, though where he acquired such an item that I had thought was forbidden, I didn't know. For Wee Thomas there was a bejewelled crown which was worn for the entirety of the twelve days, even in bed sometimes when I wasn't there to dissuade.

I felt quite dazed when the Laird handed me a small golden looking glass and comb. They were so beautiful, my eyes misted as reflected firelight danced in the glass. I had never owned anything so special; our father's house had been full of grand things, my room included, but these items were just mine, forever, and so carefully thought out, for my hair was always in need of—

"Mermaid gifts," murmured Jasper in my ear as the Laird served us all with warmed, spiced wine. "You should have sewn a bear poppet for him!"

"Shh! Brother. Hud yer whist."

"Ha! Getting into the Scots way of speaking too," he said with a laugh.

"Thomas! Ishbell!" called the Laird from behind us. "Come, I have something to show you."

So we were commanded away from the fire, through the kitchen passageway and outside to the bake house.

"Breathe it in," said the Laird as we stood outside in bright frostiness of the day. "What do you smell?"

"Oranges," said Wee Thomas.

"Cinnamon, raisins, nutmeg," I added, discerning them all in the air.

"Aye, that there is the very smell of Christmas. I used to run out here when I was a wee lad just like you, Thomas, and beg a bit of bun or sweet bread, whatever they would give me. Do you think they'll spare us something now?"

The Laird carried in a flagon of spiced wine for the ladies of the bake house and we were rewarded with soft and sticky raisin buns, which we took round the back of the castle to the walled garden. There we sat on a carved stone bench beside the sundial. Though we ourselves sat in the light of the low Christmas Day sun, the sundial was still in shadow and coated in tiny spikes of frost. The Laird said it was not well placed and told us of his plans to build other time keeping statues in the sunnier middle of the garden. Wee Thomas danced off among the bushes and beds of the garden.

"Ishbell, I wanted to give you this," said the Laird, then removing a small, ornately bound book from his beneath his coat. "I thought, better out here; it would not do to seem to be giving one more than another, but you have given us so much here this year."

I held it in my hands, then I opened it. *Venus and Adonis* by William Shakespeare. I ran my hand down the first page.

"It may be a silly story, but the words appeared beautiful and I thought you might appreciate the language," said the Laird in a bit of a rush. "I picture you reading of an evening, when this one has gone to sleep. Am I right? Have I judged well?"

"You are wrong, but you have judged well," I said, pleasure at the unexpected gift rich in my being. "For I love to read, but I brought no books with me. Thank you, sir, oh thank you so much."

"Lassie, you're welcome," he said, seeming to be relieved. "Now, we better haste back inside, so we dinna miss the feast."

The Poem

The twelve days of Christmas were intertwined with the epic poem given to me by the Laird; its words and phrases blended through the activities of the days, springing to mind at, sometimes, inopportune moments. At first I had been a little shocked at the subject matter of Venus attempting to woo, or as Bessie would say, bed, Adonis and then his refusal of her. Was I to read some unspoken message into the gift? Was I Venus? I laughed at the very thought. I, the youth, then? But no, the Laird had declared that it was the words that were of note, not the story, so I considered the work line by line and carried it through the festive days.

All the kissing. Kissing and embracing that lasted for hours. Thoughts of those passages coloured my cheeks when the Laird was near during the twelve days, and he was always near, or at least I was always aware of where he was. I didn't need to look round to know he was standing by the top table speaking to a tenant farmer or that he warmed his hands at the fire after seeing some guests out. My body warmed in ways that were unseemly, and I quivered with wanton thoughts.

When I danced during the evening revelries it always seemed I was in the Laird's arms, though I never was, for he never danced. He watched though, and his gaze caused heat to blossom in my face and body. He had been right about the new fashion among the young men for shortened, belted plaids; I saw many hairy knees and calves that festive season, but they only made me wonder what the Laird's legs were like under his trews, if the hairs were the same colour as those that were so fair on his head or darker, as was to be the way with some of the men.

"Isobell!" I mentally chided myself.

"Isobell!" said my brother, who only used my full name when in worry or distress. "Is it the wine?" he asked.

I looked into my cup, confused. I drank only ale at the dances, wine made me dizzy.

"You are all aflutter, sister," he continued, pulling me to a quiet space at the side of the great room. "Is some young man to blame? Do I have to be gallant and point a sword at some bare-legged oaf's chest?"

"In truth it is the poem," I confessed, it never being easy to deceive Jasper. On my telling of which poem and from where it came, my twin grew serious.

"He gave you that? The Laird? I took him for a good man—"

"He is a good man. He thought I would like the words and the language."

"Language of lust and words of seduction? Isobell, he thinks you of humble origin, a kitchen maid raised up to a governess in this unorthodox household, but not his equal. You know that. So what can his intention be?"

"To give me a gift I would like; he knows we are familiar with Master Shakespeare."

Jasper's voice lowered to a hiss: "It seems we have fled one man who would kill, only to find another who would ruin."

"That is not true," I hissed back, incensed.

"It is true, Isobell. I was not intending to mention this during Christmas, but it is rumoured that the two of them, Richard and John, have reached Edinburgh. Now is not the time to be drawing attention to yourself in any way. You should go sew your white collar onto your dress. Be demure and nun-like as Christen Michell would have you be. Apparently she was right all along."

"Be quiet, Jasper; you're wrong and you're the one doing the ruining: you're ruining Christmas."

"Family quarrel?" asked Duncan, strolling up beside us. "Bell, will you no give us a song? A song and a story all in the one, like you do for Wee Thomas?"

"I would be happy to," I said, marching over to my harp, mine because no one else ever played it, not because it had been gifted to me alone, because it had not. I glared over at my brother as he stood with Duncan. Perhaps a tale of lustful longing? But the Laird was watching, a small crease between his brows; he had seen us argue perhaps? So I started with a song about the virgin birth but on prompts from various people, Duncan included, I moved onto to other Christmas melodies: *Ding Dong Merrily on High* and *In Dulci Jubilo* went down very well, and there was much dancing and laughter.

Duncan brought me wine which I drank a little fast, my throat being dry from singing, and my mind troubled by the idea of Richard and John now being in the same country. The Laird approached and I saw Jasper mime widening his eyes with his fingers to let me know he was watching our every move.

"You are an accomplished woman, Ishbell," said he of the golden head and soft voice and strong arms and wholesome oaty aroma. "I have been admiring the stitch work on my kerchief." His hands had touched where mine had been. It was suddenly ever so warm in that corner of the room but Jasper was there to cool any flames that had been fanned.

"She is most accomplished and most chaste. Let's hope she gets to remain so through Christmas."

"Jasper!" I was outraged and embarrassed and horrified.

"Aye, he's nae wrong," said the Laird, to my utter confusion. "Bonny quines have to watch themselves at times like these; many men gathered together with music and drink and feasting... But rest assured, Jasper, we will look out for your sister. We will keep her safe." And with that, the Laird was off on his rounds of the room, talking with everyone, rich, poor and middling, judging none as was his way, the way of a good man.

"I am not reassured," Jasper assured me.

"Oh, Brother. Can you not see how ridiculous you are being? He does not look at me that way, and the way things are going, I am likely to stay in a nun's state all my life. Does that make you happy?"

He moved his head and hands to and fro as if weighing up the situation. "It's not an unpleasing idea," he said, a small smile appearing again on his face.

I did not peruse the poem that night, nor the next, and tried to quench the thoughts that came, unbidden, into my mind. I had been indulging in a silly story, just as the Laird had said it was, and imagining parts of it to be mine. And his. I was the one who was ridiculous I realised, as I looked at my mad hair and round face in the looking glass. I laid the beautiful book face down and tried to go to sleep in my old bed in Agnes's room, Jane being up in my usual bed in the nursery. The dark felt empty without the small boy's breathing nearby, and without the joy of beautiful words of love, and without hope.

The Twelfth Day

"Sister, all is well," said Jasper, beaming from where he stood beside the fire in the kitchen. "I have discussed the matter with Bessie and she confirms what I originally thought: The Laird is a good and honourable man. He cannot have read the thing. He saw it was by our friend and a tale that maidens may like, that is said of it after all, and he believed it to be an appropriate gift. And as to the other two rogues: there are so many taverns in Edinburgh, they are likely to stick there, sampling each and every wine and whisky as is their wont. Put them from your mind and adorn yourself in your best gown, for Twelfth Night is upon us. You are to star in a play, I am to be Lord of Misrule and the day is gay with the sheer merriment of it all!"

Irked that Jasper had not been able to take my word that all was well, and had had to hear it from Bessie before being reassured, I replied, "I am not starring in your play, Brother; it is unseemly. And I cannot put on my best gown, for where am I to say I acquired such a thing?"

"I'll see to that, dinna worry," said Bessie coming in with a jug of cream. "You go dress yersel up, quine. Hae some fun today, for it's all back to normal tomorrow."

The fact that normality beckoned seemed no bad thing. I was tired with the wine and the late nights and all the many different people I had met over a short space of time. I'd missed our cosy breakfasts and my quiet nights with Wee Thomas. Agnes was an unfriendly chamber partner, the atmosphere chill between us when she was awake, so I often feigned sleep.

However it was a pleasant activity to put on a fine dress and jewellery: I chose the red velvet and the pearls, hoping it was not too much. My clothes seemed rumpled and disturbed in the old trunk. Had Agnes been rummaging? I would happily have given her the pick of the clothing; I could not wear it anyway, but then how to explain that to her and everyone else? The kitchen maid turned governess dishing out finery to people? And she would probably not be pleased with it anyway. She had not liked my simple embroidered kerchief on the First Day; I'd seen it later, tossed aside on the floor.

I found the pearl comb for my hair and the looking glass showed a better presented Ishbell than I'd seen for a long time.

"Lassie! What a picture!" exclaimed Bessie. "You'll turn some heads today!"

"Is it not too much? Am I showing too much bosom?" I had noticed many of the ladies hereabouts did go for this fashion too, but I was meant to be lowly.

"I'd say you look perfect," assured Bessie. "Wouldn't you agree, sir?"

For a moment it was not clear that the Laird did agree. His mouth hung open for a few seconds as he regarded me, but just as it was beginning to seem as if I had irrevocably erred, he smiled and all was well.

"You look fine indeed," he declared. "Is this a new gown?"

Bessie stepped in as promised. "Every bonny quine receives gifts from admirers, and what better time to wear them than the twelfth day?"

"Indeed, indeed," said the Laird, nodding as he made his way out of the kitchen and through to the great hall for breakfast.

"And I have the perfect jewel to complete your outfit," said Bessie, with a chuckle. "You mind on that lady, back in November, the one with the baby who came out feet first?"

I nodded. That had been a long night. I'd sung songs till I was hoarse as it had seemed to give strength to the mother.

"Well," said Bessie, removing an object from her skirts. "Her brother is a silver smith in Aberdeen and I asked her to have this made for you."

At first I thought it to be an autumn leaf cast in silver, but then I recognised the thing. It was the elfin blade!

"Bessie!" I said, shocked.

"There we go," she said, pinning it to the breast of my dress. "To ward off evil. I think we'll see one ill-tricket wee lassie jump back from it today at least."

I shook my head at Bessie's own ill-tricketness but accepted her gift and headed through to the great hall. There I hugged Wee Thomas and thanked Jane for looking after him. Comments on my attire came from all directions, but happily everyone seemed to approve, except of course Agnes. She gave my chest a disdainful glare and seemed about to make some comment, but then froze with her mouth open, staring at the elfin blade.

"Red is a colour that becomes you well," said Christen Michell, stepping in front of Agnes. "How suitable for this last day of celebration. Come, we are to go below ground for your first penance."

Truly, I did not wish to go and make confession, though it was to be made in private with Father Daniel, not publicly as such things had been done in the past. And then I dearly wished I had not gone. It was one of the most mortifying moments of my life, partly because I had not understood how vague I was allowed to be and partly because of all that had been going on over Christmas. I was very glad once I was up above ground again and in the company of my brother.

"Bell, you look like a holly berry," said Jasper. "Your face matches your dress. But I dare say we can adjust it all well into my likeness."

"Your likeness?"

"I am to be you and you are to be me, no stuffy London mouths to open in aghast-ness here. Nothing like a bit of gender swapping to get a laugh."

An argument ensued. I felt I had pushed the bounds of propriety enough with my gown and my unwittingly honest confession; I was not going to act in a play, as a man no less. So Ian was drafted in and, after the broth and wine and roast meat meal of midday, much jollity arose.

The floor was cleared, tables and chairs carried to the edges for us all to sit, the many guests of the day included. They were a varied mix on the last day of Christmas: all sorts of people the Laird did business with from far and wide, the laundress, the weaver, masons, builders, carpenters; we all of us congregated together beneath the high wooden ceiling of the great hall.

"I do remind you kind sirs, fine ladies," said Ian with a wink at me from the centre of the room, "that I am a man, playing a lady (Isobell), playing a man. Such is the way of the theatre; may you enjoy!"

If silly stories there had ever been, this one topped them all. It was a tale of twins separated and lost on an island, then fallen in love with people they met there. Isobell disguised herself as a man to confuse matters further and fell in love with the duke for whom she worked. I laughed along with everyone but silently wished to strangle my brother. He, played by Ian, played as me, fell in love with the cook; Bessie Thom laughed loud and full at this, and many a nonsensical letter was passed between characters, played mainly by farmhands and dairymaids as far as I could make out.

"Do you miss London, and this sort of pageantry?" asked the Laird sitting down beside me at the ending of the play, still doing his rounds, talking to everyone as he always did.

"No, sir. Why would I? It is so much better here."

"How so?" he asked, looking to be genuinely intrigued.

So I listed the aspects I loved of our new Scottish home: the clean air, the vastness of land and countryside, the spaces so free of crowds and noise and scent of people, the stone circle, the woods, the pool, Wee Thomas and Bessie. But I could not name the biggest and most beautiful aspect. The most radiant and good. The salt of the earth and the light of my world. But he sat beside me for a while and we laughed together at the antics of my sibling. And with that, I was content.

The Lord of Misrule

The feast of Twelfth Night was the biggest of Christmas and the most merry. There were grand guests from Aberdeen, magistrates, baillies and other people who were more fashionably dressed than we had become used to. Everyone was infected with the knowledge that life went back to the usual hard grind on the morrow and was making the most of the night. Wee Thomas and I had made a pastry castle again but we were all more excited by the Twelfth Night Cake that got passed round at the end of the meal. It contained one small, hard, dried pea and one bean. Whosoever found these peas in their piece of the fruity sweet bread would be Lord and Lady of The Castle for the night.

"It'll be me," said Jasper. "It always is; that pea somehow finds its way to my hand, every year since I can remember. I'm often the Lady though."

True as that had been in England, the theory proved false north of the border. It was Duncan who raised his hand in triumph, a tiny pea between his finger and thumb. He leapt up in excitement and the Laird willingly relinquished the grand carved chair to him.

Then I bit down on the bean and held it up.

Duncan let out a cheer. "This really is my night! So the first thing I shall do…" He paused for dramatic effect, in a way that Jasper would have appreciated had he not been so deep in his own disappointment. "Is take Ishbell to wife!"

I looked round at him, surprised at his use of the Laird's name for me.

"You don't even need to move, Lassie, you're already sitting in the right place," he said with a laugh. "And you, young Jasper, can be our fool!"

Jasper perked up at this. "A proper fool? Like kings and queens have? I can say whatever truths I like and no one may be offended?"

I had a slightly ominous feeling as Duncan confirmed that this was in fact the case, and Jasper began to prance round the room. My brother was at once poetic and stark and told us it was his turn to be the storyteller. Great entertainment he did provide, though it was difficult to discern what was truth and what was fiction. Had Agnes really tried to entrap a rich gentleman with a love spell that had gone wrong? Who had that been? The Laird? I felt my own face set into as sour an expression as Agnes's and quickly corrected it to a smile. Was Bessie really the rescuer of wronged women? Did he mean me?

I accepted Duncan's offer of more wine, it making Jasper's antics easier to bear.

"Do me, do me, do me!" shouted Wee Thomas and was rewarded with a tale of how he was the great King Arthur come again to save Britain in its time of need. The Laird was left alone. I was left alone. There was a story about the dairymaids that I didn't completely hear and understand; Duncan spoke over it asking what games I should like to play as 'his Lady'.

I asked to see Jasper and Ian do the egg tossing. They took small steps back from one another with each throw and finally the egg landed on the floor with a splat. Then eggs were passed round with spoons. Duncan bent terribly close when we exchanged eggs, his face almost upon my breast, and then he broke the egg anyway. Snapdragon was played with fiery raisins; I noticed the Laird, at one of the lower tables, doing particularly well at that game.

Then came the dancing. The music got wilder as the night wore on, faster and faster, I was spun and flung around the room, every man wanting to dance with the Lady of Misrule. The most unpleasant gentleman was one of the magistrates, a Mr. William Dunn, Dean of Guild, a title he gave me several times. He was the only person, apart from Agnes, to notice the elf bolt on my dress, indeed he bent his head very close to it in examination which made me want to shudder. Though dressed with fresh looking collar and cuffs, Mr. Dunn smelled unwashed like something gone off, or rotten fish, and his hair was dark with oil. He smiled when I told him the elfin blade was a charm against evil and that it had been gifted to me. His smile made me feel I actually needed such a charm. Duncan rescued me from this man twice and I was whirled and skipped until I thought I could whirl and skip no more.

Then Jasper insisted on teaching everyone La Volta, the fast lifting dance, and got me to partner men who wanted to learn. Up and down, down and up, so many faces looking and laughing, so many dancing partners with indelicately wandering hands, and even more who were not endowed with sufficiently strong arms for the task, and I was finished.

I was dizzy. I was faint. It was not unlike the sea-sickness I had endured to get to Scotland in the first place.

"Fresh air," said Duncan. "That'll sort you out." And I was whisked across the earthen floor towards the kitchen passage.

"Far ye gaing?" The voice was rough and cross; it seemed impossible that it had come from the Laird, but it was he who stood, barring the way to the outside, to my escape from the heat and crowd and dancing.

Duncan started to tell how I was feeling the heat but was cut short by the angry Laird and sent away. I stepped into the passageway where it was cooler and leant against the wall, it being cooler still. But there was nothing cool about the Laird's eyes; they had taken on something of the bear-like expression from the day I had first seen him.

"I think you have danced enough for one night," he said to me, stern and disapproving.

"And you have danced too little," I answered, feeling undeservedly chastised.

"Well, obviously I dinna dance," he said, annoyed.

"Why not?" I replied, also annoyed.

He spread his arms to the side. "Do I look like I'm made for it?"

I surveyed the beautiful man. I saw his natural grace. I knew of his strong arms. "Yes. You do. I suppose you believe the activity beneath you?"

"No, I—Lassie. This is not the point. It is time for you to take to your bed for the night. And bar the door behind you too."

But I couldn't concentrate on the words of Thomas Manteith anymore. My attention was fixed on something terrible that I had just spied happening at the other side of the great hall. Two men were passing through the doors from the entrance hall. Two men with tall hats.

I pressed myself against the wall, so as to be hidden behind the Laird, and backed away. It was dark in the passageway. They wouldn't see. I hoped they wouldn't see, although their eyes were everywhere in the room, seeking, searching, furious and curious.

"Ishbell, dinna be feart," said the Laird. "I sounded vexed, I ken. With you I seem to forget my size and appearance can be frightening, but I would never harm ye. Quiney…"

Wicked Richard's foul glare lingered on the passageway. I cringed, longing to be able to vanish right into the very wall itself. Then he looked away. He hadn't seen. He hadn't found me. My great plan might be in tatters but it was not entirely unravelled. Not yet.

The Secret Stairway

"Lassie, I didna mean to speak so rough—"

"No." He thought it was him I fled. "Not you." But it was time to flee: flee or be caught, flee or be murdered; I sensed my time in absentia would not have lessened the wicked intent of my intended. And there was no longer any point in maintaining the lie. "The man I was supposed to marry is in there. He is looking for me. I have to run, I have to leave." I staggered back as I spoke, not knowing which way to run.

"What?" The Laird's head whipped round as he glared back into the great hall, seeking Wicked Richard. "Ishbell, wait, come with me."

He took my arm and I was led into the kitchen, where he picked up a lantern. I was pathetic. I couldn't think, couldn't adjust my plan, certainly couldn't go back through into the passageway. But the Laird took us round the side way that led to the entrance hall.

"It's safe, Lassie. Here, look." He lifted a large tapestry of unicorns and thistles, revealing a wooden panel in the whitewashed wall. This he pushed and it opened inwards. Escape! I climbed through the square hole in the wall, not thinking about what might lie beyond, and was closely followed by the Laird. We were in another passage, small and stony and grey, and after a short way it led to a narrow stairwell that was not lit by torches and sconces like the big one, but dark and shadowy and hidden. Secret. Indeed safe. For now. I sank down onto one of the steps and sat, breathing, sweating, trying to think what to do next. I could hardly stay behind the wall forever.

"You're shaking," said the Laird. "And your hands are cold." He had my hands in his. He tried to rub warmth back into them, but if I was nearing my end, what was the point?

"He's found me. He's somehow found me. We must have left some clue."

"You and Jasper?"

And out it all came. Wicked Richard's reputation for cruelty. His last wife, bruised and frightened and then dead of a mysterious malady. My decision. My plan. The boat. The farce. The rumours of York, then Edinburgh. On to the current reality: he was here.

"Well, let's see where he's gone," said the Laird, raising me to stand. "You're still shaking, quine. There's no need; he winna find you in my castle. I know all the ways of it. He disna. We're going to look through the Laird's lug."

Halfway up the stairs there was a long recess to the side: we walked into it, the lantern illuminating the coarseness of the walls and the windowless state of the small and rounded space. "Put up here by my grandfather for his own wicked ways, now we can put it to good use. Look, see if you can spot the wretch who seeks you." The Laird pointed to a triangular hole in the wall, through which sounds of music and laughter were coming.

I positioned my face close to the strange little opening and peered down into the great hall. Ian and Jasper were talking to Wicked Richard and our older brother, John. For it was he that was the second tall-hatted man. I told the Laird, and he took his turn at the peephole and gave the scene a long assessing look.

"It is a pity there is so much noise tonight; we could have made out their words otherwise, the walls of the lug are thinned in places and shaped to augment speech made in the hall. But no matter: I will hide you and I will expel him from the castle. Has there been any... Has this man ever treated you rough, Lassie?"

"Rough?"

"It will affect the manner in which he is removed."

"He did sometimes…" My hands went to my shoulders, remembering a rough grabbing and pushing against a wall and, if Jasper had not interrupted us—

"Hush," said the Laird, taking my hand again in his large and warm one. "Come, let's make you safe."

Up and up the narrow stairs we went, until finally we came out into a closet of some sort. There was a washing bowl and clothing, but we passed quickly by and into a bed chamber.

"My room," explained the Laird, shocking me somewhat, because surely I shouldn't be in his room? But then, no one would think to look for me there, of course.

The Laird knelt down and lifted up a portion of the wooden floor. "A priest's hole, for hiding," he said. "It's comfy enough, there's some cushions, but it will be dark. Do ye think—"

"It's wonderful. Perfect." Wicked Richard would never ever find me in there. I almost jumped into the person-sized recess beneath the floor, so inviting did it feel.

"Only open up for my voice," advised the Laird before he closed the door and left on his mission.

Once he had gone, taking all his light and radiance with him, it was exceedingly dark. But strangely warm. Comforting somehow. It felt like I was in a good place, a place where harm could not reach me. Sleep beckoned on the soft cushions that had a pleasant scent. How odd: to have been faced with a dreaded terror and to now be so relaxed.

It wasn't long before I heard the sound of the door and the Laird's voice, assuring me that it was only him. He helped me out of the hiding place and urged me to sit on the bed, and told me that all was well. Wicked Richard had already departed before the Laird had reached the great hall even, and both my brothers with him.

"Jasper!" I said in fear, for his part in all this would not sit well with the two rogues.

"It is good, I think," said the Laird. "He and Ian have them convinced that you have moved on from here, that you took up that position near Inverness, but Jasper has gone with them to the Inn to show goodwill before they return South. They are talked out of pursuing you further. Or at least they say they are. I think you should sleep here in this room tonight, Isobell. I will stand guard for you, in case they return."

My protests were weak. The Laird brushed them aside as he might a small flying insect. So it came to be that I slept a long and sound sleep in the soft and cosy bed of Thomas Manteith at the very top of the tall tower of the castle. Just before I fell asleep I thought I saw a shooting star pass across the ceiling of the Laird's room, but then exhaustion borne of earlier fear summoned deep slumber.

The Proposal

There really was a star, bright and large, sitting in the hollow of a thin crescent moon. The sky was still dark, though the silver light of dawn hung round its edges. It was as if I lay upon a soft and fluffy cloud, scented like heaven, admiring the celestial objects around me. I soon realised I was looking through a window in the ceiling, a shapely rounded window with many small sides, and that, in fact, I was lying in what must be the Laird's bed.

I sat up and beheld the man himself sitting in an armchair under three narrow windows, the silvery morning glow lighting half his face. He was watching me and his eyes were wild.

"I have it, Ishbell. I have it!"

"Have what, sir? Have you slept?" His appearance suggested he had not.

"No, but that is as well, for I have had much time to think. I know exactly how to ensure your safety. It has been so obvious all along really in the strange ways that life points things out. You must marry me."

My mind went blank. I looked up at the ceiling window and tried to formulate a thought, any thought. There was the moon and the bright star clear in their intention and purpose. I looked back at the Laird. I had misheard him. I was still half asleep and in shock from the events of the previous night, which were returning to mind as my body wakened.

"Sir, I—"

"Ah, no. Dinna be feart, Lassie. It would be to keep you safe here in the castle. If you were married to me, no other man could make claims on you. But life will go on the same as it is now. You're happy here, I think? You like taking care of Wee Thomas?"

I still had no clear thoughts but a sensation was growing in my chest, swelling and receding as if it didn't know quite what to do.

"So you are not asking me to marry you." That fact was clear, had to be held onto, before nonsensical notions ran away with themselves.

His eyes were still rather wild and bear-like. So was his golden hair, being more unkempt than I had ever seen it. "Aye, I am," he said. "But we can make of it what we will. Why should state and church dictate what has to be between man and woman? We are friends, good friends, and that's how we will stay. And you would be safe, Lassie. No more worries about wicked men coming after ye; I saw how frightened you were last night and I never want to see you look like that again."

I got out of the bed and stood in the cold air of the Laird's chamber. With the change in temperature came understanding. He pitied me. He was being kind as he always was to all those he came into contact with. And this was such an ultimate kindness that it would affect his life forever. And mine. It was unbearable. For the second time in so many hours, I found myself wanting to flee a man who offered me marriage.

But this was the Laird, and I had to answer him. Of course I did. I squeezed words past the painful swell in my chest. "Thank you, My Lord, but I must decline."

His brow furrowed in confusion and he looked like he was going to speak again. I had to stop him and I had to get out of the room.

"Good day to you, sir," I said as calmly as I could and walked away with my head high. My attempt at a dignified exit from the excruciating scene was spoiled somewhat by having to unlock the door with its big stiff key. I finally managed to turn the wretched bolt, just as the Laird started to make an awkward offer of assistance, and then I ran down the stairs, footsteps echoing off the circular walls as I went.

I paused halfway down to catch my breath. I was hot and sweaty with embarrassment and heart-sore from the sadness of it all. Why did he have to do that? Nothing could be the same between us now. Gone forever were our happy care-free breakfasts and interesting talks. Everything was ruined. I put my hands on the startlingly cold wall of the stairwell to steady myself and another realisation occurred. The Laird thought he could save me from the pain of marriage to a bad man. But the pain he had just caused me was worse than any I could imagine Wicked Richard inflicting. Far worse. I had no fondness for Wicked Richard. He couldn't touch my heart. The pain lessened as a grim determination grew, eclipsed like the sun by the moon on a portentous day, a day of doom or a day of reckoning.

By the time I reached the bottom of the stairs a new plan was formulated but it had to be done right. I had to dress for the occasion. Agnes was still abed in our small room.

"Where've you been?" she asked. "There was one awful to-do with fine gentlemen here looking for you."

"I've been in the Laird's bed, Agnes. And those were not fine gentlemen. And now I'm leaving."

For this, she had no reply, so I was left in peace to dress as lavishly and warmly as I could. From now on, I would take all the small comforts life offered. My green satin dress was one of them, my black Dutch cloak another. Truly, I would have rather have wrapped myself up in the warm comfort of the plaid that the Laird had given— No! Such thoughts would not help. And I would not take it with me. I struggled to maintain my angry determination for a moment – *why did he have to be so kind?* – then sat on the bed and pulled on the long-hidden well-heeled boots. They completed the outfit and were practical too; there was a long walk ahead. Just as I was combing my hair, with my old comb, Bessie appeared in the doorway.

"Right you," she said in her not to be argued with voice. "Kitchen. Now."

That was fine. That was well. It would mayhap be wise to have some breakfast before setting off. Though how the food would fit round the pulsating ache of my heart and reach the swirling pit of despair my stomach had become I did not know.

It worsened in the kitchen, the scene of so many breakfasts. I could hardly breathe. The fire crackled, recently lit, a little smoky. My eyes stung and nipped with the acrid atmosphere of the place.

"Out with it! Fit's this Agnes is saying about ye going?"

"That's right. I have to."

"Lassie," said Bessie, inspecting me more closely and wrapping her warm arms round me.

The sympathy was overpowering, tears sprang forth, trapped no more.

"I can't live a long life with this feeling," I explained, pressing my hand into my chest to illustrate the pain. "This way it will all be over sooner. Jasper can return home; I know he misses London. And I... I —"

"There has been a misunderstanding," said the Laird, striding into the room, and looking us over.

I tried to harden myself, for I knew he spoke false.

He continued to speak: "I wouldna expect anything of you, Isobell. You dinna need to be frightened like this."

I looked upwards, straight into the Laird's face, creased with concern as it was. "I understood. You suggested that we enter into a love-less marriage. A marriage in name only. A lie before God."

Bessie gasped and looked up at him sharply. "You made an offer of marriage to Bell?"

"Aye," said he.

"No," said I. "But it matters not. I am to marry the one man who does want me. I am already betrothed to him, and I shall be Wicked Richard's wife."

The Pain

The Laird and Bessie exploded with words together.

"By God, Ishbell, ye're nae!"

"Marry yon evil manny? Bell, have you lost your senses?"

I stood tall and strong, and faced them. "I think it is only now that I have awakened to sense. I'm going to the Inn to find him, and I'm going to marry him."

The Laird seemed to inflate with anger. I'd never seen his eyes as furious. "I'll take you over my knee before I see you commit such an act of foolishness!"

My own stature increased with rage also and I bellowed across the room at him, "Just try it! I grew up with brothers, sir. I can fight you!"

The room was left with the sound of breathing, heated breathing, and the odd crackle from the logs on the fire.

"I widna do it, Ishbell," he said in a much softer voice, nearer to his usual tone but spoken in such a way as to pull at the harp strings that seemed to have strung themselves across my breast. "But the idea of harm coming to you vexes me something sare."

"Aye, and me," said Bessie. "Sit doon, the two of ye. Ye'll listen to what I have to say."

It was more of a command than an invitation, so we sat, one on either side of the long table, the circular and triangular marks of mishap in the wood between us, sad now in the midst of disagreement and sorrow.

"You," said Bessie to the Laird in a cross tone that pleased me. "You've offended the wee lassie with an offer of a celibate marriage."

"I meant no offence. Isobell, look at me."

I looked at his beautiful, if somewhat coloured with emotion, face.

"My bairns are like me: huge. They tear a woman apart."

"Och! What nonsense!" scoffed Bessie. "Wee Thomas was one of the smallest babes I've ever seen that went on to survive. You were tiny yourself, Thomas. It's time we spoke of these things that hurt. Mary was a frail lassie; she barely survived her pregnancy. And then the bleeding wouldn't stop; it happens sometimes, no matter what we do. In the end God chooses the time of our passing, not us. All there is for us to do is live as best we can with the time we've got. Find as much joy and love in life as we're able."

The colour in the Laird's face had moved to the top of his cheekbones. The talk of his wife, whom he had obviously loved dearly, was causing him much suffering.

I put my hand on Bessie's arm. "Stop," I beseeched.

"Oh, it winna be like that for you Bell," she said. "You've got the hips for childbearing and the temperament of a mother. You only have to see how you are with Wee Thomas to know that."

The bench on the Laird's side of the table scraped back. He raised a finger and then made a fist as if forgetting his point. But then his voice was cold: "I will not lose another wife to the childbed." And with that, he stormed from the room.

"Aye, well," said Bessie, as if he'd merely made some passing comment about the weather. "This matter of children is an important one. They are in your future Lassie, I've nae doubt about that. If you marry yon plumped up peacock from last night, they'll be his to do with as he likes. And what will you do then? He seemed an important man, lots of other important men around him, nae doubt. What choices would be before you if he abused your child? I mean, would you trust such as him alone with Wee Thomas?"

The thought was abhorrent in the extreme. "No," I said, "but Bessie, I can't stay here. Not now." The pain was swelling again, pushing against my heart, making it hard to breathe.

"I ken you think you love the Laird," she began.

Breath left my body in a rush. "Think?"

"Bell, I—"

"I do love him, Bessie," I declared, standing, as if giving the emotion freedom through my mouth would free my heart of it. "And it's the most terrible thing that's ever happened to me! It was fine when it was just this unspoken feeling in me, I could cope with that, and be happy just being near him. But now, he's said it."

"Said what?" asked Bessie in a slow and thoughtful way, the opposite of the way in which I was speaking.

"That he does not. Love me, that is. Oh, of course I knew that really," I shouted as she seemed about to interrupt. "What a ridiculous idea. Stupid little Bell with her girlish dreams and stories. And look at me," I gestured up and down my wide frame. "But now I know he pities me enough to do this awful thing, to spoil his life, to stop his chances of ever finding a beautiful wife who he could actually love; and that's terrible in a whole lot of other ways. And I can't bear it…"

Anger kept melting to tears and that angered me and saddened me and I let Bessie guide me back to simply sitting on the bench.

"First off, my bonny quine, for bonny quine you are," she said, "I dinna doubt for a second that you love him. That's nae fit I meant at all. I walk through a veritable pink cloud in here every breakfast time. But you wait until I lay your first babe in your arms. Your idea of what love is will change at that moment, as will all the rest of your life. And if the Laird's determined in his statements, well…" She paused, head tilted to one side as if listening for something. "Most marriages are not based on love."

"I know that," I said, cross, because of course I knew that. Everybody knew that.

"There's others who would wed you in the blink of an eye. And love might grow, fondness there already is."

"Bessie, what nonsense." I felt faint. The course of the conversation and the morning was getting away from me; I wanted to be alone to think.

"Do you think your burnt bannocks tasted good, Bell? Or that the blackened ring on the table is decorative? And he tried to take the blame for you for yon." She pointed at the triangular cleft in the end of the table.

"Duncan?"

"What was the first thing he did last night on getting the crown?"

"But that's misrule. Everything's topsy turvy."

"And many a truth is spoken in jest. I've heard Jasper say that. Think on, Bell. You love that wee hoosie in the woods. You'd be happy waking up there each morning surrounded by trees and flowers."

I eyed her suspiciously; the words were strangely similar to my own imaginings on seeing the house.

Her eyes sparkled back at me. "And the way the lad looks at you, you'd be lucky to make it home through the woods from the Kirk withoot a child already in your belly!" She roared with her own special laughter. "And it'd be a bairn every year after that I'd wager. You'd be the Greeve's wife, a position of some standing. You'd get to come to the castle and see Wee Thomas still. Christen Michell would arrange the thing in a minute. She'd get to keep you near and also keep the Laird as chaste and enshrined as she wants. But before you go further down that road, ask yersel honestly: why did the Laird make his offer to you?"

It was annoying. It was far easier on my heart to stay angry with the Laird than to consider this question. I sighed. "Because he's a good man and he wanted to help me."

"Aye. Any other reason?"

I shook my head.

"You need to take your time with this, quiney. Here." She bundled a piece of bread and a lump of cheese into a cloth. "Take your breakfast in the stones. It's a woman's place, as I've told you before. Ask yer questions there."

Knowing I had to be alone, I took the food, and walked away, stumbling a little as I passed through the door. Everything was changing. That was the one certainty. It was scary and— the Laird stood in the passageway looking all white like a ghost, his face now as pale as his shirt.

So he'd heard. All of it. He knew of my love for him, and here he was, totally horrified. A confusing mix of terrible emotions fought to be heard within me, but I let cold clear anger win.

"My Lord," I said and curtseyed low. And then I fled.

The Circle

The stones stood, waiting, shining in the new light of the day, each tall megalith tipped with white frost. They seemed to curl round me, cosseting me in my anguish as I sat among them on the flat stone. The moon and star were lower in the sky now, hanging just over the largest stone where it lay on its side; they would no longer be visible from the Laird's ceiling window.

The Laird. All that he'd said. How could I have expected him to want a full marriage with me? Not that I had expected or hoped for that, but having the impossibility voiced had hurt so much. I was crushed. And confused. Because something was offered? But wouldn't it hurt all the more to live in such a way? To be so close to the man I loved, but never be really close, never intimate. Words from his poem came back, loud and crude in my mind. Why had he given me that? I may have let Jasper and Bessie believe that he hadn't read it, but I suffered no such illusion. Of course he had. He knew what it was he was giving. But why? To toy and tease and be cruel? That didn't fit with what I knew of the man at all.

And know him I did. He was kind and good and fair, in all the ways a person could be fair. In his presence I forgot my own oddities; I felt beautiful and clever and worthy, for that was how he made people feel.

I lay down on the flat stone and traced my finger round the markings on it, the centre of the heraldry of the castle, the tunnel system. Hidden secrets. Dark places. The Laird held great pain in his heart about Mary. He must have loved her so; she was beautiful and fine and then gone so young. No woman would ever compete with her, nor would I want to. After the many visits to her portrait with Wee Thomas, she felt like a departed friend of mine also.

"What should I do?" I asked aloud, to God, to Mary, or the stones, or the sky. It felt a little silly, but Bessie had said to ask my questions there, and Bessie was wise, that I knew too.

Of course I couldn't marry Wicked Richard; that was a ridiculous idea borne of hurt and anger and the need to flee. So. Duncan. But how could I possibly—

The atmosphere in the circle changed. It warmed. I looked round and beheld the Laird, standing beyond the stones but in front of the trees. He looked wilder than wild now. I felt my anger again, a surging fury that, with no expression, made me feel like I was going to burst. I leapt up onto my feet and stood, strong and defiant on the edge of the stone, as if I was defending it, or defending myself.

We both remained stock still. Eyes locked. Breathing matched, in and out, in angry tandem. I jerked my head up a little more and he moved. So swift. So quickly, he passed into the circle of stones and closed the gap between us. Completely closed the gap. His hands on my face. His mouth on my mouth. Kissing. Kissing and kissing again. Anger found its freedom. The stone made me taller; I bit at Thomas Manteith's lip and pulled at his hair, matching his wildness, meeting him there in fury and ferocity, and love.

And then we were looking at each other, me up, him down, for even with the stone beneath my feet, he was the taller. I could either cry or — I pushed him back. "What are you doing? Is this some sort of toying cruelty? Because, if so, you are a worse monster than Wicked Richard!"

"Wicked Richard," he repeated from one step away, where he had let me push him, voice cool, so much cooler than his kiss; that hadn't been cool in any way— "So after everything I heard you say to Bessie this morning, you are still considering marrying this man?"

"I'm not," I admitted at once, lowering to a seated position on the stone. That way his mouth would be out of sight. Its close proximity had become distracting now I knew how it felt on mine.

"Because I reckon," he said, "no, I ken it. Bessie is right in this. We don't know when our time will be up; we could be taken at any point by plague or fire or accident. We should reach for what joy we can before death finds us." He punctuated these last words by sitting down beside me and laying his palm against my cheek. I couldn't help but lean into it and place my own hand on top of his. "It disna mean I won't be feart if you fall pregnant, Lassie. I'll be a positive fussing nuisance!" I looked at him, unsure I had understood his meaning, or his change of heart. "Or are ye contemplating marriage to McCulloch now?" he asked, the hint of a smile just discernible at the edge of his mouth.

My mouth formed a small smile too. "Well, he does have a very nice house."

"Aye, a house that I own! We could live in it, if that's fit ye're wanting, quine."

His grin was infectious; I leered back at him like an idiot. A confused idiot. What appeared to be happening could not surely be happening. Could it?

"Lassie, you're so beautiful. And I love you so dear. I deserve a medal, or a Sainthood, for what I suggested earlier, nae a bunch o' women shoutin' at me."

I raised two very sceptical eyebrows at him, scared to believe the first words, befuddled by those that followed. "Oh?"

"I've thought this before, that most women would prefer a marriage where they weren't asked to risk their lives in childbirth. Why should they be expected to make such a sacrifice? Or to share the bed of a man that they hardly know? You always smile when you see me, Ishbell. I couldna bear for that to change, to see you look at me in horror or fear, as I thought you did last night in the passageway."

"When I saw Wicked Richard?" Words came slowly as if in a dream, clarification sought with each new revelation.

"Aye. I mean, I've had thoughts before…"

"Thoughts of marriage?"

"Aye."

"To me?"

"Aye."

"Even when you thought me a kitchen maid?"

"I wisna caring a whit aboot that," he said with a dismissive gesture of his hand. "I've din the sensible wedding, the one everybody else wanted and approved. But you were my precious Wee Ishbell, innocent and sweet and—"

"Not so innocent. Not anymore."

His eyebrows raised.

"I've had thoughts too," I told him. "Especially after reading that poem you gave me at Christmas."

He had the grace to look a little shamefaced, though he said nothing, merely reaching forward and taking my hand between his.

"I confessed these thinkings to Father Daniel," I said. "It was mortifying. He had to stop me and say he didn't have to hear the detail, that all I needed to say was 'impure thoughts'."

The Laird laughed then and the energy of the circle shifted again as I joined in.

"This fear of mine had no foundation then," he said. "You are not a woman who dreads the marriage bed. Perhaps there is no place for such fears in a love-match such as this will be."

I still couldn't quite believe it; I was tensed, waiting for more words to undo all that I was hearing. "You sound very confident," I said, trying to stick to facts. "Why did you say you deserved a medal?"

"Lassie," he said in a tone that suggested I should already know. "I would have done it for you, kept my promise to be no more than friends. But can you imagine what torture a 'marriage in name only' as you called it, would have been for me? Loving you as I do? Wanting you as I do, Isobell." His face regained some of its earlier colour as he spoke, our eyes meeting in the seriousness of the moment, and the importance of the words. Then he smiled. "You rose from the water on our first meeting, a vision of female perfection, like Venus herself, and I hinna been the same since."

My cheeks warmed at the memory. "You thought I was a mermaid!"

"Aye, well, I realised soon enough you couldn't have been Venus... and you thought I was a fearsome beast, a bear!"

"That was before I got a proper look at you. You were all wrapped up in your travelling plaid, and with a beard and your wild eyes. In the kitchen I…" I stopped in embarrassment.

"Aye? In the kitchen? Dinna hold back now, Ishbell. I've spoken my truth. I should like to hear the fullness of your story too."

"It was I who beheld a vision of great beauty."

He laughed. "Maybe you have an affliction of the eyes, Lassie?"

I reached out my hand and ran my fingers across the beautiful face of Thomas Manteith, his high cheekbones, his manly chin, then his mouth.

"I have no affliction of the eyes," I told him, before kneeling up to kiss that perfect mouth and be kissed back and kissed back and kissed back until we were both breathless and trembling, foreheads leant together in pause.

"Marry me, quiney," he said, a note of pleading in his voice now. "Fully, marry me. A joining of bodies, and minds, and souls. Will you agree to wed me this way, Isobell?"

"Aye, I will, Thomas."

So it came to be that a Mermaid and a Bear walked down the forest path to the castle, small hand in big hand, and very much betrothed.

The News

"You've sorted yersels out then," said Bessie with a sparkle in her eye as we arrived, big hand still in small hand, in the kitchen. "When's the special day?"

"You're a scheming woman, Bessie Thom," said the Laird, letting go my hand to kiss her on the cheek. "But I love you for it."

"Now, now," she exclaimed. "That's quite enough of that. Young Jasper's just come back from the Inn; you'd better be goin' through and seeing him."

I'd never seen Bessie look all flustered and reddened about the cheeks before, but there was no time to dwell on the phenomenon, as Jasper's wellbeing was my foremost concern. He sat by the large fire in the great hall, looking tired in the flickering orange light.

"Are you unharmed, brother?" I asked on our approach. "What did they want with you at the Inn?"

He rose from his chair, relief showing on his face. "It is good to see you well, sister. You did well too, to vanish. They plied me with wine all night to see if I would change my story, but I remained steadfast and true. I think they believe you in Inverness and, despite their tale to the contrary, I think they do plan to follow. And when they find out the lie? What then?"

"Do not worry," said the Laird, standing behind me and putting his hands on my shoulders. "I have asked Isobell to marry me. She declined me at first, so I asked her again, and she finally accepted."

I turned my head to look up at him. "You did not so much ask again, as amend your offer," I corrected and we smiled at one another like two Twelfth Night fools.

"This is no time for playacting and jokes," said Jasper. "Being thwarted has not improved the temperament of Wicked Richard; there is a positively demonic countenance to him now."

"He needna try coming near my wife!"

His wife. I felt melty inside, like a candle burned too long and too hot, soft and pliable so close to the Laird, my Laird, my bear—

"You two don't look to have had much sleep," Jasper noted, sharp and accusative. "Where did you spend the night, Bell?"

"Oh, upstairs, actually in…" It seemed a bad idea to continue. Jasper was not joining in the joy of this happy morning.

"Ishbell," said the Laird, "you go through and check that Bessie is quite well. We are shocking everyone this morning."

So I left them to talk beside the fire, the two men I loved best in the whole world, and walked back through to the kitchen.

Bessie still looked a little pink as she encompassed me in her arms. "I've never seen two people so right for each other," she said, with a tear in her eye. "This can be a properly happy home at last. It's always seemed a dark place to me; always there's been a creeping sadness, but this changes everything. You'll be in charge of the castle, Lassie."

"No…"

"Aye. Lady of the house. And to know that that wee laddie is always going to have you, that's a weight from my heart too…"

"So, he loves you," said Jasper from the doorway. His face was stony, bare of all emotion. Then he broke into a wide smile and opened his arms. "He's telling Christen Michell right now; I would have dearly loved to stay and watch that exchange, but it would have been unseemly to stare. But Bell, myself and Ian are your guests here now. No more blisters. And we're to put on a play for your wedding. I thought, 'Dream'. We did that for a wedding in London, and very grand it was. The great Crispin Trewelove played Oberon, King of the Faeries, and I was Puck, the mischief maker, a part written specially for me, obviously."

"Bell's marrying Faether," shouted Wee Thomas running into the room, jumping with excitement. "You're my new mother."

"Ah, well," I said sitting down at the table with him, for this was a subject I knew should be handled carefully. "Your mother, Mary, will always be your mother, just like my own mother who died when I was born will always be mine. Bessie and Christen Michell have been living mothers to me, here in the castle, and I hope I can be that to you."

"So we could go and tell her?" he asked. "We can tell my mother?"

Up in the blue room, Wee Thomas, bouncing with enthusiasm, told the serious and beautiful Mary about the upcoming marriage. I renewed my silent promise to her to always look after her son to the best of my ability, and the Laird too.

"So, this is where you're hiding," said the Laird, peeking his head round the door in seeming confusion. "Thomas, why don't you go down and see Bessie? She's got bannocks and preserves."

Off the wee boy ran.

"This was always considered to be the best room," said the Laird, coming in and looking round. "Would you like it for your own?"

"No, My Lord," I said, shocked.

"You're going to have to stop calling me that noo, ye ken," he said with a laugh. "You called me Thomas in the circle this morning. But as to the room, there are many others that can be freshened up; you can have your pick."

"I think it's important for Wee Thomas that this all stays the same," I said. "And for Christen Michell too; I know she comes in here sometimes." I paused. "And maybe for yourself too, Thomas." Saying the name felt good, right, as did continuing to voice the thought form. "You must have loved her very much."

I looked at the portrait of the sweet woman; the Laird, Thomas, followed suit. The big, dark eyes of his first wife looked down without judgement.

"I was very taken with her," he said, "but it wasn't like this thing between us, Ishbell, dinna think that. It was a sensible marriage, a joining of two families, bringing money into the castle. We met only once before the event. I hoped fondness would grow between us, but she was always wary of me, afraid even. There was always someone whispering in her ear, Christen Michell or Agnes, so we rarely got a chance to speak, just the two of us. And then, once she was with child, she was ill, bedridden in here, all the time, the women round her." He went quiet for a moment, then lifted my face up by the chin to look upon his. "I dinna want a sensible marriage again, Lassie. I want love. Fun, laughter. And for you to be happy. I never want to see you afraid. You must promise to tell me if I ever do anything to offend or cause you fear, and I will change it."

"I will. I do already, I think."

"Yes, indeed," he said with a wonderfully wide smile. "Come then, Lass, there's all manner of preparations to be made."

The Angels

The air in the entrance hall to the castle was silver with stone dust, and in the great hall too. The echoey chip-chip of tools on granite was everywhere, like many tiny heartbeats had suddenly been added to the place.

I felt myself to be inside a story, a very great and far-fetched tale of a silly girl from the city who was to marry a grand Scottish Laird. How could such a thing be true? I, who had been dismissed and demeaned all my life, not by everyone, not by Jasper, but by my father and older brother; how could this be my life? I had told stories since I was small, fictions of a better world, of kinder people and love and music and magical woodland creatures. And here it all was.

I ran my hand across a grey angel's wing and studied its serious face.

"They'll all be up and finished before the wedding," said Christen Michell, walking up behind me. "Lassie, I canna thank you enough."

"You can and you have," I said with a smile. "It's right they should be here; they suit the place."

"God took one daughter from me," she said, "but he has truly sent another to soothe my heart. And your idea to tell Wee Thomas more about his mother was true too; he is enjoying hearing about her life, especially what she was like as a wee bairn of his age."

"He's been greatly encouraged in his dancing about, since you told him she liked to dance too."

So much was happening at once; it was confusing and unbelievable at times. The Laird had decided to have the heraldry of the castle and the Manteiths redone with a mermaid and bear replacing the unicorns at either side of the labyrinth design. On the day the masons arrived to work on the new reliefs, a letter had come from my father. And a dowry, again unbelievable and unexpected, as I had thought I would have none. So pleased was he at being able to boast that his daughter was marrying into Scottish nobility that he was giving Thomas ten times the money he had offered Wicked Richard to take me, and also gifting the house and estate in the North of England.

Jasper was especially delighted with this news but his reasons were not entirely pure. "Can you imagine how much it will anger John?" he remarked. "His face will be all mottled and purple and not just from the drink. He believed that property was to be his."

"Do you think he will turn up to the wedding after all?" I asked, horrified. I did not want to see my brother John again; he was cruel and mean and so loud and offensive when drunk. Our father had written that they would not be attending the service due to the great distance involved.

"No," Jasper reassured. "He'll skulk and sulk in some dark tavern somewhere with that despicable friend of his. We're free of them now, my dear."

Thomas's attitude to the dowry was also unexpected. "It's your money, Ishbell," he said with some firmness. "It's nae fit I'm marrying you for."

"Maybe it could be our money," I had suggested. "And as the masons are here anyway, I think it would comfort Christen Michell if she could have her angels out of it." And so it was.

"Ye ken she'll put bleeding hearts and trumpets and Lord knows what else in among them?" he'd said, and he was right. Religious imagery was appearing everywhere along with the mermaid and the bear and it all added to the unreality I felt at times, like it was all an imagined story of sculpted stone that could come to a crashing end at any moment.

The only times it all felt completely real and not like a ridiculous notion I had dreamt into being, were those moments when I was alone with Thomas. We took a walk together every day: to the pool where it had all began, up to the stones and through the walled garden. It was strange and wonderful to visit a place and know that we weren't really there for the place at all but to visit with each other without anyone else around. The places just provided a pretty scene, a beautiful backdrop, for our hand holding, our hugging and all the kissing.

What an appetite Thomas had given me for kissing. I had never known it could be so sweet and feel so strong. It made me understand the ways of marriage better than either of the pre-marital discussions that were forced upon me by Bessie and Christen Michell. I could feel the need in my body, all entwined with my love for the Laird and indulged no concern that for me the marriage bed would be 'the worst thing' and something to be tolerated for the begetting of children, as Christen Michell had warned. It would be closer to Bessie's chuckling description: "Twa bodies coming together for the joy of it, quiney. Dinna worry." I wasn't worried. Truth be told I was a little impatient. It would be good to be married and getting on with life and past all the teasing remarks and knowing looks.

Only two people did not fully share in the joy of the occasion. The first, Duncan, seemed quite happy to me when he joked that he'd thought I'd been going to marry him. It was Bessie who informed me how his 'mouthie went doon' when she first told him. "Only for a second," she added. "He's a good heart, that loon; he'll wish you well. It's Agnes I'd be a bit mair careful of. I reckon she had some sort of fanciful thought the Laird might choose her one day, and she's an affa one to resent and grudge."

So to Agnes I gave my old gowns; she feigned delight but I could tell I had done wrong. Since my betrothal to the Laird she had treated me with extreme politeness but now I worried that she felt patronised, palmed off with what was no longer good enough for me. I shared some of the Laird's gifts with her and Wee Thomas and Bessie and Jasper and sometimes even Duncan and Christen Michell, but with Agnes I suspected they went down as badly as the gowns.

And gifts there were so many: each day some new thing was presented to me. A snowdrop, white and beautiful and pure. A necklace of gold and diamonds. Gowns, aplenty. A new plaid. New glass cups and goblets for the table from Italy. And sweetmeats of such number and variety that I had to share them around, or risk not fitting in my new clothes.

"Where are you getting all these?" I asked Thomas in wonder.

"Oh, some from market," he said, "but most come up the smugglers tunnels to us Ishbell; it's our way here at the castle. I have ordered many fine things for you, Lassie."

"So they really are smugglers tunnels?"

"Aye, I think smuggling was their original use."

I thought of the curved chamber below the ground, so like the stone circle in formation somehow, and suspected the original use had been long forgotten. It was older than smuggling, older than the church, something mysterious and sweet, a story from days long past.

The days of the present were filled with flowers and jewels and sweets. I loved the Laird's shy smile when he presented them; it was a new aspect of the man, something that appeared just between us, and it made my heart quicken in such a good and wholesome way.

"You have to choose one," he insisted as we climbed the stairs, stopping to inspect each and every vacant room as we went. Some were already done up in fancy ways for housing guests. Others were filled with trunks and old chairs and paintings. "Any can be made good and fresh, Ishbell. Do you want to check the views from the windows?"

I shook my head, saying nothing. Thomas had been trying to get me to select a bedroom for myself since the very day of our betrothal. Finally, I had agreed to take this tour of the tower but, in truth, my decision was already made.

"Well, this is the last one," he said, as we arrived at the room situated just below his own.

I walked into the large chamber, empty except for one bed that had carved flowers curling up its posts.

I ran my fingers over the wooden blooms, touching the detail of the petals, pausing to summon the courage to tell him what I'd been planning to tell him all along. "This is a beautiful bed," I said, my cheeks warming in anticipation as I spoke. "But the one I want to spend my nights in is located in the next room up."

"Mine?" he said in surprise.

I smiled back at him.

"Are you throwing me out of my room, quine?"

"No."

"So my room is to become our room," he said with that beautiful shy smile of his. "And my bed, our bed. That's just the way of us, isn't it Ishbell?" he said, pulling me into an embrace. "I want to give you a space of your own too though, Lassie. How about this one, the one nearest to my – our – room?"

I kissed him in answer, then left him to the business of starting to measure for furniture, as I skipped down the stairs to tell Bessie about the room arrangements.

I found her serving tea to Christen Michell in the great hall.

"I wondered if that's what you were going to do," said Bessie with a laugh when she heard about 'our room'. "I knew there was some sort o' teasing going on."

Christen Michell did not find it so amusing. "I chose the chamber furthest away from the Laird for Mary," she told us. "You'll need your peace, Isobell."

Bessie shook her head. "These two don't think they need any peace from each other. It's strange to see you in here by yourself, Bell. Ah, but look, here he is."

Indeed, it was Thomas at the doorway, asking if I wanted a seat by the windows in my own room and, if so, how high it should be. "It could be built higher to see out across the forest," he said, "or lower so you could lean back on the wall and read in the sunlight?"

"Aye, it's a gentle wooing we have here," said Bessie to Christen Michell who agreed. As I left the room to go with Thomas, I overheard them discussing whether we should be better chaperoned; apparently Christen Michell's window overlooked the walled garden.

"Ach, it's a pleasure to see young people in love; how often does it happen like this?" said Bessie. "And they'll be wed soon enough, so where's the harm?"

I walked back through the entrance hall to where one of the angels was already up and in place at the edge of the ceiling, holding a heart, watching over us, telling our stories in heaven, our lives such small beats in the grand passage of time.

The Marriage Bed

A shiver went through me as the back of my hand brushed the side of the Laird's hand again. The Laird, Thomas Manteith, my husband. He took my hand and kissed it, earning a cheer from the people who sat at the tables of the great hall. The warmth from his mouth travelled round my body as we sat at our wedding feast among pots of yellow and orange spring flowers that must have been taken inside early to have bloomed so soon.

Bessie had outdone herself in planning the food for the day; I knew Christen Michell had helped too and wondered if Jasper had been drafted in to give ideas also. There were dishes I had never seen in Scotland: star gazey pie with the little fish heads peeking out; birds cooked within birds as at a king's table. I ate some, but I wasn't hungry, not for food. My cheeks warmed at the thought and I touched Thomas's arm. Again.

It seemed odd that now we were actually married, we were more surrounded by people than ever before and further intimacy was delayed. The Laird took the lace cuff of my cornflower blue wedding gown between his finger and thumb, feeling and examining the pretty texture and pattern. The making of the dress had been arranged by Christen Michell, the chosen colour representing the bride's purity and the husband's faithfulness. The old lady had even attended church with us all that morning. She had wept during the ceremony. As had Bessie. As had Jasper. But all I could do was smile.

The day was long. The feast lasted for much of the afternoon, then came Jasper and Ian's performance, with half the castle staff drafted in to play various parts. I had assumed it would be a short version of a London play, as they had done at Christmas and during the snow. Not so. On and on it went, and amusing as it was, and thankfully it seemed to be a story with no allusions to mermaids or bears, or anything else teasing at all, I was impatient to get on with married life.

After the play came the dancing, the fiddles and pipes; Wee Thomas loved that part so, prancing round the hall, enjoying all the applause and attention his antics gained. He exhausted himself quickly and Jane took him up to bed. And then there was even less reason to stay downstairs. Our guests were merry in their cups. No one noticed us sidling away up the kitchen passage and taking the secret stairway. The unicorn tapestry gave way to the relative cool of the narrow stone staircase and up we ran, past the recess with the spyhole and onwards right up into the closet off the Laird's bedroom.

"I've a wee surprise for you Ishbell," he said, pushing open the door to his chamber. Therein stood the most ornately carved bed I'd ever seen. "It's been most affa difficult keeping you from kenning aboot this, especially as Wee Thomas knew of it."

"It's beautiful, Thomas," I said, walking into the room and running my hands up and down the dark smooth wood of the bedposts which were swirled with infinite oak leaves. Then the back panels drew my attention. One held a mermaid, the other a bear. The carving was exquisite and so detailed. The mermaid had diamond scales upon her tail and the bear was marvellously furry. The letters TM and IM were carved above. IM. I was Isobell Manteith now and how good that name felt in my mouth. It was like I had finally grown up into who I was meant to be.

"And look," said the Laird, Thomas, my husband, "Wee Thomas is here too. This is what he wanted on his panel."

At the foot of the bed, facing outwards, was a sword, a shield and a crown. I laughed. "King Arthur!"

Thomas pointed at the blank wood beside Wee Thomas's panel. "Maybe one day, another wee soul?"

I looked at his face, pleased to see it free of fear, and hoping he had truly managed to let that go and leave such matters to God, with whom they belonged.

"So," I said. "We'd better try it out." I laughed at myself. So many things said on this most special of days were coming out with a double meaning. But I sat up on the bed; it was higher than the old one.

"Aye, and look up Lassie."

The top of the bed was not panelled, but curtained, and the drapes sat open showing the ceiling window. The sky was quite dark and very starry, little points of silver dotted all over.

"My Grandfather was not a good man," said Thomas. "But some of his ideas were good. I thought you liked the window when you were here before; you gazed up at it for some time. Before you ran off in a huff."

"Before you made an offer that would not have led us up here on our wedding day?"

"Aye, then," he said with a smile.

"We have moved a long way past that. To this moment here." I touched the pillows and the bed clothes, all freshly sewn and new too.

He sat beside me on the bed and kissed me. I kissed him back with some keenness. Finally. Privacy. Our wedding night. No having to pull back and remain restrained. No having to touch only hands and arms and backs.

For the first time since our betrothal, some of the old doubt crept back into Thomas's face. "It disna have to be everything at once, Isobell."

"What if I want everything at once?"

"Ye dinna ken fit yer sayin', quine."

"I have a fair idea. Many people have been talking to me." Even Jasper had stuck his oar in, expressing concerns about the Laird's size in comparison to mine.

"Oh? Fit have they bin saying?"

"Well, I don't think Christen Michell much liked her marriage bed."

He grimaced slightly but it was in good humour; he had relaxed again.

"But Bessie said ours was a love match and that would ease the way."

He laughed. "Aye well, I think, maybe, that's right enough."

"So, what are we to do?" I asked, wondering if I should undo my clothing. Or his? The neck of his new shirt, or sark as they said in these parts, was already loosened a little. There were small hairs there, small hairs I wanted to touch.

"I want to cover you in kisses Ishbell."

And so he did.

The Rainy Day

The sky showed grey through the ceiling window and I could hear the patter of rain upon it. It formed the perfect background percussion to the Laird's deep and restful breathing.

I circled a finger round the inside of my wrist, the first place he had kissed that was not my cheek, my hand or my mouth. The skin tingled at the memory. More of me tingled. I was tired and a little achy, but relaxedly so. So relaxedly so. So floaty and soft. Like a faery, or a mermaid, I thought with a smile.

Who would have believed it possible to feel so at ease when being entirely naked with another person? But the other person was key. I turned my head to study him. Again. I resisted the urge to reach out and touch him. Again. Why had no one mentioned the sublime nature of the intimacy of marriage? In all the little pre-wedding talks I'd been subjected to, it had simply not featured. Well, Bessie had mentioned joy.

It seemed such an incredible process, the coming together of man and woman, the way our bodies fitted to one another, the way we were made for it. Even stranger then that people didn't speak of it. Perhaps men did. I had caught parts of lewd conversations between my older brother and his friends; my arrival into those scenes had always induced laughter. But their talk had not been of love. Love had to be key too.

Too late I realised my fingers had travelled of their own accord and were exploring the Laird's chest. It was so firm, so muscular, as was his tummy below, the little hairs tickly under my fingertips; I could feel the layers of hard work in his body. My husband's body. My husband's mouth formed a small smile, though he still appeared to sleep, and I jumped when he spoke, exploration interrupted.

"Would you be tickling me, wife?"

"No, I would never dream of doing such a thing. I am studying you."

"And have your studies brought you to any conclusions?"

"It is confirmed that you are the most beautiful man alive."

"Lassie," he said with a laugh, as if I had spoken nonsense. "Maybe you need a better viewpoint. Or maybe I do."

And with that I was lifted up and onto him, astride, on top, and holding his hands. I leant back slightly and closed my eyes. Just to feel. To experience every perfect detail of the moment. The inside of my thighs could feel the hairs of his legs. And the muscle. And the strength. Then there was the fullness of his desire. He always woke with that, at least he had these two past days. And I could hear the rain, loud against the glass above, sending a crescendo of water cascading down the pointed roof of the tower.

"Ye canna see anything wi' yer eyes shut," he commented.

"I can feel much," I said, then looking down at him and lowering to take my face close to his.

"Are ye sore, quine?"

"No. Well, yes, but it's a good sort of sore. A sore I could stand to have more of." I laughed at the wantonness of the words.

He turned his head and kissed my wrist. Again. And then his hands moved up my arms and into my hair which meant I lost any semblance of control or propriety. What useless and fake things control and propriety were, I thought as I threw my head back, abandoning myself to all that I felt. There was a flash of lightning as I rose and fell and thunder rumbled all around us, loud cracks and roars, tearing the sky in two as my own self broke and reformed there in the bed with Thomas, my husband, the Laird.

We rolled across our glorious land of blankets and were gentle and loving after the storm. Kisses were sweet as the sunshine that lit us from above.

I couldn't stop touching him. Before love. After love. And during. The muscles of his back rippled downwards under my hands as he moved. His hair: I loved to tangle my fingers all up in it. His growing beard was rough but delightful to rub my cheek against. I could feel it wherever he kissed me and it was like tinder to the kindling of my flesh.

Then there was food. Bessie kept leaving cold meals in the closet. Thomas told me she knew of the secret stair and would understand our need for privacy; she would not disturb us until we ourselves chose to venture downstairs.

"Why would we do that?" I asked and he laughed again. His laugh was a sound I loved, one of the best sounds in the whole world.

"To see people, to eat, work, walk outside…" He held my face between his hands and studied me. "You are right, why would we want to do any of that?"

"Are you making fun of me, husband?"

"Never, Ishbell."

"It's just…" Suddenly I felt a little shy, something I had not experienced in the two days in bed, for maybe it was not the same for him. I had to voice my thought anyway and did so quietly: "To me, us being together like this is wondrous—"

"And to me," he said at once, touching my hair and my nose and my lip.

"Then why…" I paused. Was it too stupid to say? "Why do married people not want to spend all their time in bed?"

He didn't laugh. "It is not always like this," he said. "In fact, I believe it is rarely like this. You know yourself, what Christen Michell told you; that is the common experience of women I think. Forced to lie with one you don't love. Much is wrong in our world, Ishbell. Maybe this is one of the greatest wrongs, one that spreads outwards into many seemingly unconnected parts of society. How can people be happy when they not only miss out on such joy as we have, but experience dread, or disdain or indifference in their bedchambers? But dinna be sad, Lassie. Here, have some food."

I ate a piece of the best herb cheese along with some soft white bread that must have been made specially for us. It had been baked into the shape of a wheat sheaf and very tasty it was. And I was so hungry! Too hungry to dwell deeply on all that Thomas had said. But my small thought had laid the way for his big thought. In privacy and safety our ideas grew, and maybe that was an important part of marriage too.

"Ah," said Thomas, looking at a small square of paper that had been placed under the wine jug. "A note from Bessie and Christen Michell: they hope to see us below stairs soon to welcome us into our married life."

And the world was full of good humour again. I giggled between mouthfuls of the wheat sheaf bread.

"They are obviously worried that I have brutalised you. Or," he added, "squashed you."

I giggled harder and almost choked on the best and sweetest wine I had ever had.

"And to more fully answer your question about spending all our time in bed…" It was his turn to pause and wonder if he should say it.

"Say it, tell me," I encouraged as the rain hammered on the ceiling window. Again.

He smiled and took my hand, turned it and kissed the inside of my wrist. Again. "Well, with the way we are, I think there might be places other than bed for us, Ishbell."

Pink lightning flashed through the three narrow windows in the wall, lighting us up as I spilled wine on the new bed sheets and kissed my husband upon on the mouth.

The Places

I explored all the places of my husband's body as if it were a new land to be discovered. Every mole knew my touch, every indent of muscle and out-jut of bone. His perfection evoked awe, for he was like a grand statue, though much larger in some parts. Telling him so brought forth the glorious, deep-voiced, man laughter that I loved so. Tasting him caused his eyes to widen in shock and I wondered if I had done wrong, but no: my delight was his, he assured me.

Too soon we walked down the main stairway, fully dressed once more, and back into the life of the castle. I was seized upon at once by Bessie and Christen Michell, Jasper closely in tow, and made to sit at the kitchen table and drink a strengthening women's draught. The main meal of the day appeared to be another feast and I was cajoled into trying every dish and drinking enriched wine. Complaining to Thomas helped not at all; he agreed with them that it was good to be nourished and fortified.

Wee Thomas's face on seeing us caused me joy and sorrow at once, for though he adored Jane and was well cared for by her, I could tell the wee lad had missed us sorely. I began to understand that marriage was going to be a game of balance; trying to give everyone enough time and energy and space. I wanted to stay by Thomas's side as had become normal over the last three days, but he had business to attend and Wee Thomas delighted in sitting by the fire for a story of a Prince and Princess locked up in a magical tower, invisible to anyone but each other.

I spoke to Jane about her becoming permanent governess to aid me in the new balancing act of my life. The kind-hearted girl was as delighted as her grandmother was proud.

The castle was changed. I was changed. I didn't just love Thomas; I had become part of him, and he me, and the place that was his home held his memories and his touch everywhere. The carved arms of his court chair had seen him make judgements and mend feuds; I loved the feel of the polished wood and the manes and wild eyes of the lions. Every stone step had known his feet, running when a little boy, walking sensibly as a man. Mary's room was a place that gave me pause in my thoughts; had he visited her there? Had she gone to the top of the tower? I didn't know and I couldn't ask, and in truth it didn't matter. I felt no jealousy about the beautiful woman in the picture, indeed she now felt like an old friend, who had become dear to my heart.

The angels in the entrance hall were as new to me as they were to Thomas; we would make our own memories under them. Some places were already our own. Thomas ordered that no one was to walk the pool path on the afternoon we ran down it, full of laughter and fun. But it was cold, too cold to consider wading in as he had suggested.

"Well, here will have to do then," he said, spreading out his brown travelling plaid on the ground. "How do you feel about the outside, Ishbell?"

"I love the outside, you know that Thomas."

"And to love outside, how do you feel about that? No one will come this way today; I have made sure of that."

"Oh," I said in understanding, then laughing for the utter naughtiness of it.

"It is where we met," he reminded me, solemn for a moment before I, too, removed my purple plaid and we lay between our two garments, cosy and laughing and content.

There was the sound of birdsong from the trees and the slight movement of water where the stream ran into the pool. A gentle breeze rustled the thinner branches as we loved one another in a half dressed fashion. We were natural creatures on the ground, part of the earth and the sky and the air, at one with the magical world. Nowhere was this more evident than within the stone circle.

We went there several times in the weeks following our marriage, those happy, happy, weeks. At first I was worried it would be irreverent, but Thomas was right, the place felt made for lovers. The stones stood so tall all around us, as if they were absorbing our love and putting it to good use elsewhere in the land. Thomas laughed at the notion, but he liked the echo that happened there, the way sounds stretched and bounced around us, our voices made ethereal within the circle.

The final 'other place' he mentioned to me one night, for night was the only time we could visit it for our 'wholesome marital purpose', as he called it. We crept down the secret stair with a candle, like thieves in the dark. "I am not the saintly man you imagine me to be," he said, lifting me to sit upon the kitchen table before barring the door. "This is what entered my head the first time I saw you standing there by the fire."

"Really?" I said, astonished.

"The heads of men are full of such thoughts much of the time," he said. "But this was different; it wisna just your beauty, but the way you looked at me, Ishbell, as if you wanted me, desired me even. I was instantly alive for you and then Bessie came in and dampened everything down. But when you dropped into that curtsey, I was undone again."

I thought back. "You were the most beautiful sight I had ever seen, like a vision from heaven."

"You really mean this, quine, don't ye?"

"Aye, of course I do," I said with a smile.

"The sad thing is," he said, indeed looking sad, "you dinna ken how much I love you."

"I do know, Thomas. I feel it."

"But I canna put it into words. I'm nae one for making stories and songs as you are."

"So show me," I said, pulling him in a little closer by his belt.

So the poor table had spilled candlewax added to its litany of imperfections, each mark a story of our home, and our family, and our marriage; each dent and gap a song of work and food and love.

The Mistress

I awoke ensconced with the Laird, snuggled in his big warm arms. My face was near the inside of his elbow, the rest of his beautiful self being behind me and asleep. It was a cuddly scene, happiness and contentment should surely have been all there was to feel, and yet… Something lurked, hidden and forgotten in sleep. I turned in my husband's arms and looked up at the ceiling window; it showed billowing clouds of dark grey, travelling fast and changing, storms ahead.

I remembered. He was leaving. Going on a journey to where and for why he would not say, but his eyes contained a glint of mischief whenever I asked about it. I smiled in mischief myself; I would catch him before he had fully woken and he would tell me the facts of the matter before he thought through the need for secrecy.

I leant up on one elbow in the soft bed and kissed him lightly. No response. So, again. And again. And I sensed the change, though he did not move; I had succeeded in calling him back to me. I kissed his ear and whispered in it: "Tell me where you're going, Thomas, and for what reason?"

I knew by his smile that I was too late. I had not won the game.

"I am going for delight," he said.

"You need this trip to make you happy?" I replied, slightly petulant.

"It is for happiness, yes." He turned and cupped my face in one big hand, touching my lip with his thumb. "And, I hope, excitement. Surprise."

He gave nothing away in bed, or over breakfast and then he disappeared off to sort out secret details with Duncan who was not going on the trip, and Rab the stableman, who was. I sighed as I corrected Wee Thomas's writing.

"Are you quite well, My Lady?" asked Agnes. "Do you need anything?"

The 'My Lady' thing was irksome, but I did not like to criticise her. Bessie said the reason for it was that Agnes had hopes I would make her my lady's maid. That was never going to happen. But I could be friendly and I could be honest: "I am saddened by the Laird's leaving, that is all."

"Oh yes, it is a hard time for a wife. Mary was always upset too, though she hid it well."

"Oh, really?" I asked, interested to know more of Mary.

"Aye. I think it was mainly the thought of what she might be like. Is it the same for you, My Lady?"

"Of what Mary was like?" I said stupidly, not understanding.

"No. Her. His mistress."

There were a few heartbeats of silence.

"Agnes, the Laird does not have a mistress!"

"I beg your pardon, My Lady. I have said too much," she said and seemed intent on scuttling away out of the door.

"Agnes, come back! Say more of this, whatever it is."

"I would rather not," she said and I knew it was not true. Agnes Milne was thoroughly delighted to tell me more. She licked her lips as she did so, looking at me often for my reaction. She told of how it was well known that Thomas Manteith kept a woman in Edinburgh. His many business trips all passed that way. His many absences from the castle were for that reason. "If you need anything," Agnes added at the end of her detailed spiel. "I have helped one lady with this before; I know how it is with the thoughts of what she might be like, a woman like that, all the tricks she would know. Mary became so good at feigning ignorance and pretending to be happy."

"Enough!" I said. Agnes's excited eyes seemed to intrude into both mine and Mary's thoughts, our lives, our marriages. "You may go about your business."

With a curtsey that was more of a quick bob, she was gone. And of course it was all nonsense! Malevolent gossip. Bessie would have told me if such a thing were going on. Of course she would!

But Agnes was the only one who really gossiped. Everyone else was besotted with the Laird, Thomas Manteith, my husband, and spoke no ill of him.

But what a piece of nonsense the talk had been! I banished it from my mind.

Wee Thomas's story writing was all over the place but I couldn't see how to fix it.

He'd said he was going for delight. Thomas had said that. Happiness. Excitement. The things he couldn't get here? Obviously he couldn't get them here if he felt a need to go away for them.

I wandered through into the great hall, Wee Thomas in tow, and sat at my harp. Not my harp, the castle harp. As I was the castle wife. A person to look after his child. I was good at that. She must, indeed, be better at other things. She would be tall and slim and glamourous. A treat to visit. The glint in his eye should have told me all this. How could I have thought— I mean, me! Fat, stupid, little Isobell! Storm clouds gathered across my belly as I sang a song written by a king for his lover when he was stuck with a wife he didn't love. Jasper had told me that wasn't true, and that the song had actually been written by someone else, not King Henry, that great user and killer of women, but it felt true to me.

"It is too sad to make a dance of, Bell!" complained Wee Thomas.

"It is a morose ballad," agreed his father from behind me, having come in at some point during the song. "Is something wrong, Ishbell?" he asked, brow furrowed.

"Everything is quite fine," I replied. Feign ignorance. Pretend happiness. However, a smile refused to be summoned to my face. "Is everything in order for your trip, sir?"

"Sir?" he asked with a frowny smile, then nodding. "All is ready."

I sat down to the main meal with everyone. I nodded and attempted to smile but I could not eat. Bessie and Christen Michell all but pounced on me afterwards in the kitchen, examining and questioning in such a way that it was obvious they thought me to be with child. Maybe I was? Who could say? I did feel sick, though my breasts were not sore. I had had no monthly courses since my marriage but I was not sure if they were due. I could not think.

It was important that I did not think. In the evening I told my husband that I wanted to sleep in my own room, that I needed my privacy that night.

"Of course," he said at once, though he followed me to the foot of the stairs. "Ishbell, if I have done something wrong, I would have you tell me."

I shook my head. No thinking. No explaining. Men had mistresses. It was accepted. It was allowed for them. "Please allow me my privacy, My Lord."

He inclined his head and I turned and walked up the stairway, holding my grand gown up a little so as not to trip and fall. It was best I was in my room with its new silvery décor and plainer bedstead. I would not think of the room above with the mermaid and the bear and the ever-changing ceiling window. The mermaid and bear were a figment. A pretty story. But what had happened up there was sacred to me. I could not let it be diminished by imaginings of what might be better, or similar, in Edinburgh.

No. I would lie in my grey bed and stare at the grey ceiling. No one had lit a fire or a light in the room for some time. That was fine. I did not need them. As I'd said to the Laird, Thomas Manteith, my husband: everything was quite fine.

The Fire

I did not sleep that night. My mind went to all the places I had determined to avoid. I sat up on my seat by the three thin windows and watched the first golden shafts of morning light creep over the tops of the trees in the forest. I lived in a place of great beauty. It was a place of great friends too: Bessie, Christen Michell and Wee Thomas who I did love so dear. There was much to be thankful for, so many blessings. The Laird would never harm me. Not physically. And this? This recently learned news? Surely it was not impossible to bear? Many wives bore such a burden; some looked upon it as a blessing too, though how that could be I did not know.

I loved the Laird. He was surely fond of me too. I could be a good wife: ignorant and happy, or feigning both. I could try. Maybe Bessie would be in the kitchen by now; I could confide and talk it through. She might have a calming draught of herbs to help.

Down the stairs I went, a small song beating in my head as I walked: a good wife, a happy wife, ignorant and sweet. Across the great hall it continued: a good wife, a happy wife… and down the kitchen passage into the room itself. The fire was lit under the great archway; I recognised the crackle and steamy scent of kindling that had not been completely dry. That was careless of the kitchen boy, he knew to—

It was the Laird who knelt before the lacklustre fire, poking at it with a stick. In the smokey air of the kitchen, all notions of goodness and happiness evaporated. A tremor grew in the very centre of my being and quickly spread out to my legs and arms and face. Breathing quickened as I got ready to burn with the kind of fury that was missing from the grate of the fireplace.

His head turned. "Ishbell." He stood.

The tremor became a more violent shiver, rising to the surface, ready to burst free and wreak havoc.

He approached. He tried to wrap me in his arms but I was a stone, a stone with a molten core. To allow anything else through would be to crumble and fall. I marched over to the fire, and threw some dry straw from the bucket on it, and some dry twigs. It flared.

"I am so angry!" I said and the fire leapt higher.

"Good. Good," he said, nonsensically. "Then maybe you will tell me why."

"You have all the facts, sir. I was the one kept in the dark. Well, no more!" I flung a few bigger sticks on the quickening flames.

"It is about my trip? I wondered this in the night, Ishbell. I thought of coming to your room to tell you all. I canna bear that I have somehow lost your love through this."

He sounded so sad, so soft and gentle and tired. I wanted to hold him and lay him down in bed. And weep. It was pathetic. "You have not lost my love; it is not conditional. And there is no need to furnish me with details of your destination, as I already know."

"Did Bessie, or McCulloch—"

So they knew? "No. It was Agnes who helped me with this as she did Mary before me." I knew as soon as the words were out of my mouth that they were too much, too cruel. I should not have mentioned Mary. We looked at one another in the flickering yellow light, both serious, both sad.

He did not speak for a few moments. "You will have to explain, Ishbell. I have no understanding of what you say."

I shook my head, wishing I had been able to be good and happy and meek and mim and whatever else I was supposed to be. "I know where you are going, Thomas, that is all. It was a shock."

Again, there was a pause. "I will truly not be gone long, no more than a week or so at the longest," he said. "And then I'll have her with me when I come back; I thought it would make you happy."

"You're bringing her here?"

"Aye, of course."

"And, where is she to stay?" The fury was returning, churning and turning in my belly, sparking and dangerous.

"Why, in the stables; where else?"

It was my turn to pause. With my mouth open. "You're going to keep your mistress in the stables?" It should really have been funny, a humorous interlude in a play, but my mind was trying to find a way round the concept; how, what, why—

"Mistress?" The Laird found it funny. The Laird was laughing. "Lassie, fit are ye talking about? I'm bringing you a bonny wee horse, she's white and feisty and just perfect for you."

"So… you're not visiting your mistress on this journey?"

He sobered. "Ishbell, I dinna hae a mistress. I have never been a man for such ways. I was married once before, as you know. That is the totality of my dealing with women, in any romantic sense."

Again we looked at each other, a healthy blaze at our side, illuminating half of each face. He smiled. "You thought I was to keep a woman in the stables?"

The emotions of the past day and night morphed then into mirth and I laughed with almost as much gusto as Bessie was prone to do. But not for long. It soon turned to tears and a telling of all I'd felt. I curled up on his knee and breathed deep of his salty aura. He told me all he felt. How he loved me, how I was like all the weathers of the world rolled into one powerful storm in his heart and there could never be room in there for another. And how I must always tell him any worry or bad thing and we would work it out together.

"I never expected my life to hold such a passion as we have between us," he said. "My perfect Venus, my mermaid, my wife. The other reason for my journey is to visit my solicitor in Edinburgh to change my will in your favour."

I felt stupid. I felt relieved. And I wept some more.

Then Bessie came and exclaimed at the size of the fire. There were jokes about us creating 'an affa heat' in the kitchen. There was breakfast. And Wee Thomas and Janet and Jane who all marvelled at the fire too. And then Duncan, asking if the Laird was ready for the road.

"No, we will have to delay a day," said Thomas, still holding my hand, squeezing it between his two. "Set up the hall for Barony Court. There's been a poisoning and I will not leave till it's sorted oot."

The Court

"A poisoning?" I asked.

"Aye," said Thomas with great seriousness. "Of mind. A slandering against myself. I'll treat it like any other event of its kind, by questioning those involved to get to the bottom of the matter."

It was rather alarming. Through in the great hall, I sat at the Laird's side and told all that Agnes had told to me. She had not said where she had heard the untruths against him and only in the second telling did I understand the full implications of what it might have meant for Mary: a sadness in her life that need never have been. And great sadness can make a person ill, and weak, and unable to fight for their life.

Bessie was aghast. Duncan was aghast. Jasper was apoplectic. Thomas was so well thought of and respected. They had not heard these rumours. Christen Michell seemed to take it personally: "As if I would allow my daughter to marry a man of such low morals!" And Mary had never mentioned it to her. It was to be hoped Mary had never believed the tale, if, indeed, it had even been told to her.

"We fled to avoid a bad marriage," added Jasper. "We travelled hundreds of miles away from it and I am certain we did not arrive at another. I've been in among everybody here; no one has a bad word to say about you, brother."

So, the one source of the tale was summoned and stood before us, looking most uncomfortable. Thomas did not soften his words to her, though he spoke in his usual low and kind tone.

"You told my wife I had a mistress, Agnes."

There was a prolonged silence, during which light from the morning sun travelled from bottom to top of the twelve tall windows, until they cast twelve slanting shapes on the earthen floor, like twelve fingers pointing at the accused.

Agnes's face appeared to be full of many thoughts. She looked at him, the Laird, and then she looked at me. "I was only trying to offer support to My Lady."

"By inventing this story?" asked Thomas.

"No, sir! I mean, it is said of you, it is well-kent of… about…"

"Said by whom?"

"Many, sir. Here in the castle and round about."

"Be specific, Agnes," my husband warned her. "As it stands, we have only you that has spoken of this."

"Everybody knows it!"

"Are you accusing Duncan of lying when he says he knows nothing of it?"

Agnes looked at Duncan; he looked back at her, stony faced.

"No, sir."

"Bessie? Christen Michell?"

"It was Mary!" she cried out. "Mary who told me!"

"The one person who cannot speak for herself here today," noted the Laird. "Are you sure it was not you who told her? To poison her heart against me and keep yourself topmost in her affections?"

Agnes gaped. The Laird had hit home. It was the truth, we all of us there saw and felt it.

Christen Michell spoke up. "If Mary had believed such a thing, either before or during her marriage, she would have spoken to me of it. We would not have connected with a Godless family. I would not have let Isobell make such a mistake either. And I should not have listened to your whisperings of impropriety between the Laird and Isobell last year!"

"I didna make it up! Nae any of it!" said Agnes, her face crumpling up with tears. "I was trying to help you, My Lady." Her swollen eyes beseeched me.

"Dinna you try your wiles on our Bell," said Bessie. "She believed you right enough but she confided in her husband and learned of the falsehood. If she'd have come to me first I'd have had clouted yer lug and put you oot! In most houses you would be put straight out! The Laird and Lady are giving you the chance of a fair hearing, Agnes. If you invented the story yerself out of jealousy or spite, as I've a mind you did, confess it now and make amends."

For some reason Bessie's words got to Agnes in a way that the Laird's had not. Her face hardened and she pointed at me. "I'm nae the een that maks up stories! Why are ye all so keen to believe the great Lady Isobell? She who was a kitchen maid? Oh, she tells a tale of being a fine Lady from London, but who's to say if that's even true? She's just a jumped up little whore who—"

Everyone moved or flinched and exclamations of horror were made, but it was the Laird's thunderous face that halted Agnes's speech as he pushed back his chair and stood and looked at her. "Go and pack your things," he said, and she did.

So Agnes was dismissed from her position at the castle, but Thomas, ever a kind and thinking man, gave her wages for six months and arranged for her to stay at the Inn for a few nights. A reference he did not give.

"It's like the lancing of a boil," said Bessie. "She didna fit well here wi' us."

But through in the kitchen, I did feel bad. I had believed such a nonsense of my husband, a man I should know better.

"Ach, dinna put this on yersel, quine," he said, pulling me into his lap at the table. "I thought about the words I had said to you to explain my journey: delight and excitement and surprise. They backed up her tale. But I meant for you, with your new horse!"

"Yes, well, I know that now."

"My delight and excitement is in you. And you've always some surprise."

I buried my head in his neck, relief and tiredness combining in the moment to make me relaxed and pliable in his arms.

"So let us reclaim the missing night and day of our marriage before I go," he said. "And once I'm back, I have many rides out and about planned Ishbell, many places to show you when we have the wee mare for you. There's beaches of golden sands, hills with old ruined forts atop, and many more ancient stanes you might like to explore."

So he carried me up the stairs and into bed where we slept and loved, and then it was time for him to go, which still hurt and felt all wrong. The castle was a darker place without Thomas in it; it was like a big stone lantern that had been extinguished. Bessie and Jasper and Christen Michell could not make up for his absence. Wee Thomas's games brightened the air for a time, but the nights were cold, as if a bitter ice crept up from deep places in the earth and through the dungeon before entering the rooms and penetrating the walls of the great keep, or perhaps it had always been there waiting to be set free by sadness and tears.

Part Two:
The Steeple
Witches

The Five Men

Bessie was in the kitchen. Christen Michell sat at the long table murmuring her penance and prayers as her fingers counted them out on her beads. Wee Thomas was outside playing with Janet's children, and I sat at my harp. For it was my harp. My dear love had bought it for me, before. Before we were married. Before we had spoken of our love for one another. Before he went away and everything felt so wrong, so dismal and doomful and like he might never return. He had said he'd be gone 'a week or so' but ten days had passed. What if something had happened to him?

I dismissed that dreadful thought immediately but could still hear the melancholy tune of my heart in the strings of the harp. I had meant to cheer us all with songs of love and happiness to help us look forward to Thomas's return but the notes always descended into minor keys that led to tales of sadness and woe.

"Aye," Bessie had said, with a frown and a troubled look like she might have said more, before she departed to the kitchen.

So much could be said with that one word. This I had learned since coming to Scotland. 'Aye' could mean: 'what nonsense'; 'look at what you've done now'; 'what a mess'; 'oh dear'; or sometimes simply, just 'yes'. It could also mean 'I love you' and at that memory I smiled. With the addition of the word 'right', as in, 'Aye, right,' it was sarcastic and really meant 'no'. There was humour in that thought, and more memories of Thomas, so there actually was a smile to be banished when Agnes walked into the great hall with the five men.

I had heard no horses, no footsteps, no door, even though I was constantly on the alert for such sounds that might be Thomas arriving home, but then I had been singing. I stood and smoothed my gown, confused and worried. This was the doom I'd been feeling; somehow I knew it. The arrival of these six people was the true source of Bessie's frown, Bessie always being one to sense and know when something was amiss or when bad weather was coming. They were the wrong thing, the dreaded thought; it was upon us, bearing down in the dark atmosphere of the castle, squashing, hurting, squeezing, making it hard to breathe.

"That's her," said Agnes, a smile on her face too, but not one born of love or anything akin to love.

"Aye," said the one man I recognised, and it meant, 'A-ha! I have her now!'. "I remember her," he went on. "The worst of the harlots from Twelfth Night." He snapped his fingers and two of the other men, two particularly large men, came forward and took hold of me by my arms. I tried to step free of their grip; how could such a thing be happening in my own home? I had been sitting and singing, nothing that called for the sort of arrest that was taking place.

"What are you doing?" demanded Christen Michell, shock delaying the formation of the same words in my own mouth. "That is Isobell Manteith, the lady of the house, unhand her at once!"

"That's the Papist!" shrieked Agnes. "She helped. She was in on it all too!"

And Christen Michell was seized.

"Let her go!" I shouted. "She's an old woman, and you're hurting her."

"An old woman, is she?" asked Mr. Dunn, who still smelt like fish gone bad and slimy, as he bent his face close to mine. "A woman like you? A witch?" He spoke the last word so loud that it echoed about the ceiling. They all looked up and then they all looked back down at me as if the acoustics of the place proved something.

I started to explain that such an accusation of either of us was nonsense, but then Agnes jumped up and down with excitement and pointed towards the kitchen passage. "There's the other one. She tells women how to get rid of a bairn from their belly. She killed her husband and helped them two kill the Laird."

The world seemed to slow, to become thick and sludgy and strange. Bessie's eyes were huge in her face and then she was gone. Just gone. There was a small delay in the men's reaction to this, because four of them were already occupied in the holding of us two who had been captured. But the delay was enough. They didn't catch Bessie. By the time they had decided that one man each was enough to restrain a wee lassie and an old woman, Bessie had fled. I knew she would fly through the woods and into Duncan's hoosie and down the secret tunnel to the secret chamber where she would be safe. They would not find her.

"Has something happened to the Laird?" I asked, because the words 'kill' and 'the Laird' had been used together and the day had taken on the feel of a nightmare, something that could not be real, but seemed to be so. No one answered. Agnes showed them the back stair down to the dungeon, and there we were dragged and chained.

I was frightened for Christen Michell as she stood against the dark, damp wall, hands held up above her, as mine were, but she looked resolute, determined and grim. I was worried for Bessie, for if the men took the tunnel they might find the chamber and, though it did not open from this side, they might find a way; there were five of them to push the boulder. But these were but background thoughts to the main terror: Thomas. Was Thomas dead? They would not tell me. They ignored my repeated entreaties to elaborate on their earlier words. Instead they told evil stories, egged on by Agnes who nodded and filled in gaps with lies. So many lies.

The Lies

I had tricked the Laird into marrying me, so said Agnes. Bessie had helped me to enchant him and seduce him. Christen Michell was known to take part in black mass when the moon was full; I had attended too.

"I've seen 'em go into the Papist chapel together as well," said Agnes, which of course could have been true. "And when they came out, their eyes were all sneakit like, you could see they had been planning something, plotting."

"No, we weren't, we—" I started.

"So she admits it," said Mr. Dunn, Dean of Guild, who smelled of fish gone bad. "There is a chapel; we'll need to do something about that." One of the other men wrote something down.

"So," continued Mr. Dunn as the men brought down a chair for him to sit on. It was Thomas's court chair; I was outraged. They also carried down a table and wine for him. Christen Michell's fine wine. I was so furious.

"Where is my husband?" I demanded and they all, except one, the shorter one, the younger one, laughed.

"That's for you to tell us," said Dunn. "But let's start at the beginning. With your step-son's illness."

"Aye, aye," said Agnes, cheeks flushed with excitement. I looked very hard upon her as she started the new tale of wickedness. "He came doon wi' some enchanted disease. It came out of nowhere, right after Isobell gave him some cheese which she did say was magical. Then

164

Bessie was giving him herbs, the papist had that blessed bread and she…" Agnes turned and met my look. "She was with him all the time, that's how she went from kitchen maid to governess and that's how they got the Laird to come back here, so they could bewitch him."

"Is that right?" asked Dunn with a smile, thoroughly enjoying himself.

"No, it is not right," I said. "Wee Thomas was ill and Agnes did not recognise it. It was Scarlatina. We three of us nursed him back to health and of course the Laird returned on hearing his son was ailing. Now, will you please tell me where he is and why you have stated that he has been killed?"

Dunn laughed. "Tell us the rest, Agnes."

"They started to work on the Laird. They tricked him into eating with them in the kitchen, like a servant, every day. They put things in his porridge, magic things. Then at Christmas, Bessie told Isobell to 'learn fae the best' about how to enchant a man. And after twelfth night, all of a sudden and with no warning like, the Laird said he was marryin' her." Agnes's bony finger pointed at me, quivering with excitement or hatred, or perhaps both.

It was a shock when Christen Michell spoke. "You always were a jealous and dishonest wee girl, Agnes," she said. "I should have discouraged your friendship with my daughter long ago. Perhaps she would have been happy then. She would certainly have been better without the vicious sin of your lies in her ear. Perhaps she would be alive still if I had seen you for the disgrace to all that is holy that you are."

"Maybe that was Bessie too," said Agnes. "She gave Mary her draughts."

"You silly, silly child," said Christen Michell. "Do you think God doesn't hear you? You think he doesn't see the truth of all that is in your mind? You wanted Thomas Manteith for yourself. That is what this is all about," she explained to the men.

Dunn looked at Agnes with raised eyebrows. "I'm giving you them," she said, as if reminding him of something.

"Give us them, then," he said.

Agnes, still shivering with some sort of sick exhilaration, went on, "Isobell seduced Thomas in the pool first. She had all her clothes off and made him believe she was a mermaid. She took on the appearance of a mermaid wi'a fishes tail."

I laughed because it was so ridiculous. "We mistook each other through the mist," I explained.

"So you confess to being unclad like a doxy in the pool?" asked Dunn.

That was unfortunate. "I like to bathe, to be clean..."

"Lassie, you could have had a bath made up for you," said Christen Michell, shocked.

"I was a kitchen maid then," I reminded her.

"But not for long," said Dunn. "You weaved yer devil's spells and curses, and got rid o' wee Agnes here, and got yerself into the Laird's bed."

"Aye," said Agnes, all eager and agitated. "She spent Twelfth Night there. She told me herself."

"That was to hide from Wicked Richard, as you well know, Agnes Milne," I retorted. "The Laird was not in the bed with me. He is an honourable man, an honest man." I glanced round the dingy room that was filled with men of a very different calibre to Thomas Manteith. "Where is he?"

"Buried in a shallow grave roundabout here, I'd warrant," said Dunn. "We will conduct a search."

Experience simplified into solid physical feelings that were known to be true. Stones at back: cold and wet. Earth under feet: dry and hard. Metal at wrists: sore and dark, bloody, rusty, dirty.

Dunn was still speaking. "So," he said, 'so' clearly being his favourite word. It meant: I am important; I matter; what I say goes, here and in all places. "A man changes his will to include his new wife and then disappears. Convenient that, wouldn't you say?"

"This is an outrage," said Christen Michell. "Isobell has been here since he left, and she loves him as he loves her. They are a devoted pair, a besotted couple. Is a love match a thing so rare that it invokes accusations of witchcraft?" The incredulity of her voice was great.

"Oh aye, Papist," said Dunn, approaching her, holding out his wine glass, one of our wedding glasses, for her to see. "Is it wine? Or is it blood? You take part in black mass and drink blood and eat bodies. That's right isn't it? Confess and it will go better for ye. Name others and it will be better yet."

As Dunn turned his head away from Christen Michell to pour the contents of the wine glass down his throat, Duncan burst into the dungeon.

"Fit the hell's goin' on? Bell! Mistress! Undo them at once!" He looked from us to Dunn and the horror in his face increased. "William Dunn," he said as if he knew what a very bad man that was and what a very bad thing for all of us his presence in the castle was.

"Ah, the young man from Twelfth Night. Didn't choose you in the end, did she, laddie? You must have a few tales to tell of her sorcery?"

Duncan stood tall, taller than Dunn. "You canna do this. You need a commission from the king."

Dunn reached into his jacket and withdrew a folded parchment. "The king is as keen as us to rid this land of the whores of Satan. We have a five year commission to do as we will, to catch and burn all the witches as we find them, no delay, less time and expense wasted. I've stockpiled wood and tar to dispatch the creatures in their multitudes!" He brandished the document at Duncan and then re-pocketed it. "So. We'll leave the devil worshippers down here to contemplate their lot while we get ourselves some deserved and needed rest. There can be a whore of work involved getting a confession out of such as these, lads. Agnes Milne, you know your way around; you can find refreshments for us."

The Dungeon

"Find Thomas," Christen Michell instructed Duncan, when the five men and Agnes had gone to help themselves to food from the Laird's kitchens and larders. "That's the best thing you can do now. Murder is the greatest charge levied against us: prove it wrong. You won't free us, Dunn has the keys."

"That little bitch Agnes," said Duncan, examining my fastenings to see if they could be loosed. "I canna believe this."

"Find Thomas," repeated Christen Michell. "And take Jasper with you; I dinna want to think about what they might do to a boy like that if they got hold of him."

"Because he's my brother?" I assumed. "Duncan, why are they saying Thomas is dead?"

He stopped then and looked at me. "I dinna ken, lass. He should rightly have been home three days ago, but there's been no news of anything untoward happening. Weather's bin bad. 'Tis probably all it is."

My stomach churned. I wanted to run about in a panic, searching for my dearest dear but there I was, chained to a wall. "Find him, Duncan. And Wee Thomas—"

"Janet's taken him hame wi' her; he'll be safe there. Jasper's up at the farm; I'll find him and set off. Once the Laird's hame, it'll all be sorted oot, you'll see. Try and get them to keep you here as long as possible."

The darkness gathered around us once he'd gone. "What did he mean, keep us here?" I asked Christen Michell. "Where else would they keep us?"

"With murder being spoken of? Aberdeen, Isobell. The Tolbooth."
She shuddered, making her chains tinkle like small bells as if it were
Christmas, a time of merry and bright celebration again. "He's right;
we're better off here."

And there we stood. In chains against a wall. It was not Christmas.
The one candle they had left spluttered out after a while and the place
fell into total darkness. The thick blackness that swirled around us in the
dungeon took on its own evil life; it gusted sharp breaths of hatred
towards us as if it took a cruel delight in witnessing the harming of
people, maybe especially the harming of women. The air below the
castle stank and smelled of a base loathing built deep into the very
foundations of the place.

Physical discomfort grew. It was so cold and so damp and so very
painful to be still standing after all this time. My hips ached. My knees
hurt. And I was young. We were too far apart to touch or hold hands
but we could speak.

"How are you doing, Mother?" I asked, my voice sounding alien and
harsh in the dark.

"I am alive, Isobell, and so are you. Given our predicament, we are
doing well. I would suggest we sing a hymn, but it might only make
things worse for us; these Presbyterians are obsessed with witchery and
popery, as they call the one true faith. But we should pray; they canna
hear what goes on in our hearts."

So we prayed, but I didn't know how much good it did. It felt as
though the dark walls and ceiling were barricades to light, as if our
prayers bounced off them, unable to get through to God or angels or
any good spirit or soul. But we couldn't give up. I prayed for Jasper and
Duncan: let their journey be safe and fruitful. Let them find Thomas,
safe and well. I imagined my husband riding his fine horse through the
woods before dismounting and walking into the castle. He would rain
down his fury upon the bad men and see justice upheld. Maybe William
Dunn would know the cold of the wall and the confinement of chains.
I prayed for Wee Thomas and hoped he wasn't frightened with the odd
change in circumstances. And I prayed for us three accused, Christen

Michell and Isobell Manteith and Bessie Thom; let us be spared, let us be laid down in our own cosy beds soon, let the light come.

"Ye're nay to sleep," said a rough voice.

I jolted awake, astonished that I had managed to fall asleep in the shackles. My arms rang with hurt, my wrists stung, the dried blood on them scratchy and sore. The man set a lantern on the table and proceeded, in turns, to poke at us with a stick and sit in the Laird's court chair. It would have to be cleaned after this, freshened with cleansing herbs. Bessie could— Where was Bessie? How could she have deserted us so? She could not, that was what my heart told me, that was what I knew of her. She could do more unchained than she could if she were caught. That must be it. Bessie was rallying forces to fight for us. Seeing Wee Thomas was safe. Making sure the Laird was found. I said another prayer for Bessie, for her safety and the success of her endeavours.

Surely it was the most tired I had been in my life. I remembered the boat that had brought us to Scotland, with its constant motion, and how I could never properly sleep. But I had been lying down. There had been caring hands and voices and an end to the journey in sight. I tried to hold fast onto the vision of Thomas, alive and well and galloping up to the castle door, but the dark encouraged other pathways of thought. Death: his; mine; Christen Michell's. Bodies underground. Stones up above.

I stared at the huge stone in the ceiling of the dungeon. It became the focal point in my line of vision. If I were a stone I would feel no pain, I would attract no attention. I would be heavy and strong, a giant block up above. The strangeness of the new subterranean world swam and blurred before me; a hard poke in the stomach stopped that. No sleeping, no sleeping ever. Stones didn't need to sleep.

Footsteps in the dark, feet on the stairs, not the secret stairway of Thomas; oh, to be able to run up that way now, to fall into bed, to sleep in my beloved husband's arms—

"So, ye pair of stinking, festering whores; time to confess before God and your betters!"

William Dunn had spent some of the night sleeping and much of the night drinking. Drinking our wine and our ale, eating our food, and now he was well rested and raring to go. It was morning.

The Questions

The questions had changed; they contained new allegations. In fact, they were no longer questions but statements of untruth that we were urged to admit to.

"Confess! Confess! It will go better for ye. Look at yer long mermaid's hair," said Dunn, tugging at it with his filthy hand. His odour had grown stronger overnight; he stank of truly putrefied fish now, mingled with whisky. "Ye take the shape as well, don't ye? De it for us noo. We'd all like to fuck a mermaid, isn't that right, men?"

They all laughed and stamped their feet, all but that one younger, shorter man.

Dunn slapped my face. "Ye de it for him though, don't ye? The Deil? In the pool? Is that his place? Ye open yer legs in there for him, don't you? Just like yer queen, English whores both."

I stared at him who spoke such foulness as I had never heard before. If the Deil, devil as I knew that meant, was anywhere, it was in front of me; the stench of the man could have risen from hell itself.

"Dance for him too, don't ye?" He crossed to Christen Michell. "Danced at the Fish Cross and at the Mercat Cross in toon, didn't you?"

She laughed at him. "Accuse myself and Bessie Thom if you wish, but wee Isobell has never even been to Aberdeen, so your allegation is nonsense, a Godless fabrication of lies."

And then Dunn hit her so hard across the side of the face that she fell forward, unconscious, arms wrenched so violently in the shackles that the bones were surely pulled out of their joints, such old joints were they, so frail and tender.

"She needs a doctor," I said, for a brief moment, glimpsing a small hope; perhaps the doctor would come and undo all this evil, put things right, let everything be good and well and fixed for when Thomas came home.

"A doctor for a witch? Are you mad as well as wicked?" Dunn marched back over to me. "It's why ye wouldna dance wi' me at Christmas; ye only dance for him, only service him. Got yer husband's money for him too, but that'll be put right now. Canna hae doxies like yersel running roon the country thinking they can control things, owning money and castles? Have you ever heard the like, lads?"

The choir of louts laughed, all but the one, again.

Dunn sat down in my husband's chair. I assessed the facts of the situation, the physical truths as I could understand and feel them in my unslept state. My cheek stung and ached where it had been slapped, but that was nothing to what had been done to Christen Michell. The Laird was missing. These foul men had come. We were accused of witchcraft. It was unbelievable, but it was true. I had heard of others being so accosted, mainly from Agnes, but had always assumed they were guilty. Why else would the Crown and State take such action against them?

Agnes entered the dungeon, looking a bit the worse for wear herself. The front of her dress was hanging loose, torn at the neck, as she carried a bowl of porridge across to William Dunn, Dean of Guild, and laid it on the table beside him.

We were not witches, Christen Michell, Bessie and myself. We knew nothing of spells and potions and wickedness. But Agnes…

"Agnes wanted to use a love spell on the Laird!" The words burst out of my mouth, as if they could do good, as if the men would hear them and understand the whole thing was based only on a silly girl's jealousy and then take their leave. "She wanted him for herself," I continued. "She asked Bessie for a love spell, but Bessie, not being a witch at all, didn't give her one. Agnes spread lies about the Laird having a mistress and she was dismissed from her position at the castle. This is what it is all about. There are no witches here." There. It made sense. It was true. And now all would be well.

William Dunn flicked his fingers and two men seized Agnes, who now looked very small and poor, between the two of them. It was established that there were no more shackles in the dungeon and rope was found to bind her wrists and her ankles.

"No!" she cried. "My master winna let you do this. He's going to marry me."

Her short speech produced peals of laughter from Dunn. "A gentleman like John, marry you? Now, I've heard everything!"

Agnes was gagged with a dirty piece of cloth and thrown into a murky corner of the dungeon to lie on the floor. "One less detail to be taken care of," laughed William Dunn, Dean of Guild, as he stood under the huge stone that had been stolen from the stone circle.

If I really were a mermaid and a witch as they said, I could make it fall, the stone, the crushing stone; it would crash down from the ceiling and squash Dean Dunn as if he were a small bug under someone's shoe. That is what I envisioned as they questioned Agnes. That is what I envisioned as she, then bloodied and bruised, confessed to having danced at the Fish Cross and the Mercat Cross and to having sung songs for the devil.

"That's her wi' her harp," she shouted at the mention of music, after readily agreeing to their accusations – "Aye, aye, I did…" – but they had forgotten me; their cruelty had found new prey, new fun, and I was so, so sorry. Agnes was poked and prodded and slapped and hit and even bit. I seemed to have been the luckiest in this regard, the recipient of the least violence. So far.

The stone, the stone, I could make a song to bring it to the ground, it could go back to the circle and make all things right. I worked it with my mind but it shifted not. Night came again, indicated by the one candle and the one man. But it was the younger man and he gave us water; even Christen Michell took some, though she did not reply to speaking.

Agnes was gone. Agnes they had taken with them. The walls of the castle were thick but I could feel her cries through the earth under my feet and knew I would never forget them. They would live in my heart for the rest of my days and remind me to only ever speak words that had been thought through, words of love and kindness that could do no harm to any person, no matter what wickedness they had done.

The Good

Time passed in the dark. Mornings? Nights? The questioning seemed
to be over, the young man gave us bread and ale and the place soon
began to stink. We could compete with William Dunn in that respect,
Christen Michell and I, for it was just us, hung by our wrists there in the
dungeon. Wee Agnes never returned. Pain became the normality of
life. I looked at the young man, our keeper, our guard, and wondered
at his easy movement, how he could use his arms and move his head
without flinching or moving stiffly. He looked back at me and did not
smile, but his eyes contained the light of sympathy.

On the first day of the inhuman incarceration I would have been
glad to have had my chains lowered and to have been freed from the
wall. But when it happened, it was an agony of body and mind. I
couldn't lower my arms, I had to hold them at half-mast like a mad
person. I was accused of casting a malediction. Oh to have known how!
To have been able to bring down God's wrath down upon Mr. Dunn,
Dean of Guild! For he was no servant of the Lord, no good man.

I had my wrists bound as had been done to Agnes and was dragged
up stone steps and then wooden steps into the castle, both by the rope
and by my hair. Christen Michell was carried by the young man and
I was glad for it. Down the passageway, through the great hall, past a
great mess of drinking vessels and bowls and wasted food, and on to the
entrance hall, where I stood under the angels. I communed with them,
the angels, those messengers of God; I asked them to intervene for us.
They looked down, stony faces observing the actions of the five men.

The chapel door was broken; the statue of Mary, fallen upon the floor, her back turned to us. It was bad that Christen Michell had been so wounded but it was good that she did not see the Lady in that state.

The world became divided into those two simple categories: good and bad. Being pulled down the castle steps and falling onto the ground surrounded by laughter was bad but I sought the good with my heart, for if it could not be found, what was left?

We two accused were innocent and so: good. The young man had a kindness in him: good. It was raining, and while this might hasten our death of cold which may or may not be good, I could not tell, it was most definitely good to feel the clean water on my face and feel the freshness of the air all around. I sucked it in to my body to replace the fetid atmosphere of the dungeon. I could hear the wind in the trees; that was so good it was almost musical. The same wind would be blowing all around the stone circle. They had never mentioned it, the bad men, in their questions and statements of evil; they did not know about it so the circle was safe, protected from harm. Good. Good.

The cart floor was softer than the compacted earth of the dungeon and we were permitted to sit, just us, no men to guard, as we were tied. Finally, I could move. My joints and bones creaked over to Christen Michell and I held her against myself as best I could, looping my tied wrists over and about her shoulders. I was her pillow, I was soft and kind and that was good.

The cart was noisy as it set off through the trees; the two men up front did not hear me sing in my grainy voice. I sang all the hymns I could think of, all Christen Michell's favourites, and I prayed out loud. I prayed to God, I thanked Him for all the good in our lives and asked Him to spare us, to save us, to make the evil men desist in their plans. I said a special prayer for Agnes, who I felt was no longer living. She had paid for her lies, the poor damaged wee lassie that she was. I prayed for her soul.

I prayed for Thomas and Wee Thomas. Let them be safe. Let them be happy; whatever happens. And Bessie, let her stay safe and not be caught.

It rained on and on, cleansing, chilling, numbing the pain away. I sang and I prayed. I beseeched the Goddess of the circle for help, for why not? She was only good, whatever these men might say and I could guess what they would say. And then I slept and fell into a deep slumber where I dreamt of the stones and the sun and the Lord of all. Salt of the earth. Light of the world. And for a while it was as if the Laird was with me, as if we held each other, and I loved him and he loved me, and all was very very well.

The Mither Kirk

"It's the Mither Kirk," said Christen Michell, her voice waking me.

I stared up at the high steeple and it did not feel good. We were so wet, soaked through to every bit of us, but Christen Michell was excited. I didn't know how long we'd slept, or how long it had taken to get there, but we were in Aberdeen outside St. Nicholas's Kirk. For what exact reason I did not know, but it could not be good.

"There's been a delay, they're not ready for us," said my dear mother and friend in a happy tone, as if we were on a country outing with the Laird and Wee Thomas. "The Smith is to come and then we are to go inside."

Christen Michell spoke on and on about the Kirk, as if it were still a place of the one true faith. She said it was renowned for the great number of chantry altars and paintings and statues contained within it. They surely could not be there now; Mr. Dunn and his ilk would have torn down anything they could call idolatry. They loved to see evil where it did not exist, mayhap to disguise the darkness of their own souls and hearts.

There was a gathering of men round the cart, faces and hats kept bobbing up to look, to see, to gawp. Then, with much fuss and comment: the Smith! I raised my head to peer out at this seemingly great personage; ah, he carried new chains for us. So we were to be kept in the church. Was that good, or was that bad? It could be hoped that there might be Godly people about to stop the worst offences, or were we to be placed in a town stocks or pillory situation? To be mocked and have things thrown at us? To be pinned to wood with nails through flesh?

It soon became clear that there was disagreement among the gathering of men. Not everyone present liked that I had been dragged from the cart by my hair. That was another good thing, for it meant that Christen Michell was lifted with more care, by the younger man, and carried into the church, and even permitted to sit upon a chair.

There were many churchmen present. Dunn, puffed up with his own importance, talked very loudly at them, saying that we had already been questioned and merely awaited trial. He stated that Christen Michell had confessed but that I had yet to do so; it was ongoing work and naught to do with them. There was much discussion as to whether we should be placed in St. Mary's vault, below ground again. Another witch had been kept there, a man. Dunn said the Papist would like it overly much and that it was not the place for us.

In truth he was not wrong; Christen Michell was deriving enjoyment from being present in so impressive a church. She stared round like a wee child, taking in all the sights of windows and altars and archways and screens. There remained some carvings, and these she stared at in earnest, as if she were unaware of the discussion taking place around us, or the reason for our being there in the Kirk.

More self-important men arrived and looked us over as I swayed on my feet. Provost. Chancellor. Friends of Dunn. Yes, yes, they all agreed. Witches, witches, they all agreed. Dunn said he had known there was witchery in the castle the moment he met me at Christmas. He spoke of the elfin blade that I had worn. In truth I had not seen it since. Had he taken it? Had William Dunn, Dean of Guild, stolen it? It was well I had not thought of the wretched bolt earlier, else its story might have burst forth from my lips and things would have been worse for Agnes. Not that they could be worse. That thought made the world shrink and grow all about me and I staggered there in the Kirk, in front of all the important men of church and law.

The young man put out a hand to steady me.

"Dinna touch, dinna touch!" was the cry that went out among the legal men. "Dirty! Filthy! Fornicators! Ye might catch something, might be drawn in, caught by the demons in their skirts!"

The churchmen didn't much like such talk in their holy house but they took no action to stop it or to help us. For a short time, I wondered if they might and let the hope be spoken. I tried to tell them about the Laird being missing, and Agnes being harmed, but Dunn struck me as he had struck Christen Michell in the dungeon and my face met the floor.

The floor was stone and it was grey. It was not warm and friendly like the stone floor of the castle kitchen; that homely floor was messed only with food splatters and spills, twigs escaped from kindling and some ash from the fire. Blood speckled the floor of the Kirk; my blood, blood from my head, pooled in one place, dotted in others. Foul art. A story told on rock for all to see who would look, but none did. They let me lie there though, that was a relief. They let me lie there while they expressed deep concerns, such caring concerns, about the well-being of their church building. It must not be damaged. Must not be misused. The Tolbooth was the place, the place to do some things that must be done, not there on the sanctified ground. But the walls would be able to contain our evil, yes, that was agreed by all. The holiness of the church would suppress our abilities to work magic and curses and spells.

If I had been able to do such things, I would have turned those bad men into toads or worms or snails, creatures to be stepped on and afforded no respect, creatures such as they had transformed Christen Michell and myself into. They had wrought an obscene magic upon us, by their actions and their words. True malefic was theirs, not ours as they said, as they kept saying, those men that claimed to be of God, but were actually Christ-less beings who kept no image of the Lady in their Kirk.

The Steeple

I was kicked until I got to my feet. It was not easy. I managed up to hands and knees and was kicked down again. So I moved quicker, cowering away from the attacker like a puppy that I remembered my brother John beating: curled over, first hands, then knees and finally feet connected with the floor till I was standing, standing in the church under the high roof, higher even than that of the great hall, in front of the churchmen, so many men, so little knowledge between them, so little sight, and no compassion.

The one good man, he who was neither churchman nor sycophant of Dunn, lifted Christen Michell without commenting or asking, he just did it, he just carried her. I blessed him, but silently, in my heart; it was good to have such a thing to do, for I was close to cursing people as they said I was wont to, close to damning Dunn to hell. But there was no need; where else could such a soul be headed? Fiery pits awaited William Dunn, Dean of Guild, as they awaited the Provost Alexander Rutherford, and the Chancellor James Stewart. I would never forget their names. I knew that it would be impossible not to curse them, not to wish them ill.

The steps into the steeple were many and difficult to navigate, being very narrow and wooden and rickety. I stumbled and fell several times but Christen Michell was carried up them and for that I was glad.

New shackles. Shiny shackles. Tinkling like Christmas bells or wee bells on the harness of a horse that pulled a magical sleigh. Better shackles. Ones that allowed us to sit upon the floor, beside one another.

I thanked God for His mercy in this happenstance in His house; it was no small thing, such a great difference did it make to our state of living.

They went away soon, the many men, to their homes and their firesides and their wives. I hoped they didn't have children, small innocents to inflict cruelty upon as the fancy took them.

So we were left. In the dark. In the cold. I could hear the wind howling round the tall steeple. I had glimpsed a chapel lighted with candles below through a gap in the floor of our new prison, the room in the steeple; I had seen the view of Aberdeen through the wooden slats in the rough stone walls and thought it a very grey place, full of empty people like the church. But there were no kicking feet in the dark of the kirk tower, no fists or cruel mouths. We were alone with the sound of breathing. Mine. Christen Michell's. Hers was laboured, scratchy and sore.

"How do you fare, Mother?" I asked of her.

"I am at peace, Isobell. God will take me soon. It's you I fear for. That wicked man has you in his sights and what can be done about that?"

I could give no reply, not because I didn't have one – I wanted to soothe her with platitudes, tell her we would live and all would be well, Thomas would come, we would go home to our warm beds and big dinners and listen to gentle music on the harp – but hell itself had exploded all around us, right in my head, in my legs, my feet; my whole body shook with it. Hands on ears did nothing to drown out the bells, for that was what the great tonal clashing must be: bells to call people to church to hear the scriptures and holy words; bells to announce marriages and deaths and births. Bells to torture witches, to keep them from sleeping. Bells instead of a stick. Bells.

There was no musicality in the sound. My brain bled with it, my ears burst with eruptions of agony but they continued to function, to let the noise in. And then it stopped. The bells stopped, but the ringing did not. In our heads, through our shaking bodies, the damage rang on, glorying in the harm it did to flesh and sanity.

The young man came with a candle and bread and ale. He spoke to me. I could not hear his words but his faced showed concern when he looked at Christen Michell. She was unconscious again but she lived still, I could feel a pulse where she lay against me. It was life. The life of someone I loved. Someone who loved me; such a person still existed in the world. The dark came again and with it the bells, evil metal objects forged by the devil to split a soul in two. Clang, clang. Clang, clash; each crash of clapper resounded round the walls and blended into an echoing cruel whole, a collieshangie, an uproar in the sky that no angel could silence, though I prayed for them to do so. I prayed for God to smite the tower and send the evil chimes plummeting to earth, for fire to ravage the steeple and finish the game of torture played by men.

I covered Christen Michell's ears for her as she was asleep and unable to do so. She was old. And so much smaller than I. The bells could hurt her more. Then it was quiet, or at least still. The ringing persisted, a permanent state of internal banging and drumming and screaming, and all from a bell, or bells, as there was in the pointed space above us. There was wood between. Did it muffle the ringing at all? Maybe so. Maybe we would have been dead without it.

It grew light and still no bells. Had they forgotten us? Or was our sentence to rot away in the steeple until we were no more? Like the bodies of rats that no one wanted to touch. They left us so long in silence that other sounds started to exist again: birds outside on the sloped roof and words, human words, kind words as we had for each other. Christen Michell would wake sometimes and speak of the church and the great bells above us. She told me their names: Mary and Laurie, those were the bells. East and West, that was the kirk divided. Rich and poor. Good and evil. Dark and light.

The grey light of Aberdeen showed brighter through the wooden slats in the window. Christen Michell's pulse grew weaker, her voice faded away and I knew I would soon be alone for a while, before we were reunited again.

At first I thought I was hallucinating. Because how could Bessie Thom be standing before us? Looking down at us and smiling? How could her glorious laughter have replaced the demonic clanking from above?

But there she was, hands on hips and looking quite pleased with herself. "Aye, aye, quines! Fit like?" she bellowed.

The Witches

Bessie sat down and studied us, me first, then her examination of Christen Michell brought a look of sad knowing to her face. "Aye," she said, and it meant many things. And then she told us how she came to be, unfettered as she was, in the steeple.

She had hidden up the secret stairway in the castle, not down in the chamber as I had thought. And then, as I had known, she had ascertained that Wee Thomas and Janet's family were safe and hidden, and that the search for the Laird was underway, before slowly making her way toward Aberdeen.

"On my own terms," she explained. "They'll have me and they'll finish me, but I chose the means of entry. I walked right into the middle of the kirk session. They didna ken fit to de wi' me, just asked me to sit at the side!" Her laughter pealed round the steeple again. "No witch-hunters present, they're off haranguing other poor women, so the church mannies just put me up here. They're nae right pleased aboot their bonnie bells being used to keep you twa wakened. Ye may get a fair trial yet, quiney. Yer man may appear yet; there's a world of hope for you."

"And what about you, Bessie?" I said, aware that my voice came out too loud, over the ringing in my head.

"Aye, well, I've confessed such as I have to confess and admit to them. I'm hoping they'll satisfy themselves with me and let you eens off."

"Bessie, have they tortured you into some nonsense of a confession?"

"I'm as close a thing as they're going to find to a witch. I notice things. I ken things. I know the ways of herbs and people and I work to arrange the world a little better where I can. And I did have full intentions of killing my husband. He was not a good man like yours, Bell," she added, seeing my shocked face. "Ye mind I once asked you fit ye'd de if ye were married to an evil man and he touched your bairns? Well… I didna ken if Janet would ever manage to make a happy marriage, or to have children of her own, but see? She did, she's happy and healthy and full of love. There's nothing so bad as we can't recover from it and go on to live a joyful life." She squeezed my hand. "You remember that, Bell. I prepared the poison and waited for my moment, but before he came home that night, he drank whisky till he was bleazin' and then he fell in a burn, knocking his head on a stone like the fool he was. His brothers found him the next day. But I would have done it; I admitted that to them downstairs. And I've told many a woman how to prevent or get rid of a pregnancy when it is in her best interests to do so. There are some women it would kill to go through that again. They won't always take the draught that stops a babe planting in the first place. I told them church bodies that too. They didna like it: playing God, they said. Not my place, they told me. And here we all are."

"I made my Mary get rid of the baby," announced Christen Michell from where she lay at my side. "I often wonder if she would have lived if I hadn't done that."

"But Wee Thomas——" I began.

Bessie silenced me with a hand on mine and shook her head. We were to listen to Christen Michell, who was awake and keen to tell her tale.

"Not Wee Thomas," she continued. "Before Mary was married to the Laird, there was another, a most unsuitable boy, that she loved. She wasn't like you, Isobell, she didn't go to her marriage bed a maid, nor willingly." Her chains clinked as she tried to raise her hands to her face. "If I hadn't forced her, if I had just let well alone, she would have eloped with that boy and——"

"She would still have died in the childbed," said Bessie. "A little sooner, is all."

"But she might have been happy!"

"Aye, life's full of 'might haves'," said Bessie, patting the old woman's arm. "And there's no point to any of them. We all did the best we could at the time."

"She was so angry, Bessie. She kept a gift from the boy, a wee pink stone, and she threatened to present it to the Laird and tell him all, thereby undoing the marriage. We fought over this and she hid the thing from me, somewhere I would never find it, so she said. This dispute between us was ongoing when she died."

"Ach, these are just the disagreements of daily life," said Bessie. "All families have them. Ye'll see her soon enough, My Lady, and ye'll see that she's got nothing but love and forgiveness for you."

"But with no priest to issue Last Rites…"

"You forget yourself, madam; I am a midwife. We all do baptisms, permitted by your church and all. I've heard your confession here just now under this hallowed roof, and who's to say I canna do Last Rites as well? There's many a thing that men think is their own domain that we women can do just as well, if not better."

So, in the dirty grey light of the steeple in the great Mither Kirk of Aberdeen, Bessie spoke the Latin words and anointed Christen Michell and we held hands as she began to pass from us to God. Tears ran down my face but my companions stayed peaceful. Bessie said Christen Michell would fly straight through purgatory, no stopping on the way; her angels from the castle would see her right. Christen laughed at that; she laughed there in the steeple, right before she died, and then she was gone.

It seemed so terrible that she had passed in such a hard, cold place. In chains, no less. "She died among friends," Bessie reminded me. "With folks that she loved beside her, and with a wee laugh to see her off. Not many can say that. And she's the one who's got off the lightest. You have to prepare yourself for what's to come, quine. It's nae going to be easy. First things: they'll take her away and her body willna be treated with the respect that it should be."

I was horrified at this thought, the poor old lady, and it started me crying again.

Bessie took my hands. "Your knowledge of Scotland extends to your bonny Laird's lands. You're in Aberdeen now and it's not a place of fair dealings and justice for all, or kindness and thought for others, or any of the good things. An accused witch dies in prison? She'll be dragged through the streets for all to see and then buried in an unmarked grave somewhere; her family will be sent some enlarged bill for it all too. But the body that is left is nae her. That was her vessel in life, she's free of it noo, mind on that, Bell."

Bessie proceeded to tell me how Aberdeen was run by men who thought themselves important and how, behind every atrocity, lay money or expectation of money. These men stole trade from the country areas, but their deserved downfall would come, if not in this life, in the next. It was important for me to remember that, she said, and indeed, it did help to think of it when they threw Christen Michell's body down through the hole in the floor, and when they spat upon Bessie as they fastened her into the newly vacated shackles.

"Judgement cometh," she said, and the bells began to ring.

The Blood

We became used to the noise and the dark and the slow changing of night to day, Bessie and I. There was grey light and black dark, and an occasional golden glimpse of sun which I took to be midday. We were weakened by the noise and the dark and the changing cruelty of men: sticks and spittle and foul words that we could not hear for the perpetual ringing in our heads.

Our own speech to each other we understood, for it needed not words. We held each other in the dark, during the bells and after and before. We were given little to eat, some days no food or water at all, so there was almost nothing to pass through our bodies. My courses came, but there was not much of that either there in the prison in the high parts of the church. Bessie said it was the small blessing of starvation.

In dreams my blood ran down the bell ropes, flooding the chapel below, washing away the bad men, the men of the devil, for who else could it be that they served?

Then he came again, speaking words of filth and bile and he unlatched me and took me down the stairs. Bessie screamed and hollered at him and fought to get out of her chains, but powerful woman as she was, she could not stop him. He stopped me falling down the steps by holding my hair, I felt it rip out in places, bloody places, and then he tied me to a metal ring by my wrists and left me in the quiet.

The chapel was cold but I was beyond shivering, my body had long since ceased to react to simple discomforts like cold. The window above was ornate but I was beyond noticing colour or beauty or pictures of saints as had suffered in various ways. Maybe the pictures were of angels. Maybe of men. Probably not of women; not there in that place. No picture could be as handsome as a portrait of my husband would have been: his blue eyes, his mischievous smile, his strong arms and perfectly formed face. I closed my eyes and was comforted by the internal image, painted by my love for him. That he had never come, I would not think of, nor the whys or wherefores of that situation.

Time passed. Light changed and there were no bells. I started to hear again: footfalls and muffled voices. Men's voices. Then one up close: "Well, sister, what a pretty sight you do make here on the floor of the church!"

"John!" It was my brother John. My own flesh and blood. Did this mean we were saved? Were Jasper and the Laird present as well? They were not. I knew it as soon as I thought the thought. Their bright lights were not within the thick walls of the kirk.

"What a conniving little bitch you are," said my brother. "Stealing my inheritance? Murdering your husband?"

"I never stole anything and I never murdered Thomas. He will come, you'll see."

John laughed and the sound echoed round the chapel with its effigies and knights and grey stone. It was a joyless sound, holding none of the lust and goodness of Bessie's mirth.

He spoke again: "No, he won't, not after what we did to him."

"What? What…"

"He won't be coming back from that, sister. You'll be escheated and I'll petition to get back what's rightfully mine. My house in the North? My money. My own castle even, depending on the contents of that will."

"What did you do? Where is Thomas?"

"Dead by now, I should think."

No, no, that couldn't be true. It was just an evil lie told by my evil brother. My evil brother… "You did this? All this…" I recalled something, blurry and strange as if from a nightmare. "Agnes!"

There'd been a mention of a 'John' around all that happened with Agnes. "Where is Agnes, John?"

"The same place you're bound for, Isobell." He snarled my name in my face as he spoke, his spittle spraying my cheek. "Take her," he said to someone in a room beyond. "Do what needs to be done."

I flung myself after him as he walked away. I wanted to grab hold of my wicked brother's legs as he tried to leave but, tied to the ring as I was, I only fell awkwardly and hung there, flailing like a fish, or mermaid, out of water and unable to function. I wanted to drag him across the floor, as my dear friend and mother had been dragged through the streets of Aberdeen, and then beat the truth out of him. He strolled away to his freedom outside the church and left me in the stinking hands of Aberdeen's finest: William Dunn, Dean of Guild.

Dunn freed me from the ring only to tie another rope to my wrists, binding them together but leaving a long part for him to hold. This he used to haul me to my feet, to pull me through the church and then down the wide steps outside. He laughed when I fell. So much joyless hilarity was expressed that day. But I didn't really hear it, for I was not completely there. Part of me was fading away as John's words about Thomas being dead crashed round and round inside my head like clanging bells in a hollow steeple. Agnes was dead. John knew all the facts about that. So Thomas must be dead too. And John had done it. John was a murderer. And Thomas was dead.

Whatever the immorality of the man, Dunn was a magistrate of sorts so I told him what John had said. He laughed some more. He didn't care. Down more steps we went and I fell and rolled and got tangled in the rope. That angered him but I had formulated a chant and I repeated it till he kicked me in the jaw. "John said he killed Thomas. John is a murderer. John Killed Thomas. John is a murderer."

My words drowned in the metal taste of blood, blood that flowed from my mouth and face and dripped onto the cobbled street as we walked. Dunn kicked me in the back every so often and told me what a useless little whore I was. The king could not be bothered to come for one as worthless as myself; even the witch pricker was not coming, so he, the great William Dunn, was bound to take the duty upon himself. The great things he did for God. The great service he did for mankind.

William Dunn, Dean of Guild, took me to The Tolbooth, a tall building, a prison and a court. It was dark. It stank of shit and piss and blood and terror. Someone cried out. I don't think it was me, for I was only part there when I was put in the wee cell and pricket all over to find the mark of the devil. A three inch nail he had, and he drove it into my shoulder, my arm, my chest. I heard it break my kneecap after I had fallen on the floor. He tore my dress and stabbed and stabbed.

Surely I would be all the way dead soon, no blood left inside, all poured out onto the floor. The cold and hard floor of the Tolbooth became sticky with the actions of the devil who drove the nail in and drove himself into a frenzy of bloodlust. I watched his face in the candlelight as he took on the form of the Deil himself, malice shining out of every pore as he tore me apart. I saw his delight in a grin so wicked as to rival any evil I had ever imagined in story or song. Dunn was unimaginable. Dunn was bad; badness was he, and he had me.

The Host

Agony was me, what was left of me. I was blood, more blood than skin, more meat than bread. And then, right there in front of me, I saw it: the Host, the bread that was become the body of Christ. And then a great golden chalice filled with the light of heaven and earth, filled with goodness and kindness and charity, all the qualities man should aspire to embody in this life.

Man. And woman. For it was a woman who raised the Host and held the chalice aloft. She was Mother Mary and Christen Michell and Bessie and Agnes and me. She was all of us, past, present, future. She was all in white, clean, safe, whole, and she shone with the Christ light. The Host. The Chalice. The body and blood of Christ; the sacred Eucharist was ours to raise as much as any man's. Our right. Our truth. Our power.

Such wonders filled my heart and mind as my flesh was defiled. In the filth of the prison, my body had been turned to face the floor so that William Dunn could carry out foul deeds of his liking.

I lifted my face out of the blood. I found power in my arms to push up and swing round to look upon the piteous creature who believed he had authority over me. He spoke and I heard his words: "Confess witch! You fornicated with the devil!"

"Aye," I said and it meant many things. My arm was straight and strong. My finger pointed true. There was no waver or weakness to be detected in my voice as it enunciated words of power: "You took the form of the devil today and committed the mortal sin of rape. Christen

Michell was here with Mother Mary and their sainted forms bore witness as they raised the Host high above your act of evil. One such as you cannot stand in the Christ light. Seen by God and all the angels of heaven. Damned for eternity for your sins. Step away William Dunn, Dean of Guild, or God will smite you where you kneel!"

He staggered to his feet, breathless from his sinful exertions, and frightened by the speech that had flowed through me. He looked round the cell, up at the curved ceiling, into the darkest corners of the dark, in search of angels or demons come to get him. William Dunn, Dean of Guild, hater of women, was a coward, afraid of shadows and wee lassies, and he was gone.

Many locks turned and ground within the thick door after he exited. Afraid I would follow, or that ghosts would chase him. William Dunn was stupid; walls and doors were no barrier to spirit and he would be hunted down and ended. I knew it. And I was glad. And I slept.

Another man came, but he did not hurt me. He took the rope and led me like an animal through the streets of Aberdeen. Grey streets. Stone houses. Wooden houses. People staring. Horses tied as I was, led and whipped. Grey skies. Rain to wash. Through the Kirkyard and into the Kirk. We climbed the steps together, the man and I, back to the shackles and back to Bessie.

Power flowed through Bessie as it did me, and all womankind, and she used hers then to shout and rage and pour anger down upon the man.

"It was not him," I told her. "He just led me here. Dunn is the devil. Christen Michell raised the Host high above him."

She was not comforted by my words and my appearance distressed her, I could tell. I tried to explain that it did not matter; we were powerful beings and soon we would be free of these earthly vessels.

"Aye, quiney, I ken. And you've got to be prepared for the manner of that. This is nae London where they chop heads off in the tower, all quick like. In Aberdeen they both strangle and burn a witch. It'll be a town show."

"We have not fear in us, Bessie."

"Fit a strength you hae, Bell. We'll show 'em, Lassie. Noo, let me fix yer dress."

Golden light shone through the wooden panels in lines, lines of pure goodness, like Bessie's heart and mine. Bessie tore a piece of her own gown and wound it tight to tie mine together over the chest. Through the holes, her fingers worked hard as they had done all her life. So many souls saved by her herbs, brought into the world alive by her knowledge and skill. I told her this and she laughed. We both laughed there in the Steeple and we brought light into the dark.

We told such stories as were left in us. Bessie spoke of babes born covered in hair and one in a mermaid's purse, and little ones delivered still and cold who then revived when their mothers wouldn't let them go. I took my dear friend on a walk through London that Jasper and I had once walked, down past Tyburn, the place of hanging, and out into the greener places. By Hyde Park, Queen Elizabeth's private hunting ground, we saw a rider upon a horse and a flash of orange hair. We fancied it was the queen herself and perhaps it was.

Bessie told me the sad story that she had seen and heard through the Laird's Lug in the castle; she had not been able to say it while Christen Michell was still with us, for fear of distressing the old lady. But Bessie and I were made of metal and stone and all the strong things of the world and I needed to know. Dunn had dragged Agnes across the great hall and, by sound, Bessie had divined, into the chapel and there he had defiled both woman and place with his evil. I shed a tear for Agnes while Bessie cursed Dunn.

Thunder rumbled over Aberdeen and lightning flashed through the wooden slats in the steeple room and I recalled how, some years before Jasper and I were born, the grand spire of St. Paul's Cathedral had been struck by lightning and the tower and bells had fallen down into the church itself, setting fire to the roof. They'd rebuilt the roof but never the spire. The notion became a humorous one as thunder crashed above and white light flashed through our prison. We clung to each other and roared with laughter, the elements joining us in glorious release as rain took over from thunder. We laughed until our middles ached with it, but it was a good pain, wholesome and human and pure, like the pounding of the rain and the fading thunder rumbles, sounds and actions that were in the natural order of things. We settled to sleep, cuddled up together like bairns or kittens, in a warm haze of comfort, approved of by God, souls safe in his keep, and for a while all was quiet and still in the steeple of the Mither Kirk of Aberdeen.

They took Bessie first, before me. We did not cry or wail. We kissed a temporary goodbye; we would see one another again soon.

So I sat. In the church. In the Steeple. There were no other people. No one to ring bells. No one to cause hurt. Just me and the grey light and the dark and I knew I would soon be with Thomas.

I remembered the first time I had seen him and then saw the light of the second time too. Our breakfasts. That first kiss in the stone circle. Our wedding. Our bed. Oh, to be in his presence again. Thoughts of Thomas did something to ease the stiffening of my form that had taken place after Bessie had gone. My body was already half-dead, the blood from the nail wounds dried and scratchy on top of deeper injury, deeper bleeding.

Bessie had fixed my dress with a cord made out of her own dress. I could do that too. Make a cord. I looked up at the splintery and dirty wooden beam above. The chains of the shackles were long. I was short. The means to speed my reunion with my husband were there. God would not judge it a mortal sin, God would forgive. I would only be quickening the way to Thomas and Christen Michell and Bessie and Mother Mary. Only removing the task from low men. Choosing the time to leave. Choosing the time to go. As I had done before.

The young man appeared then, interrupting my contemplation. He held out bread. It was to me, the bread of life. First in his hands. Then in mine.

The Mermaid

The young man told me of processes to be gone through, roads to be travelled. He loosed the chains and took me to the steps; there were so many of them and they were harder this time, power seeming to have left my legs. I was not pulled up by the hair when I fell. The young man lifted me gently by the hands, the two parts of me that were least hurt, only grazed and bruised from many fallings.

"You're nae finished yet," he whispered in my ear on the steps as I faltered again with my footing. "The pricking didn't prove it, so they're going to dook you. Try and relax and hold yer breath when ye go in—"

Another man shouted then to him to make haste, and he stopped speaking. There was a cart again but no rest: I was made to stand, or sway about and be held up as was the case. People followed the cart and shouted foul things and threw foul things and were foul things. The road went downwards, I fell forward against the front of the cart and then just stayed there, leaning, resting.

The sea was close, I could smell it and then I saw it, large and grey and flat it did look as it splashed along the edges of Aberdeen. The way I had entered Scotland was to be the way I would leave it. The Mermaid would swim one last time and then the sea would have her way; she would kill me and take me from these low ones to be in the light. And with Thomas. I filled my heart up with him, the salt of the earth and the light of my world.

So I was full of love when they tied my thumbs and bound my big toes together. Like a mermaid. Like a fish's tail. But it would not help me swim. I knew that. I was at peace with that.

More chains. Big ones. Oily and fishy smelling, but still less putrid than Dunn who was not there. Dunn who was afraid. Not brave like Bessie. Not strong like me.

It took much time to tie me up and to tie more ropes to me, and to then tie them to the chains that would test me for a witch. The crowd grew impatient. "Dook her!" was their cry, repeated, over and over, till it rang like the bells in my head. Yes, dook me, I wanted to say but speech had departed. Dook me and have done. Dook me and let me fly away from this dark town and place and people. To be with Thomas. To be happy. To be free.

Finally they were done with their tying and fiddling and fussing, those men that thought they were of import, those men with the jangling pockets, those worshippers of gold. Though what gold they could get from the torture of women I could not fathom, but it mattered not. The sea approached.

I watched the harbour walls as I was lowered, oh so slowly, toward the dark waves. Better this than to be consigned to the flames for all time as those on the dock would be. Better this cold and watery grave.

I would swim to Thomas. Dance when I saw him. I would play my harp and laugh and watch over those who still lived on the earth. Wee Thomas, who was safe with Janet and Jane. Jasper, who had Ian. His dear friend would help him through this loss; I understood that in a deeper way than I had before and my heart overflowed with the love that I felt there.

The chains stuck at one point. The crowd roared its disappointment. "Drown the Witch!" had become their chant. But if I were a witch I would float and then be burned; they were ignorant in their excitement to see harm inflicted. The harbour walls were slimy, worse even than those of the dungeon back in the castle. Green bits of weed hung here and there, growing on stone, rootless but clinging on to life.

A jolt went through all my bones and I was dropped, faster, down and down, it could not be long and then: there! Cold – such cold! – all around me, taking my breath, taking all of me lower into the dark and dank sea, oily and fishy, and then I saw a pair of bright eyes. A seal! It swam all about me, its big brown eyes meeting mine in the murky depths of the harbour. The eyes were wise and warm and I stared back into them, glad to have a friend there at the end, glad that innocence and goodness and a smiling, whiskery face were the last sight I would see in life.

The animal travelled with me as I went lower; sinking, so not a witch after all, spared the flames, the pyre of pain built by base men, cowards and rapists and thieves. No. I had my friend the seal; his face nudged mine and it was soft and gentle, a loving caress, an unexpected kindness in the deep.

So it came to be that the second time the sea killed me, a seal kissed me goodbye and waved me on my way. My eyes closed and it was a relief. My mouth closed against the water, a natural instinct, but it did not block the pathway to Thomas, for I was soon in his arms, safe and warm, all the mortal life gone from me, drained away into the sea.

The Wakening

I was free. Free to sleep. To rest in peace, those words made so much sense now. To be at rest was so glorious a state of being, such comfort was mine. All was softness and kindness and loving goodness. Thomas's salty, oaty scent was all around, holding me, rocking me, enveloping me in love and warmth.

The dark was not black, more purple with a promise of pink. A transitional phase, that's what it must be, I thought as thoughts began to form again after the time of just feeling. Could it be Christen Michell's purgatory? If so, it was sweet and safe and not at all like the conditions Father Daniel had spoken of. In the chamber. Down below. But not a low place, a high one, sacred and of the light.

I remembered the chalice of gold and the light that had existed within and without in that seeing. That was important, to hold on to that, to not forget. That mattered. I must have floated near to the earth, a ghost, a mist, a visiting spirit, for I heard voices other than Thomas's soft tones; there was Wee Thomas, high and excited, and Jasper, Jasper soliloquising works of Shakespeare. Romeo's words to Juliet, of love and the sun, more light and roses.

Roses, so many roses. I could smell them. Like the salve Bessie had given me at Christmas. And then on my wedding day, she had used it to anoint points on my forehead and my temples and even between my breasts with a wonderful chuckle. She must be near, also in a quiet state of being, but we had the communication of scent between us. It was all we needed. We hadn't needed words in life, not near the end. We had understood one another and been brave together. But I floated away from that. The time hadn't come for that sort of consideration.

There came an interlude where I could hear Bessie and see her; she caused me to open my eyes with the smell of leeks. Leeks in a broth, salty like Thomas, hot and nourishing before my eyes closed again.

Senses sharpened. There was the soft feel of the bedclothes against my skin and the sound of Thomas's sleeping breath. The need to make water was strong. In heaven? Heaven had a replica of my marriage bed and my room in the tower and, thankfully, Thomas's closet. It was quite astonishing. There was the door to the secret stair and Thomas's clothes and chair and our bed. I got back into that quite sharply, as sharply as stiff limbs and sore knee allowed, and snuggled into my husband. He roused and turned and spoke and I could hear him quite clearly.

"Ishbell, my little Ishbell, you are come back to me at last."

"I'm here Thomas," I said, trying to reassure him. We had been separated for a while, and that had been bad for us, but now all things were mended.

"Lassie, I shouldna have left," he said.

I could feel my face moving as it had not moved for some time, crumpling into some sort of frown. His words pulled at something in the dark, no, from before the dark. A memory. But it would not come. I touched his face, his most beautiful face and rested my head beside him and together we slept.

"You'll be wanting a bath," said Bessie. "We've hauled water all morning to get it up here. Come on, out of bed with you."

Bessie was not one to be argued with so I acquiesced without complaint, though I had been enjoying the restful sleep so much. The water was warm and, again, there was the scent of roses. Bessie rubbed me all over with the rose salve after the bath as we sat beside the fire. She rubbed my pocked skin, for I was covered in round scars as if I'd had the pox. Something tugged again from beyond a thick veil, from the other side of warm and cosy.

"Aye," she said, the many meanings word. "Life goes on, Isobell. There's a new one growing in you and I reckon that's what will save you."

"Am I not already saved here in heaven?" I laughed up at her round face. "Are not we all, Bessie?"

Bessie knelt down beside me and wrapped a blanket about my shoulders. "My mother never believed in softening the truth," she said. "It has to be faced. Yer nae in heaven, Isobell."

I looked around at my marriage bed, the floor, and then up at the window in the ceiling, currently showing silver stars against a dark blue sky. Beauty all around. The fire was there but only to warm, only to dry and comfort a body, not to burn one.

"Ye didna die," continued Bessie. "The Laird arrived at the harbour just in time, and proved he was not murdered. They pulled you oot and he took you hame, here, to us. Ye've slept for six weeks, but I think it's time to waken up now."

"I didn't die." The words existed but held no sense. "I'm not in heaven."

"You lived, Bell," said Janet, for Janet she was, not Bessie, though she was squeezing my hand like her mother used to do. "Time to get on wi' living. Bessie would want you to. Christen Michell too. Now let's get your clean nightdress on."

My limbs were limp like that of a wee poppet that had not been properly stuffed. Janet pulled and pushed floppy arms into sleeves and wrapped me up in a soft shawl.

"There, now," she said. "Another few months and you'll have a bonny wee bairn in yer arms."

"Bessie said she would put a bairn in my arms one day," I said for I could remember that.

"Aye, well, she'll be looking down on you."

"Bessie died." And I did not.

Janet spoke on in her practical and informative way. "She was found guilty at her trial and executed."

"Executed." A strange word. Only one meaning.

"Burnt."

And then I was the one to hold Janet as she cried. I stroked her hair and told her Bessie was so brave and so strong, how she never showed any fear in the prison, for all those memories were there to be called up for a cold kind of comfort in front of the fire. I spoke more words that told how Bessie had helped Christen Michell, how she had given the Last Rites to make the moment of the old lady's death easier, and how she'd helped me, how she'd sewn my dress back together when it was torn. We'd kissed goodbye with no tears. I told of that too.

Janet went then and I sat at the hearth a while longer, studying the orange red depths of the fire. Bessie had gone into the flames while I'd gone into the blue green depths of the sea. And come back out. I'd imagined Bessie to be here with me, but I had actually just been conjuring what I wanted to be true. It had seemed as if Thomas was here with me too when the truth was that my husband and Bessie were in heaven, the only rightful place for such good and heroic souls. I pressed my hand to my belly and wondered: where was I?

The Innocents

Only a midwife, or the daughter of a midwife, would have known, I thought as I flattened my nightdress down over my belly. The flesh underneath was flat too. I was thin, as I had never been, not even after the voyage to Scotland. My breasts swelled, though not as they had before as a part of general wideness. They were different. Everything was different. Different from before. Before the dungeon. Before the Steeple. Before it was said that we were witches.

Bessie had herbs that would remove a child from the womb, I knew that. They were only to be used in exceptional circumstances. I believed I had those. There was danger in them of course, but did I care? Did it matter? What was sin anyway? It did not exist in the way those base men had defined it. In the manner of our prayers or bathing in the woods or falling in love. Bessie had thought to kill a man, to rid the world of an abuser. Would I not do the same if given the same situation and chance? To that obscene creature who had put this child in me with force?

The face that looked back at me from my mermaid's looking glass was strange and new. Big eyes, small face. Like Wee Thomas. An innocent. Like the babe that had started within me. And like the Laird that stood before me.

I gasped in shock and put my hands out to see if he was real, if he was flesh. He was. Thomas Manteith, my husband, was alive and well. Of course he was. Had Janet not told me that he came to the harbour? And that he took me home? His middle was solid, balancing me in my befuddlement, and his smile, so full of love. Gazing upon him was balm to a wounded soul. He was true goodness embodied in a man. But he knew naught of the great badness that had happened, and of that innocence I had to rob him.

"I am not what I was, My Lord. You must put me aside."

"Ishbell," he said and moved forward as if to touch me.

"Dinna touch! Dinna touch!" I heard myself shrieking the words that had been shrieked earlier like an echo from the dark. "You know not with what you would connect," I added as an explanation.

"I didna mean to distress you, Ishbell. Why don't you sit?" He indicated the bed. "Put the covers aroon ye? Nae get cold?"

He was offering me my place back in our marriage bed, that beautiful and lovingly crafted piece of furniture. But that couldn't be. He would understand. He would not inflict any added cruelty, such a good man was he.

"I am with child," I explained, holding the bedpost for support as I spoke, feeling the many carved oak leaves under my hand, so smooth, so polished.

"Lassie!" His face lit up. "Dinna be feart. We will look after you, make sure all is well—"

"You don't understand, sir. It is not yours."

"Of course it is mine."

"No, Thomas," I said, informality creeping into my speech in accident. "My courses came in the steeple. There was no child when I went in. I was then defiled. As part of the witch pricking, I was defiled."

Silence rang loud as bells, but not for long. "The child is mine, Ishbell."

"Did you not hear my words? I spoke the truth."

"Aye, but I'm the father o' the bairn."

I stared at him in confusion, gripping the wooden oak leaves with both hands. Something had happened to him too. Something terrible. It had not killed him, but perhaps he had been knocked about the head and had lost the ability for clear thinking.

He touched then; he didn't seem to care that I might be filth or dirt or that I had fornicated with the devil. He took my hands off the post with great gentleness, and led me round to where I could get into the bed.

"You are my Bonny Quine, my wife, my wee mermaid from the pool."

"That was one of the things, one of the accusations; they said I took on the form of a mermaid."

His face lost some of its innocence then; it twisted in something akin to hatred. "Such ignorance exhibited in the name of God. In their desire to create a Godly society, they do all manner of ungodly things. What do these men know of goodness? Have they even read the good book? So keen they were to get it in English so they could." He quieted as he looked at me and said my name soft: "Ishbell, Ishbell. You are the mother of my son, Wee Thomas. It matters not that he came from another womb."

He spoke truth, this good man, this hero of men.

"I am the father of your child too, if you will let me be this. It is a child of your flesh and are we not made one flesh? Does our marriage and our love not make it so? I would raise this bairn to be a good man, or woman. I would do my best by him or her, and you. Will you let me?"

I felt a familiar pulse in my heart, not a great swell like it was before, but a beat, a note that had been stifled by the dark. "You are a good man, Thomas. You did not deserve any of this."

"As you did not also," he said. "But we are lucky, Ishbell. We have each other. We have our love." He tucked me up all cosy like a wee child, a bairn who was loved and cared for and cherished.

Then he strode to the fire. He poked it with some vigour, attacking the logs as if he might burn them in some sort of reversed fiery violence.

"It was Dunn?"

"Thomas…" I said, not wanting to answer, sensing danger could come from the words, more danger, to him, to dear Thomas, my husband, the Laird.

"I ken it wis," he said, turning back to face me. "It is costing me dear not to ride out and kill him, Lassie. But what would come to us then? I would hang. You would be left on your own. You might be accused again. He's a slicket beast of a man, nae fit to look upon one so fair as you! No, we will have to trust to God, as Bessie said, He who chooses the time of death for us all. And may that cursed wretch know pain and suffering before his time is up."

I sensed it had gone by us; the danger, and the speaking of foulness. We would not revisit it. It was confined to the past and now the future had to be created. Thomas busied himself with the practicalities and questions of the moment: how much pain still existed in my limbs and body? Would it cause me distress for him to sleep beside me? Maybe tomorrow I could see Wee Thomas and Jasper and my bonny new mare who had saved his life.

The rest of the evening was filled with the telling of that tale, of John's great devilry and attempt to get my money and property. He had taken Agnes into his employ, and paid her to accuse us. So said Duncan, who had investigated the matter. Thomas had been thrown down a well and nearly starved until my wee horse alerted a shepherd's boy to his plight. I felt roused to do some of my own killing. Bessie had herbs for that too... but no, this was not the time for such thoughts.

Here I was, snuggled against my lovely husband as I drifted off to sleep, and, for this night, that would do.

The Selkie

We galloped for miles and miles, and at great speed; the trees and fields and wee cottages flashed by like lightning, there and gone all in a second of time.

My wee Selkie horse was white and small and pretty, but so strong, so brave, like a Kelpie come straight from the sea to dance on land with her mermaid friend. Her eyes were large and brown like those of my seal friend from the harbour, for thoughts of that still came, unwitting and sudden and cold. So I mixed tales of water horses and seal people in my head and my Selkie kept me safe as we flew through the countryside, as we moved too quickly to be seen or heard or looked upon at all; we moved too quickly to be bothered by sounds, unless we chose to stop and listen and sometimes we did. Nothing scared her, my bonny mare who had saved Thomas's life, and was helping me with mine now.

Lapwings flew up out of the purpling heather, peewits shouted at us for venturing too near to their nests, but those sounds weren't bothersome. Not like the clang of pots from the kitchen where I never went, or the sound of men's voices from the great hall where I tried to spend as little time as possible. Out in the fresh air of the world, we revelled in the fast thudding of hooves through the forest, in the screech of a white owl and the mating calls of foxes and stags; though those last held the hint of nightmare, it was not a true one, not one that could harm. Even the two boxing hares we came upon did not distress us; it was not a cruel violence we witnessed but a natural one, a competitive combat of wild creatures in the light of the sun.

When the sun shone upon the gorse it created a scent so sweet it seemed to come from heaven itself. I leaned down and touched it as we passed, letting the softness of the flowers comfort the sting of the thorny branches.

We walked along grassy clifftops and looked out at the sea, a sea that was some days brilliant blue, others stormy grey; green and pink stones showed in the shallows by the craggy bays. We saw dolphins. We saw seals. I waved and called out to my brown-eyed friends.

The wind swept us clean, leaving the taste of salt on our lips and our manes wild and unkempt. We only went down onto the sandy beaches; I would risk some things, but not Selkie feet on rocky shores. We found places where waves crashed so high they shot out of the very land itself. They roared in celebration of their watery power; I instinctively hugged tight to my horse's neck then as she reared up with the waves in some Kelpie joy of her own. There were pink rocks and grey, all mixed up in some places, white shining lines cut straight through them here and there. I felt their texture with my bare feet and stuck my toes in the little streams that ran down into the sea.

If we saw boats or people, we turned for home. It was a rule made in my heart: don't take that risk. Don't let them see you and think you strange, or mad, or worse. There were other rules that had formed themselves: don't go to the pool, the boarded over chapel or the stones. Things will happen if you do, uncomfortable things, thoughts you're not ready for, memories that were kept at bay by the air and the sea and the wind, would rise. And there was Thomas's warning: if it starts to get dark, I will set out to search for you.

"You will be careful," he said, worried, as he brushed my hair free of salt each night.

"My Selkie keeps me safe." She did. No matter how loose my grip was about her neck at times.

"Aye," he agreed. "But if you should fall, quine, mayhaps far from home—"

"Would it be such a bad thing, Thomas?"

Alas, this honesty, after eliciting yet another assurance that he accepted the child in my belly as his own, ended the wild solitary rides.

Every day after that, my husband accompanied me on his own large brown horse, and the excursions became sedate and much shorter. They were still delightful in their own way, still distracting. In fact, to walk our horses slowly through the woods together felt like an almost happy occupation, certainly companionable, and it made me notice the many small natural beauties that existed close to the castle. Tiny birds building nests. Baby rabbits jumping out of our way, chased on by their worried mother. A family of deer who froze on seeing us, then bounced off through the forest, white bottoms bobbing up and down until they were far from danger, together and safe and happy again.

Janet was pleased about the change in riding arrangements. Jasper was pleased too. The two of them had previously taken to making a big fuss and show of relief each day when I had come home. Janet thought some cooking would be good for me, though she kept the key to Bessie's special store on her person at all times, never leaving me alone in there. Jasper encouraged me to read: he had sent for new books from London, but they held no interest for me, those bound pages of words written by fine men, men who thought they were important.

Wee Thomas just wanted cuddles. Cuddles by the fire in my room with him were good. We worked on his letters and he told me stories of knights and princes and dragons. I couldn't summon tales like I used to, though I told him about the Selkie and the places we had visited. He wanted to go too and I talked to Thomas about getting a small pony for the boy. It was a happy idea; it pleased Thomas. I liked to see the smile on his face and the interest and keenness in his eyes as we got into the marriage bed.

Since the brutal removal of innocence that had happened in Aberdeen, we spent our time together in bed like innocent children. It was so warm lying beside Thomas, either my body curled to the shape of his or his to mine. It was safe. And so greatly comfortable, and soft, and entirely lacking in anything cruel and grey and bad.

But there was no sweet forest air, or baby rabbits and deer, to distract me in the dark of the night, warm and safe as I was. I knew parts of me had died when I thought Thomas dead and those parts had not yet revived. What if we were both truly dead? Wasn't that more likely than the Selkie filled dream I lived during the day? What if the nightmares of sleep were the truth and I was still in that place, chained and stinking and alone? Or what if I had taken my own life there in the steeple, not knowing that my circumstances could improve, or that Thomas lived, and I was only watching an existence that could have been? That thought made me cling to Thomas in the night, Thomas who was warm and with me, and breathing, and very much alive.

So many others were dead, how could it be that I, and the child in my womb, both lived? Why should we have survived and not them? What justice was there in that? What Divinity?

The Lady

The chalice was golden and carved with emblems of beauty, such as I had never seen on any physical cup or goblet. It reflected white light outwards, beaming it out to the world. The hands that held it aloft were mine, and I was the Lady and Christen Michell and Bessie Thom and Mary who had died so young. I was young and old and wise. I was innocent and pure and Godly. I was in the stone circle, turning, spinning, the stones flying by at great speed. I was down below in the belly of the earth, the chamber, singing and shining with the light. The one true light of the world. It was mine. Mine to hold and mine to give.

I was staring at blue. One silver star, pulsing, beating, twinkling. I was in bed. Beside Thomas.

I sat up with a start, for it had been a dream of great meaning, that was clear. Great meaning, but what meaning?

I told Thomas of the dream and he listened carefully, and then I told him of the vision from the prison, my seeing of Christen Michell and the Lady and all of us raising the host. He frowned.

"It was real, Thomas. Not some hallucination brought on by lack of sleep; it was real."

"I know, Lassie—" he started, but I quieted him with a hand on his shoulder for a realisation was taking place.

That moment, that vision, had given me light and love and beauty right there in the midst of the unspeakable. And that was where my child had come from, not the dark, nor the rape, the aggression and filth, but this. Mother Mary, Christen Michell, God. The great weight I had been carrying along with the baby lifted from me then, and I smiled in relief. I knew that I would love the child, an innocent child as we all were, but this one had protective light around her, light to cast away any evil that might have clung there in the Tolbooth. Had not Mother Mary herself been protected from original sin at the time of her own conception? I was aware that was a unique event, and that it was probably blasphemous to believe it could happen again, but I had no doubt that the Holy Spirit had blessed my babe in some way at that moment.

"It was a healing vision," I said.

"Aye," agreed Thomas. "But it seems to me to contain elements of both the old and the new ways of religion. Maybe that has just come from your life here. You've celebrated the Mass of the old faith down in a place of older rituals yet. And ye've visited the stones wi' Bessie Thom after a birthing. Aye, I ken aboot that." He smiled.

"What meaning would you divine from it, Thomas?"

"I think only you can decide that. Kings and governments and churchmen are all very keen to tell us which is the right path to God, and they change their minds often enough. When I travelled to the East as a younger man I saw other ways, ways of sitting in silence to listen, to expand the soul. I have wondered since if that was close to the old ways that were once practiced here, the ways respected by Bessie in the circle."

"She said it was a woman's place."

"And these were female visions, Ishbell. Dinna fret, quine, sit with it, the sense will come."

So I sat. At first in our room, and then, in the stone circle. The time had come to return there, to a place untouched by unclean hands as other places had been. I no longer feared what thoughts might appear; in fact, I welcomed them, keen for wisdom and answers. The ancient circle was blessed by nature, all around tiny pink and white flowers dotted the grass, twinkling with dew in sunlight, as if the stars from the night time sky had caused a pretty echo on the ground. I felt peace and love and yes, a feminine energy. Hadn't Bessie spoken of the Goddess here? A female God. A burning offence to speak of such a thing surely, again blasphemous, but then those were just the ideas of low men.

As ever, I was drawn to the flat stone with its small carving of the underground tunnels. The sun had warmed the stone and I lay down on it, feeling myself grow drowsy, thoughts of the vision from the prison and Christen Michell and Bessie floating through my mind. I'd come here with Bessie. But not Christen Michell. Of course not. She would never come to—

I sat up quickly, all drowsiness gone, recalling Christen Michell's confession before she died. This was a woman's place. And a place of secrets. We came here with the greatest hurts of our hearts. Mary would have come here to be by herself, away from her mother and Agnes and even her husband; I was sure of it. I felt a strange desperation to uncover the secrets and the pain, and let the light of the sun shine on them now.

But where to start? I looked around the circle and down at the grass beneath my feet. There was only one place to begin. Right here. The turf that ran up the side of the flat stone already looked dry and loose and was easy to pull back a bit, then a bit more and then...

It wasn't even buried deep, the small teardrop shaped stone from Mary's portrait, the gift from her first love. It was pink and shiny once the soil was brushed off and it had been polished up on my gown. A small rainbow shone inside it as I held it up to the sun. Mary had held it while sitting for the painting in an act of defiance, presumably unnoticed by Christen Michell. Had she been pregnant at the time? With her lover's child? Or Wee Thomas? I felt a flicker in my own belly at that moment, like a faery had just unfurled its wings. The babe, my babe, knew it was welcome to stay now and was stretching its tiny limbs. My heart hurt and it was hard to breathe as I felt the sorrows, and the joys, of all us girls and women, and all we went through on this earth. No wonder we needed places like this, sources of solitude and solace.

For a moment I wondered if the information about Mary's life before her marriage might help Thomas, but no. It might only distress him. This truth could never be spoken. It had been told to Bessie and I in confidence and must remain secret, unheard by any but us two chosen confessors.

I reburied the small stone in this place of healing, wishing I could give it back to its owner, wanting to press it to Mary's heart and mend all our deepest hurts. My fingers felt other objects in the earth as I put the wee stone back: one was a hard round ball, carved with a pattern, and there was also something made of metal, a brooch perhaps? But like Mary's stone, they were not for me, so I left them there, undisturbed.

I asked Thomas to invite Father Daniel to visit the castle, for I wished to speak to him too. In truth I had not studied the Sacraments with the diligence I should have, but maybe some answers could be found in Christens Michell's 'one true faith'.

"He will probably only tell you that yours was a vision of the Blessed Virgin," said Thomas, before sending for the man. "Or... he may get quite excited about it."

Father Daniel did express excitement; he was most taken with the fact it had seemed to be Christen Michell as I'd looked upon the vision in prison. "Christen Michell was truly devoted to Our Lady," he told me. "You'll have seen the statue in your own chapel here of course?"

The last time I'd seen it came strongly to mind and the old man must have discerned something of the sort in my face.

"I know they destroyed the chapel," he said, laying a hand on my own. "But they cannot touch the faith in our hearts. Christen Michell contributed both money and personal effort to save the statue from the reformers. The one here is a replica, the original hidden and sent to the Low Countries for safe keeping. Some like to say it is the other way about, but that is nonsense of course, for the original was made of oak and the one here is stone.

"I have no doubt Our Lady of Aberdeen interceded with her son on Christen Michell's behalf and that in death, that good woman was transfigured by Our Lord. She died a martyr to our cause, our faith. Then she held out the blood and body of Christ to you, Isobell. You, yourself, were shown grace in this. But Christen Michell was a brave woman, providing the means for true worship here in this corner of Scotland. She was fearless, a true warrior of the faith and I think it is for me to take action now."

I smiled and nodded, and did not give voice to the thoughts that were in my head. I remembered the lesson learned about thinking through what is said, and not saying words if they might bring hurt or harm. That this was not the time for action, that that time had passed, was not something I had to say to the old priest. That the respect and concern that had been shown in the rescue of a statue should have been shown to Christen Michell herself, that fearless and true warrior of his faith, that could remain unsaid too. If he had spoken up for her, he would have told me. If he had tried to help us in our hour of need, he would have enunciated pretty and poetic words about that too.

I wished him well and waved goodbye and then told Thomas what had transpired.

"Christen Michell, a Saint?" said Thomas. "Well, good luck to him, it'll give him a focus to try and pull that off!"

And then, as Father Daniel rode away, another horse approached, at speed, from the track in the trees. Thomas stood in front of me, to protect. Indeed, he ushered me towards the great hall and beyond, but I could not tear myself from the face of the rider. It was the young man, the better man, the one who had shown kindness in a time of cruelty. Despite his goodness, his appearance into our day so soon after all the talk of my dear friend and mother had me shaking and trembling. For I only knew his face from that time. Why did he dismount and approach the castle? Why did he reach inside his jacket and withdraw a packet, something wrapped up in paper? And why did he smile when he saw me?

The Rubble

I held the great golden cross in my hand as the young man spoke; the beads of the rosary were bruised and battered, disrespected, as if they had been flung about the streets of the dark city of Aberdeen. As they had. Even the thought of the name of that grey place gave me cause to shudder.

"How did this come to be in your possession?" demanded Thomas of the man. "Her body has not even been returned to us. They say it is not to be found, yet you have this?"

"It was my last job there, working for them. I took it from her after," explained the man, then turning to me. "I knew you should have it, My Lady. I'm glad to see you looking so well."

I could not speak to him, I shook too much, but managed to mutter, "He was kind," to Thomas before walking through to the great hall and kneeling by the fire.

On the wall above the fireplace was our crest: the bear, the mermaid, the same network of tunnels as on the cross of Christen Michell's, and the heart, that symbol of her faith, though not mine. I had not been received into the old faith, had not taken the true body and blood of Christ into my body, and I knew I never would. But what signs was I being given this day? The movement of my baby, the quickening, followed so closely by the sudden return of the most precious belonging of my friend, my mother and sister.

A realisation came: I had seen the original Lady of Aberdeen leaving Scotland. Within moments of my setting foot on the shore, she had left.

She had been carried away to safety. Father Daniel had swung the smoking censer while a mysterious and dignified hooded woman, had watched. Christen Michell.

Water dripped onto the cross. I looked up, suspecting a leak had sprung in the ceiling and Duncan would have to arrange to have it fixed. But it was my own face that leaked, my own eyes. I was crying. How long it had been since that had happened, I thought, feeling the wet on my cheeks, tasting the salt. I had cried when Christen had died. I remembered it in vivid grey colour. Bessie had been there. Bessie and Christen Michell who were no more, and this fact was all at once so real and so unthinkable and so terrible.

I put the necklace over my head and the beads crossed my heart. That's where they were, those two good women, right down deep in the very inside of me. The cross itself hung low, over the top of my belly, as if symbolising a divine protection placed over the child. Of course. Had I, myself, not been safeguarded throughout this pregnancy by those around me, from my own dear husband to my wee Selkie horse? The man at the door had played a part in keeping me alive too.

I could not stop crying. I was full of horror that I could have considered ending this baby's life, this child that was obviously important and special to be as protected as she was. This pain mixed together with grief for my mothers, Bessie and Christen, even Agnes, sisters all, and the emotions could not be contained. The Laird held me and said it was a letting out of what had been kept inside and that I should not be ashamed of the tears.

Ashamed I wasn't, but I knew it was time to be strong and face all things now. "Thomas, show me what they did to the chapel. I need to see."

I could tell he was not keen, but we went outside, round the side of the castle and beheld the pile of rubble that had been the chapel. Beauty destroyed. A holy place desecrated, made unclean. I sat amid the devastation and prayed and cried and tried to make some sort of sense of it all, but none came.

"Where is Our Lady of Aberdeen, the stone one, the replica?"

"I don't know," he said, properly worried, looking around. "Maybe in the pool? They flung many things in there and they blocked off the stream."

"Show me."

"Ishbell, I think you've had enough shocks for one day—"

"I need to see."

So we stood by the pool, declared to be a place of the devil by those intent on doing his works. They had torn down trees and dug up soil and, indeed, thrown sacred objects into the water. I waded in. It was not as deep as it had been when nature ruled the woods. I pulled out the tall crucifix that used to stand in the chapel, and the golden angel; these I laid on the shore. Thomas came in with me and he quickly found The Lady.

"She is heavy. I will need McCulloch to help," he said.

"No," I replied, knowing a great truth at that moment. "Leave her be. The water will keep her safe until such time as it is right for her to be found. Time will cover her over; leaves will fall and form earth and she will sleep here until a good man raises her to the light once more."

"As you wish, Ishbell. People are afraid of this place now, so quick such nonsense and rumours do spread, but it means she will indeed be safe here."

The two holy faces looked up from below, the water rippling them, giving them the appearance of movement and life. The sun blasted down between a break in the clouds and we were illuminated by grace there in the pool that last time of our visiting it, that last time of looking upon The Lady of Aberdeen, or The Goddess, for Thomas was right when he said old and new were mixed up together in me. The two Ladies were becoming as one in my heart and mind, the image of mother and child as ancient as people, surely? A sacred image. A sacred Lady.

The wind moved the trees as we climbed out of the watery resting place. Branches with new and bright green growth upon them rustled and parted, the sun inviting and we ran up a new pathway, an opening where it had only been wild before, until we came to the stone circle. There, everything was intact, the hallowed space untouched by evil hands. But I was aware, acutely aware, of absences in and about the place of the castle. There was a missing stone and a missing person and I stood in the place where one had been and spoke of the other: "Was Agnes's body ever found?"

The Laird, who had been gazing at me as if in a dream, jerked to attention. "Agnes is dead?"

"Aye," I intoned. "After she accused us, I explained about her dismissal, thinking, so stupid, that it would make things right, that they would see it for the nonsense it all was, just a jealous silliness. But they took her and hurt her and I knew she was dead, Bessie knew it too. I did a great wrong, Thomas."

His words came out tightly. "In such a time, to men such as those, there are no right words to say. They came here determined to have their fun. It was I who dismissed Agnes with no reference, I who caused her greatest bitterness. We will put the word out, have people look for her. It may yet be that she escaped."

I shook my head in the empty place, knowing it was not so. But maybe another wrong could be put right.

"Thomas. Could we not put the stone back? The one that stood here? It was stolen from the circle long ago and Bessie said there was a curse put upon it."

"Aye," he said and it meant nothing positive, nothing life affirming and nothing good.

The Dark

We stared upwards at the great stone in the ceiling. It was not a regular shape. In fact, now that I studied it carefully it seemed to have been carved to resemble part of a man.

"I dinna ken how they put it up there and got it to stay," said Thomas. "And I dinna ken how we could get it back doon without asking men to risk their lives in the doing of it. The whole floor of the storage area above could come crashing down and bury them."

"That's no good then," I said, disheartened and disappointed. It had been good to have a hope of righting a wrong for as many minutes as it took us to walk together down the path between the trees and then back into the castle. Thomas had come down into the dungeon with great hesitancy; I had assured him that it was important for me to visit it, not just to see the stone, but also to further face the dark events that had occurred in the place and help lay them to rest.

His court chair was still down there. I took out a kerchief and polished it up with spittle while he watched. "All clean now," I said, glad to have fixed something, and sat down in it.

"Ishbell," he said and his voice was strained. "What do you really think of the castle?"

"It's a wonderful place; it's big and strong like you!"

His face was stony. "And neither it, nor I, provided you with a whit of protection when the worst happened."

"But you weren't here. Thomas, you cannot blame yourself for these things. Nor the castle, big and grand as it is; it is just a great pile of stone in the end."

Though, as I looked at the wall opposite me, I recalled the cold feel of it against my back, how the damp had travelled right through my clothes, and the chains: the bite of those metal links, the sting in my wrists, the ache in my arms, and how I had thought that was real pain when it had been but a starting point, a soft initiation. I looked away and examined the table in the corner. Upon it sat knives and swords and a chained ball with spikes. It was a wonder none of those had been used on us. But then all Dunn had needed had been one of his own hands. That blow had killed Christen Michell, slowly, gradually, over the following days.

"It's a dark place, Lassie. Oh, I dinna just mean doon here with all yon." His eyes had also found the table. "Though they were the belongings of my grandfather, a man like those from Aberdeen, with their lies and their hatred. He took me down here once when I was as small as Wee Thomas. He didn't really hurt me, not so as I was left damaged, but he frightened me, let me know what would happen if I displeased him."

I got up and wrapped my arms round my husband's middle, pressed my face to his chest and felt a tremble. My big Thomas was moved by big emotions and fighting to maintain control. I led him to the chair where he sat and I curled up on his knee, arms about his neck. I kissed his cheek. How long since I had done that? Had kissing become a thing of the past, somehow forgotten when I went into the water? Ended with the kiss of a seal? I took my husband's hand and kissed that too.

"I never used to stay here at the castle much after I inherited," he said. "It seemed full of misery and I longed to be away. Even after Wee Thomas was born, maybe especially after, I felt it best to be gone. Until you came. You lit the place up, made me want to stay, made me want to be a good man, a good Laird, worthy of your love."

"For me, it's you that lights the place up," I told him, touching his flushed cheek, and studying his shiny eyes.

"All the women of my household were taken. Abused or killed. I did nothing to stop it then and can do nothing in retaliation now, for it would bring all manner of trouble down upon our heads again. I'm fair bursting with frustration at it. And I canna bear what happened to you, quine. I canna."

I had seen Thomas look wild before. I had seen him disturbed and in pain. But I had never seen him cry. The dungeon was hurting him. Oh aye, it was all the terrible things too, but the place itself was reaching around and trying to stifle his breath, to strangle the life out of him. I could see the dark as I had never seen it before. It was at its worst in the dungeon but it existed everywhere in the great castle we called home. It lessened as I kissed Thomas on the mouth with all the desperation I felt in that moment, and he kissed me back with the same, but I felt the ghostly whispers of it again as we ran up the secret stair; dark, dark all around. It was in the very walls of the place, seeped into the floors and the ceilings, running down the wide staircase of the tower like blood, blood spilled in cruelty, blood that tasted of iron and dirt and salt.

Perhaps only the salt was our own. There was salt in the tears that flowed as we travelled from the lowest place in the castle to the highest, and returned from the worst happenings to the very best.

We fell into our marriage bed together, children no more. The bed was new, it was clean and fresh and free of darkness as we filled it with a furious love born of suffering and loss, a love that could wipe it all clean and start again, a love that could turn the babe in my womb to his, to the trueborn child of Thomas Manteith, my husband and dearest dear.

Love lit our day or our night, for I knew not which it was after that visit to the dungeon. Together we were bright enough to eclipse any moon or sun or star that twinkled over us, bright enough to cancel out the dark, for dark cannot exist where there is light. We were fiery and new and old and wise and silly and sweet. And spent. Poison lanced. Passion rested.

The Light

"I once tried to set fire to the place," Thomas told me, as we lay in the bed under a black and much be-starred sky. "When I was a boy. After my grandfather took me to the dungeon and all that I had been told there, for he detailed the uses of the objects you saw, the mutilations they caused when used in battle, and many battles there have been on this site in the past, so he said."

"You actually tried to burn down the castle?"

"Aye. I gathered up kindling from the kitchen when no one was looking and laid it all round the outside of the hall and tower. Little good it did. By the time I got back to where I had begun, the wind had taken it all!"

It was so long since I had laughed that it hurt my throat and chest to do so, but laugh I did, and merrily at that.

"I have often thought of this mistake since," he went on. "The proper start for a fire to destroy the castle would be in the great hall itself. That wooden roof would blaze up nicely and spread to the tower, I'm sure of it."

"You've often thought of it?" I asked, no longer laughing.

"With every bad thing that happens here, and those have been many."

"Maybe we can rid the place of its ghosts, Thomas," I said, sitting up and looking down upon his bonny face, and chest, and tummy that twitched as I ran a finger down it.

"Seeing you like this, I think 'Aye', but Ishbell, it's a mighty big task you're talking of."

"I know," I said, letting kisses follow my finger's path. "But you're a mighty big man, husband."

He laughed and I loved the sound so I went on: "With a mighty big... laugh, and a mighty big... heart." My kiss found its mark. "And everything needed to banish badness from any place."

I revelled in the vibration of his humour as he laid me down and gave my mouth a thorough kissing. "You are with child, we shouldna push our luck wi' this, Lassie, grand as it has been."

I made a noise, a noise I recognised as Bessie's special tut to denote that someone had spoken nonsense. "I heard Bessie telling women it was fine to lay with their husbands when they had a bairn in their belly, as long as it felt good to them. She said the church had its own reasons for naysaying the practice, and it was nothing to do with the health of women or babes."

"I've no doubt she was right," agreed Thomas.

"Mighty right," I said and we both laughed again before bringing some more light down into the old dark walls of the castle.

So light, the seeking of it, the grounding of it, became my great task and I expanded upon the concept the very next morning.

"Jasper, you should stage a play, soon, a comedy that will have all who see it laughing and filling this place with merriment."

"Bell! You've come back!"

"What do you mean? I've been back for an age."

"Aye," he said, having learned how to use the word well, "but some of you has only just now returned."

I did not want to speak or think of that; it would dilute my new motivation, so I simply said, "Are you passing up the opportunity to put on a play, brother?"

"No! I am not. Indeed, I am not."

"Wee Thomas would love to be included too, I think."

"Oh, absolutely. The boy is a born show-off. I hope you let him come to London when he's older, to walk grander boards than he treads here. In truth this play will be a good diversion for Ian too. He was left alone here to look after things when Duncan and I went to search for the

Laird, and you were in Aberdeen… He has not fully recovered from how useless he felt then."

"Poor Ian." I could well imagine him, not knowing what was happening to all those he loved. Unable to do anything but wait in this dark place. I sought him out and he did, indeed, appear diminished. I hugged him, and thanked him for all he had done. Being left in charge of the castle was no small task.

And then I found Wee Thomas and I found my stories too and filled the kitchen, the hall and bedrooms with them. There was one of a Lady who lay in a pool.

"The Lady of the Lake," Wee Thomas interjected with excitement.

"Not quite, this Lady came from Aberdeen and will lie under the water until the world is ready and good enough to look upon her again."

There were tales of witches, for why not play with the truth, twist and turn it into something more manageable, something actually magical, after all? Three witches stirred a pot and made a man king.

"Oh that's good, I can do something with that," said Jasper.

One witch sat in a pool and took on the form of a mermaid, enchanting all those that saw her, until a great bear found her and loved her and claimed her for his own.

So we brought the light back in. Wee Thomas danced on a well-made stage in the great hall. Jasper and Ian acted up a storm, quite literally; there was lightning and hail against the twelve windows that night.

"The power of a great performance!" declared my brother.

I asked Thomas to invite musicians to the castle, and played my own harp often. All these activities made the place brighter and kept the cold from the dungeon at bay.

I went below ground and sat in silence in the ancient chamber, the way Thomas had said they did in the east. I went above ground, between my stones, and gave the Goddess and Mother Mary a sacrifice of wine. I would honour both my mothers this way until the day I died. And that was a long way off; I had complete faith in the truth of that.

I prayed to the Lady and read of the lives of Saints, but on my own; I neither needed nor wanted any churchman to guide interpretation, though I did enjoy discussing my ideas with Thomas in the evening, in the privacy of our chamber only. I also confessed to him that Mother Mary was becoming all mixed up with the image of Mary from the portrait; when thinking of one I saw the other. He found this interesting, rather than disturbing as I'd feared he might, and told me of ancient cultures that he had read about, those that honoured a Mother God. But these ideas and conversations we kept secret, known to just us, like the Lady in the Pool, our part of the world not being ready for such thinking.

I learned the old ways of worship from Bessie's herb book and was delighted and amazed to find how often the dates of festivals and feasts coincided with Saint's Days and I celebrated them at once. Above and below. Bessie and Christen Michell would live in my heart until we were all reunited in death, as I knew we would be in time.

Then one day I walked along the back passageway from the kitchen and beheld a sight so tragic that it changed everything.

The End

As a child I had once been swinging high in the air on a tree swing when the fastening between wooden seat and chain broke and I was flung to the ground. I had been happy and carefree, flying through blue skies, and all in a moment I was down low and in pain and sad and crying. Jasper had rushed over to see if I was hurt. John had laughed and jeered.

The same sensations occurred that morning as I looked from passageway to hall and saw the Laird, head bent over some record he was writing up, brow furrowed, shoulders hunched like those of an old man. The weight of the castle walls and all that had taken place between them and below them sat heavily upon him. He was not blind to the signs and spaces of sadness as I had become. He sat upon the plain bench at the table; he had never taken his court chair back above ground and I knew he never would. He didn't need another reminder.

The swell of my belly had been accompanied by easy dreamy feelings; they had made it simple to ignore the truths that were all around us. There was a large hole in the kitchen, a gaping void, in the absence of Bessie Thom. Her laughter had beaten back the dark. The gap, the space where she had been, fair screamed the reason she wasn't there anymore. As did the space at the top table where Christen Michell had so often sat.

I fingered her rosary. I'd worn it every day since it came into my possession but I hadn't thought about it, hadn't let it in. I leant against the wall of the passageway, that cold, cold, wall, and let sorrow have its way for a short while. No amount of plays or love or laughter would lift this place. I knew it. And Thomas knew it; it was marked in the very position of his body, his unhappy stance. He'd been waiting for me to see or maybe, thinking I never would, he had resigned himself to living in the dark with me.

No more. There were such obvious means to fix, not the broken parts of our hearts, but the situation we lived in. He smiled and lightened as he saw me approach. He pushed back the bench so I could curl up on his knee. This was the Thomas he let me see every day, the happy man, the light-hearted soul.

I spoke softly to him. "If there's one thing I'm good at sensing, and good at making decisions about, it's when it's time to leave a place. And it's time, husband. I have that house in the North of England. It's nice. We used to visit it sometimes in the summer when I was a child. There's a great swing, hopefully now mended— Oh!" Other dim and murky memories surfaced. "Thomas! Was I escheated? Did I lose all my possessions?"

"No, my love, you were not even tried, being proved innocent by both your sinking in the water and my arrival at the harbour."

"Oh. Good. What happened to John?"

"I do not know," he said, and I could hear the heaviness in his voice. "Jasper punched him on the quayside and knocked him into the water, but someone fished him out after a bit, while I was trying to petition for Bessie. Ishbell, I didn't try hard enough. I wanted to get you home. If I had just—"

I silenced his lips with a finger. "In the hands of God. Isn't that what she said about the time of our deaths? She had confessed. Without torture even. There was nothing you could have done, Thomas. But we can do what she said we were meant to do. Live our lives as best we can, find as much joy and love as possible. But we cannot do it here."

"No, Lass, I don't think we can. But England is beset with similar problems to those we have known here. I have lands to the West, an island home that I have visited much in my life. It is peaceful and safe. The people are gentler than those from Aberdeen; the troubles we have here have not reached that far out. I would like to go there." He placed his hand on my tummy. "And when our brood is older, we could travel.

There are many sacred stones in this world, Ishbell; the isle of Lewis has hundreds, all placed together in a shape like this." He touched the cross around my neck. "My island has beaches too and pools that have never been changed by the hands of men."

"Then, let us go there."

No one tried to dissuade us. It seemed that people had been waiting for such a decision to be made. Duncan happily accepted the extra powers that were added to the title of Greeve; he was to stay there at the castle, in charge, until Wee Thomas or any other of our children returned to take up the reins again.

Jasper left before we did, a tear in his eye. It was hard for twins to part and I said so.

"Bell, I lost you a little bit from the first you set eyes on your handsome bear, and then a little more all the time until you married. But I am glad you have him."

"And you have Ian," I reminded him, our eyes meeting in a smile. "And I'm glad for that too."

I kissed Ian farewell. "Goodbye, brother."

"If things had gone differently," he replied, the old spark of humour returned to his face, "you would have been calling me husband."

"And what an interesting marriage that would have been!" noted Jasper, and we all laughed and hugged together there in the foyer of the castle.

They would visit. We would write. My family might visit London. Wee Thomas certainly would. "I'm going to suggest a Scottish play to young William," Jasper promised. "With a Manteith for a character; it'll be the greatest yet!"

We packed such items as we needed to take with us and gathered together other precious things to be placed where they would be safest: the priest's hole in our bedroom floor. Mary's portrait was to go in there and the thoughts that Thomas had encouraged me to put on paper as I tried to make sense out of all that had happened during my time in the castle. Small relics found from the chapel were also to be hidden away under the floor. Like the Lady, these things would be found when they were needed, if they ever were.

I reached down into the hole to move the cushions to the side and gasped. There on the floor was the Elfin Blade, shining bright in its silver casing. It must have fallen from my dress on Twelfth Night when I hid there, before proposals and marriage and witch accusations. I reached in and picked it up, finding it cold to the touch, this object of hurt and secrets and lies. It was of Agnes and Bessie, and me. And I knew just where to bury it.

**

The big sky of Aberdeenshire grew pink as we climbed into the coach, Jane with us, very much excited to be going. Bessie would be glad for her granddaughter, I was sure, and proud. Her old herb book went with us too. Contained within its pages was a recipe for The Speaking Tea, a drink that encouraged people to reveal the truth of their hearts, even to those they had only just met. I'd had a wee chuckle to myself when I found that and I fully intended to make pots of the lemony drink to welcome new visitors to our island home.

We trundled toward the track in the trees and I looked back, knowing it would be the last time I looked upon the castle with the earthly eyes of Isobell Manteith. The pink granite was alight in the sunrise, not on fire as Thomas had once wished, but glowing with a fiery light nonetheless; better times to come, a hope for the future.

Our future lay elsewhere. Wee Thomas jumped up and down on his seat, staring out of the window, as excited as Jane in his more exuberant way. I held the Laird's hand and leant back against him. I would die an old lady surrounded by the sea, not killed by her as I had once thought, but in love with her, counting her and her inhabitants as friends, as any good mermaid should.

We passed through the gates, the Mermaid and the Bear with their wee dancer, toward the pink sky, the blue ocean and a life full of joy.

Isobell's Story

Once Upon a Time, in the Days of Auld Lang Syne, on the mainland of Scotland, there lived a mermaid and a bear and they knew all manner of troubles.

There were those who did not like that a mermaid and a bear should fall in love and be happy and prosperous living in their castle home, surrounded by a magical forest and sacred stones and the mermaid's pool. It seemed too perfect, too good and too loving, as if it were possible for there to be too much perfection, good and love in the world. But evil was sought and seen where it existed not.

There were lies told of witchery and sorcery and murder. There were monsters in the form of bad men who smelled foul and spoke fouler. The bear knew the cold dark of a well for a time. The mermaid and her mothers were chained in a tall and pointed church tower and made to listen to bells that had been forged in hell itself.

A Selkie saved the bear and the mermaid. To the bear she came in the form of a horse. She swam round the mermaid as a seal, and soon the couple were free again. But they were sad. Salty tears were wept for those who were gone, for the mothers and grandmothers as had been lost.

In time the mermaid and the bear took their little boy, as was called Wee Thomas, to a new island home in the West. There, they lived in a fine house and swam in a warm sea and danced with their Selkie on the beaches. There, they healed their wounds and new babies were born. There was Wee Elizabeth Christen and Wee Jasper, both bonny bairns with good hearts.

The years wore on and Wee Thomas, wee no more, took flight to London town to dance and act and sing on the stage. Wee Elizabeth Christen, having grown to be a serious and strong woman, who was very much concerned with doing good, went back to the castle on the mainland to raise more mermaids and bears and to bring light back into the haunted old walls of the keep. Wee Jasper found a good woman to love on the island and there he stayed, in a cottage not far from the mermaid and the bear, bouncing babes on his knee in the evenings.

The mermaid had once been afraid of the sea. She hadn't understood. It had never wanted to kill her, but merely transport her and surround her and keep her safe. The bear took great delight in catching fish, as bears are wont to do, from the sea to feed his large family. He rowed his boat home to the mermaid every night, and they lived in their bonny island home till the end of their days, till together they soared high above into the endless celestial ocean of the starry sky.

If you look up on a clear night, you may see the splash of a mermaid's tail or the shape of a great bear, for stories, like people, only change and take new form; they never really end.

Historical Notes

Isobell Manteith, Bessie Thom and Christen Michell were real women, all accused of witchcraft in 1597. I have changed their stories somewhat, what is known of them, but hope that they might not be displeased with the resulting tale. I like to think they would have enjoyed living in a castle too.

Of the three, Isobell is the one of whom least is known, as she committed suicide in prison and so did not stand trial. It is said she hanged herself in the steeple of the Kirk of St. Nicholas. People accused of witchcraft were imprisoned there at that time, and they were often taken to The Tolbooth for examination or torture. She is mentioned, as already dead, in the trial records of Christen Michell.

Christen confessed to dancing at the Mercat Cross and to meeting the devil, who hit her so hard across the face that she was bedridden for several weeks. She named both Bessie and Isobell as having been at the same dances.

Bessie was fugitive for some time before being questioned in the kirk, where she denied all charges, including those of murdering her husband and others.

Bessie and Christen were tried and executed on March 9th 1597.

Agnes I invented, though parts of her tale have basis in fact from another time and place. In 1590, when David Seton, Baillie of Tranent, initiated the famous North Berwick witch trials with the torture of his servant Geillis Duncan, he may have been trying to escheat his rich mother-in-law Euphame MacCalzean. Geillis named Euphame as a witch, but then, just before her own execution, recanted the accusation, saying she had been persuaded to say it all by David Seton.

The Laird, Thomas Manteith, is also my own invention, but aspects of his character were inspired by the wonderful life and letters of Alexander Forbes, 4th Lord of Pitsligo, who lived about a hundred years after the time of this book. He believed in education for women and girls, and religious freedom, and at age 67, fought in the battle of Culloden, after which he lived as a fugitive. Such was his popularity that no one gave him up to the government troops, despite the large reward offered, and the hardships that were widely suffered at that time.

The financial accounts of the city of Aberdeen show that in September 1597 William Dunn, Dean of Guild, was awarded, £47 3s 4d (the equivalent of £6000 in today's money) for taking 'extraordinary pains in the burning of a great number of witches'. Details of the costs of barrels, tar and ropes needed for burning people are detailed as is an account for a blacksmith to make two pairs of shackles for the steeple of the kirk. Also fully accounted is the cost of dragging the body of Isobell Manteith through the streets of Aberdeen.

'Dooking' or 'sweimming' a witch to test her was not common in Scotland, in fact 1597 seems to be the only year to have recorded cases of the practice and those were mainly in Fife. James VI's witch-hunting book *Daemonolgie*, published the same year, recommends the method. However, there is a place at the edge of Aberdeen harbour that is said to have housed a crane that was used to dook people into the water, witches included.

The following resources proved invaluable in writing this story.

Books:

Goodacre (ed.) *The Scottish witch-hunt in context*, Manchester University Press, 2002

George F. Black, *Calendar of Cases of Witchcraft in Scotland*, Bulletin of the New York Public Library, 1937, 1938

J. Stuart (ed.) 'Trials for Witchcraft, 1596-1598', *Spalding Club Miscellany*, vol. I, 1841

King James I of England (James VI of Scotland), *Daemonologie*, 1597. Reprint by Aziloth Books, 2012

Geoff Holder, *The Guide to Mysterious Aberdeen*, The History Press, 2010

Catherine Brown, *Feeding Scotland*, National Museums of Scotland, 1996

Peter Brears, *Food and Cooking in 16th Century Britain*, English Heritage, 1985

Fiona Macdonald, *Scottish Tartan and Highland Dress, A Very Peculiar History*, Book House, 2013

Ian Mortimer, *The Time Traveller's Guide to Elizabethan England*, Vintage, 2012

Online:

Julian Goodare, Lauren Martin, Joyce Miller and Louise Yeoman, 'The Survey of Scottish Witchcraft', http://www.shca.ed.ac.uk/Research/witches (archived January 2003, accessed August 2014).

Places:

The Tolbooth Museum in Aberdeen, a medieval prison, built just a few years after the one mentioned in this book. It was there I first learned about the witches in the steeple.

St. Nicholas Kirk, Aberdeen, is now open to the public every weekday afternoon with wardens on hand to answer questions. The original steeple, in place at the time of this book, burnt down in 1874 and a replacement tower was built.

The Museum of Scottish Lighthouses in Fraserburgh includes a lighthouse that is built inside a castle and a 'wine tower' which was actually a post reformation secret Catholic chapel. The wine tower was built by the Laird of the castle for his Catholic wife.

Provost Skene's House, Aberdeen, dates from 1545. The rooms are laid out in the styles of various historical eras and the chapel ceiling boasts some most unusual religious paintings. There's also a cellar (dungeon in my mind) café with an underground storage room topped with glass that you can walk over. It used to terrify me when I was a child but I rather like it now!

And of course, the many castles, stone circles, caves and beaches of Aberdeenshire: so many, so varied, so inspirational.